The Blues of Atlantis

Book One

Patricia Elliott

ISBN 978-1-0689534-1-5

Published in 2024 by Patricia Elliott

Also by Patricia Elliott

Her Lover's Face

Her Ghosts Reborn

Not You Again

Her Prison, His Game

Beneath His Hands

Her Blue Treasure

This novel wouldn't have been possible without the help of my incredibly supportive and amazing partner. Thank you, Matt. I love you to the moon and back.

Prologue

July 2007

Nerina Winters bounced up and down with excitement. Her long, pure white ponytail was swinging back and forth. She had lived in San Diego all her life, but this was the first time she'd ever been to SeaWorld.

"Meet us back at this sign in an hour." Her dad, Kyle Winters, pointed to the *Dolphin Point* sign next to them.

As they stood there, families walked by and stared at her, whispering to each other. Something she had grown accustomed to over the years, but it still caused butterflies in her stomach.

She knew she was different. Not only did her white hair stand out, but so did her pale skin. It was almost void of any color at all, making her look like a ghost. Only her eyes, which were as turquoise as the waters in the Caribbean, brought color to her features.

"Yes, Dad." She gave him a quick kiss on the cheek before bounding towards the dolphin tank. It took forever to convince them to come to the park. They never let her go anywhere, let alone disappear on her own. It was only because it was her thirteenth birthday they relented and agreed to come. They were too darn overprotective, and it drove her crazy.

Thankfully, she was here now. The ocean and its sea life made her feel alive. Something about it made her body sing and fill with excitement like nothing else could. She belonged here. She could feel it. Approaching the dolphin tank, Nerina looked around for an opening in the crowd. Seeing an empty spot by the gate leading to the trainers' area, she walked up to the wall of the tank. The dolphins, which were on the other side of the tank, flipped in the air and started swimming her way.

When they reached her side, she expected them to keep on swimming, but they stopped. They peered up at her with their gorgeous eyes and started singing, slapping the water with their fins. One kept flicking his head, as if telling her to join them. Her palms itched to reach out and touch one, but she was afraid she'd get into trouble.

She ducked down behind the concrete wall and jumped back up. The dolphins seemed to get a kick out of it. They ducked under the water and jumped up when she did. Time flew by and before she knew it, it was time to go back to the sign. She began to walk back the way she came.

The dolphins' cries of excitement turned to a heart wrenching sound of anguish. They followed her as she walked around the tank. It broke her heart, but she had to go. If she didn't, her parents would never let her come back again.

"They seem quite enamored by you," a male voice said from behind her.

She turned and saw an employee, dressed in a blue neoprene suit, walking towards her. Nerves rattled in her chest. Had she done something wrong?

"Why are they crying like that?" Nerina asked.

"Looks like they don't want you to go. I've never seen them act that way before."

"Really?" Why did they care so much about her? She wasn't

anyone special, just an odd-looking teen that everyone ignored, except to bug her about her looks. The outcast and the school yard freak.

"People come and go all the time. They are usually so playful and give everyone a show. But with you, it's like they forgot anyone else was around."

"They are gorgeous."

"And super intelligent. They must sense something about you. Would you like to feed them with me?"

Nerina looked down at her watch and sadly shook her head. "I'm afraid I have to go. My family is waiting for me."

If she wasn't back at that sign in two minutes, her parents would never bring her back. With one last glance at the dolphins, she whispered, "Sorry." She wanted to stay and say to hell with the consequences, but her parents were strict. More strict than other parents. And she planned to be back.

"Bye," she said to the employee and raced towards the Dolphin Point sign.

Her family was already waiting for her. When her mother, Maggie, saw her, her hand flew up to her chest, and she let out a long breath. "We were so worried."

"Geez, Mom. It's not like I'm late or anything." Nerina sighed. They never gave her a chance to breathe. That was why coming here was such an amazing surprise, especially as it helped her realize what she wanted to do with her life. "I know what I want to be."

"What's that?" her dad asked, as her mom took a sip of coffee.

"A mermaid."

Her mom spewed the coffee everywhere. "What? What did...you just...say?" she asked between coughs.

Rolling her eyes, Nerina repeated herself. "A mermaid."

Her parents exchanged a look, and she wondered what silent thought passed between them. Their gaze held a secret, and they appeared to be at a loss for words.

"What? Why are you guys looking at me like that?"

"Nothing. Let's just go home," Kyle said, patting his wife on the back, who couldn't seem to stop coughing. He took Nerina's hand, and they quickly left the park. No one said a word on the ride home.

Whatever. She knew what she wanted to be, and nothing would stand in her way.

Chapter One

July 2018

"There. All done." Jenny placed the last sequin sticker next to Nerina's eye, perfecting the look for her next performance. Her make-up assistant swung the chair around so she could look in the mirror. "You look awesome."

Nerina examined her reflection. "Only because you're such an amazing artist." Half of her hair had been pulled back into a ponytail and secured with a seashell clip. The rest was still free to flow down her back, nearly touching the seat of her chair.

"The blue highlights definitely bring out your eye color."

"I actually look alive for once," Nerina said, laughing. She had tried all sorts of dye jobs to offset the white hair over the years, trying to get the kids to stop bugging her. During her final days in high school, the walking dead craze swept through the halls, and she became known as the walker. But now those days were behind her, and she had the best job in the world.

"Pale or not, you have skin to die for." Jenny's hair was dark red, and her face complimented it with unending freckles. A blatant contrast to her own. "It looks so pure."

"Thanks." She smiled at her friend before heading over to the round pool of water, which was in the center of the room. Reaching out, she grabbed the next part of her costume off the rack—a silver silicone mermaid tail, with a tinge of blue around the scales and the fluke.

The show organizer poked her head in the door. "Neri, you're on."

"Wish me luck." She slid into the water and with a flick of her tail, she disappeared beneath the surface into a tunnel that led to the open tank. It didn't take much to convince the president of SeaWorld to go for the idea of a mermaid show. Of course, her parents hated her passion for the sea and did everything they could to keep her from the ocean. However, she was twenty-four years old now and could do what she wanted with her life.

Working with the architects, they'd designed a pool with an underwater viewing area. Below the water's surface, it looked like an exotic coral reef, spanning the colors of the rainbow. There was a cavern towards the back which hid the tunnel entrance. It also concealed the breathing tubes used by the merfolks that entertained the crowds.

Not that she ever needed them. Her body appeared to hold oxygen better than most people, allowing her to stay under the water longer than any of the other mermaids in the show. She poked her head out of the cavern and ducked back inside. Kids gathered around in the viewing area, hands resting on the glass.

In her earpiece, she could hear the announcer talking. "It looks like another mermaid has come for a visit. She appears to be shy, though. Maybe if you wave and give her a great big smile, it may encourage her to come out."

The young ones began jumping up and down, waving their

hands with all their might. Their energy was so contagious even the adults joined in. She poked her head out again and slowly left the confines of the cave.

"Look everyone, it's Mermaid Neri. What a treat! She is the most elusive of the merfolk and doesn't come out for just anyone. As you can tell by her appearance, she doesn't visit the surface much. I wonder what she has up her sleeve."

She rolled her eyes as the announcer cashed in on her looks. As Nerina executed a perfect underwater backflip, a dolphin swam out of the tunnel and joined her in the tank. This was her favorite part of the show, frolicking with the bottlenose dolphin, who adored mimicking her every move.

Gasps of delight came from the crowd as she rolled on her back and created bubble rings. They watched as the dolphin swam up through the rings. The two of them made a great team.

"Maybe if you guys point upwards, she may swim to the surface, and you can have your picture taken with her."

The kids all pointed to the surface. She glanced up and then back towards the viewing glass, swimming closer to them. She tilted her head sideways as if she didn't understand their request. They began to bounce up and down, both hands pointing towards the ceiling. A huge grin spread across her face, and she made her way up top.

A young girl, with shoulder-length blond hair, was next to the tank when she surfaced. "Daddy, Daddy, look, it's a mermaid. Is she real?"

Neri slid onto a perfectly angled rock, careful not to snag the silicone tail. The child pulled her dad towards the rock and others gathered around.

"Hi there," Neri said to the youngster. "What's your name?"

"Lauren," the girl said quietly, partially hiding her face behind her dad's hand.

"Well, Lauren, it's nice to meet you."

"Can I be a mermaid?"

"You can be whatever you want to be," she said, with an elegant wave towards her tail. "You just have to believe."

"Would it be possible for us to take a picture of you with my little girl?" the dad asked.

"Feel free." Neri helped Lauren onto the rock beside her, and the girl climbed on her lap, making herself comfortable. An ache grew in the pit of her stomach, and sadness filled her heart, but she forced a smile for the sake of the picture.

After snapping the picture, the dad helped his kid down and turned back to her. "How can you hold your breath for so long?"

Before she could respond, the little girl piped up, "Don't be silly, Daddy. Mermaids can breathe underwater."

Just another oddity about her, but it surprised the heck out of the audience. One time, when she was younger, her parents took her to the recreation center. She'd given the lifeguards quite a scare when she went to the deep end and stayed on the bottom with her eyes closed. Neri never paid attention to how long she'd been down there for and ended up being scooped up by one of the male lifeguards.

They thought she'd drowned. Needless to say, her mom and dad lectured her and refused to take her back, much to her displeasure. How was she supposed to know that wasn't normal? It was just something she could do. After taking a few more pictures, she said her farewells and launched herself off the rock, disappearing back into the cavern.

Wade Douglas watched as she swam back into the cavern, glancing down at his watch. There was only an hour left until Nerina had to be at the *One Ocean* show. That didn't leave him much time.

Making his way through the crowd, he slipped under the chain link rope and entered the employee only area. If he was quick, he'd catch her in the change room. He planned to be quick in another way, too, and take her by surprise.

Various employees walked by him and said hello. A few stopped to talk with him, but he excused himself politely. His mind and body only had one agenda, and it didn't include small talk. He entered the outer dressing room. After locking the door, he walked towards the door on the left side of the room. As he approached it, he pulled his shirt over his head and undid his belt, slipping out of his pants.

By the time he got to the door of the change room, he was stark naked. He took a deep breath before quietly opening it. Nerina was sitting on the bench, sorting through her bag. He bit his lip as she stood up, praying she wouldn't turn around.

She reached around her back and untied the seashell top, placing it on the bench beside her. Wade stifled a groan, as he caught a glimpse of the corner of her breast. She hooked a finger in her bottoms and pulled them off. Fully aroused, he snuck into the room, trying not to make a sound. However, when he went to lock the inner door, she heard the click and spun around. But he had her up in his arms before she could say a word, walking towards the showers.

She shrieked and giggled at the same time, pushing against his chest. "You! I'm trying to work here."

"So am I." He grinned as he released her legs, letting her body slowly slide against his arousal as her feet came to rest on the floor.

"What if someone comes in?" She tried peeking around him to check the door, his lips pressing against the nape of her neck.

"They'll see me making love to my wife," he said huskily. "Don't worry, I locked the door."

When he turned on the tap, water cascaded over their heated bodies. He took her hands and wrapped them around the shower head above them, feasting on her body with his lips. Even though they'd been married a few years now, her body was still like an aphrodisiac to him, his own personal siren. Her scent, her looks—everything about her—called out to him in a way unlike any other. Stealing these moments with her had to be his favorite hobby.

He swallowed hard as she opened herself to him, eager to take what he offered. Sadly, there was no time to spoil her in the way she deserved, but he couldn't help taking a little longer than he had planned. He kneeled before her, sliding his hands down her bare body. The water hit her breasts as she leaned back, nipples hardening. Whether from the force of the water or the administrations of his hands, he couldn't tell.

"You are so hot," he murmured, moving his fingers teasingly towards the mound between her legs. He separated her womanly folds and leaned forward, breathing in her scent. His body ached to take her then and there, but he took a moment pleasuring her with his tongue.

"That feels so good," she said, her body shaking beneath his hands. When he slid two fingers inside her, she couldn't contain herself anymore, and her muscles contracted around his hand, almost pushing him out of her.

Teetering on the edge himself, he stood up, lifting her leg to his waist. She reached down and guided him into her. She was still pulsating from her orgasm, and it was nearly his undoing. Struggling for control, he pressed her up against the wall. "Don't move."

With a knowing grin, she wrapped her other leg around him and used the shower head as leverage, then ground into him. Wade didn't want to come yet, so he grabbed her hips. "If you don't stop, it will be all over."

"But I'm so close," she whispered into his ear. That was it. No longer able to hold back, he plunged deep inside her, and she cried out in ecstasy. He muffled their cries with a kiss as they reached the peak together.

They stood there for a moment, neither moving, breathing heavily. Slowly, she unlatched herself from his waist and tried to stand up, her legs trembling. He wrapped his arms around her so she wouldn't fall.

As her head came to rest on his chest, she said, "Wow."

"You can say that again."

No other woman ever rocked his world. But then again, all this was still a new experience for him. He hadn't been with a woman for a long time before her. This wasn't even supposed to happen, or so everyone kept telling him, but it felt too good to be a bad idea. As soon as he met her, he knew she was the one. Screw everyone else.

Chapter Two

Weeks later...

The smell of bacon drifted into the bedroom, where Nerina was sitting on the edge of the bed, trying to clear her foggy brain. Her stomach churned and rolled, bile rising high in her throat. Clamping a hand over her mouth, she rushed towards the bathroom.

Lifting the toilet seat, she lost the contents of her stomach as her muscles contracted with a gut-wrenching heave. The acid burned her throat as she doubled over repeatedly. Wade walked up behind her, pulling the hair out of her face.

"Again?" he asked, rubbing her back.

She tried to say thanks, but her stomach clenched, causing her to lean over the toilet again. After a few dry heaves, she sat down on the edge of the bathtub while he grabbed a cloth. Upon wetting the cloth, he handed it to her.

"Thanks," she said in a raspy voice. A lump settled in her throat, which was currently on fire. He appeared to sense her need and filled the cup beside the sink. Grabbing it, she downed the water in one gulp.

Her stomach gurgled and rolled. "Ugh, that was a bad idea," Neri groaned. Leaning on Wade, he helped her back into bed.

"Just sleep, darling." He kissed her on the forehead and then left the room.

Lightheaded and nauseous, she laid herself flat on her back, afraid to move a muscle. *Healthy as a horse, ya right, Mom!* Whatever this illness was, it had put her down and out for two weeks. Thankfully, her boss was nice and allowed her to take as long as she needed, providing there was still a show.

Wade poked his head in the door. "I'm about to leave for work. Is there anything I can get you before I go?"

"Can you tell him I'm sorry that I couldn't make it in."

"Will do."

A few minutes later, she heard the front door close. Tears pricked her eyes. It wasn't fair. She wanted to be in the water with the rest of her team, surprising children and adults alike. Things never felt right when she was away, even more so now because her body craved water, like an addict craved their drug of choice. Her mouth was dry and parched, throat still aching from her earlier activity. Reaching over, she grabbed the glass of water off the bedside table.

The liquid did little to moisten her dry mouth, which felt like she was sucking on a cotton ball. She set the glass on the table and flopped back onto her pillow. Picking up her cell, she called her mom.

"Hi, dear, how are you?" her mom asked.

"Blah," was Nerina's only response.

"What's wrong?"

"I've been sick for the last two weeks, and it just won't go away." She sniffled into the phone, tears rolling down her cheeks. God. She felt like a weakling.

"Maybe you need some of my homemade chicken noodle soup."

Nerina grabbed her stomach as it rolled again. "Don't mention food, please!"

"Your father and I will be right there," her mom said quickly and disconnected the call.

She regretted making the call immediately. Now they would come over and treat her like a child. They would probably lecture Wade on not taking better care of her. For some reason, they didn't think she could take care of herself. If her parents could chose, they'd make her live at home or they'd move in with her. When she married Wade, she talked him into only getting a one bedroom, just so they wouldn't be able to pull something like that.

True to her mother's word, they were there in less than an hour and with chicken soup to boot. The smell had her racing towards the bathroom again, slamming the door behind her. When she came back out to where her parents were, her mother was busy picking up the clothes that were strewn about the apartment.

"Sorry, I haven't had a chance to tidy up lately."

Cradling the clothes in one arm, her mom walked over and placed the back of her hand on Nerina's forehead. "You don't feel warm."

"Honey, she isn't a child. Come and sit down." Her dad motioned for his wife to sit beside him, and she appeared torn between coddling Nerina and going to sit with him.

"I'm not gonna die, Mom. It's safe to sit."

Her dad grabbed his wife's hand and pulled her down beside him, making her drop the clothes. "Have you been working while sick?" he asked.

She shook her head. "I can barely get out of bed, let alone swim. Every time I move, I end up puking."

"Can we convince you to come home till you feel better?" she asked.

"Wade is taking good care of me."

Her mom looked around the room at the mess, lips pursed. "If this is taking care of you, I'll eat my hat."

"Just drop it, Mom," Nerina said, exasperated.

Struggling with her upset stomach, she walked over to the heap of clothes and deposited them in the laundry basket in the bathroom. When she returned, she saw the two of them whispering to each other which stopped promptly when they saw her.

"You two look deep in thought."

Her mother opened her mouth to speak, but her dad gave her a warning glance. "It's nothing for you to worry about, dear," he said.

"Okay, what's going on?" Nerina asked sternly, placing her hands on her hips.

"I—" her mom started to say.

"We better be going," her father interrupted, and all but pulled his wife out the door.

"Wait, I..." she tried to say, but it was too late. They were gone.

Well, that was bizarre.

Her parents had been cryptic before, but that took mysterious to a whole new level, even for them. If she had been feeling any better, she'd have followed them and checked to see if they did anything else suspicious.

"Oh no." The familiar churn rocked her stomach, and bile snaked its way up her throat. "Not again." She rushed to the toilet for the umpteenth time.

Wade walked into the bedroom and saw her fast asleep. The sheet was down at her ankles, and she had on a pink teddy bear t-shirt that was bunched up to just under her breasts and was wearing matching underwear. Her right leg was bent, giving him a good glimpse of the sweet spot that was waiting for him.

Hoping she felt better, he removed his clothes and climbed into bed beside her. He brushed the hair away from her neck and licked his lips hungrily. A spark of desire shot through his loins, and he hardened at the sight of her bare skin. Even in her sleep, she was as enticing as anything. They hadn't done anything for two weeks, and it was killing him. He wanted to bury himself deep inside her, but she'd been too sick.

Leaning in, he brushed his lips against her neck and slipped his hand into her underwear, cupping her mound. She stirred slightly and nuzzled her face into his chest, letting out a cute little moan. Her eyes still closed.

"Wakey, wakey, sleepy head." He bit her earlobe gently, as he slowly moved his hand back and forth over her clit, dipping a finger deep inside her. Even in her sleep, her body prepared for him, swelling up to welcome him. Moist and wet. He moved down to taste her, to make love to her with his tongue.

He loved waking her up this way. Often times, this was when she became the most abandoned in their lovemaking. Not fully awake but fully aware. She arched under his touch.

Nerina's eyes popped open. Wave after wave of nausea made her stomach roll, muscles contracting ferociously. She tried to get up, but something was weighing her down. She shoved at whatever was stopping her and raced to the bathroom.

As she was puking in the toilet, a loud groan emanated from the bedroom, and then something banged against the wall. She didn't...that wasn't? *Please, don't tell me that was Wade.*

She knew he was getting annoyed with her being sick, despite how helpful he was when she needed him. Tomorrow, she'd go to the doctors and see what the heck was up with her body. After cleaning herself up, she went in search of her husband.

"Wade?" she called from the doorway.

The cupboard doors in the kitchen banged open and closed, and she could hear him muttering away to himself. Sheepishly, she walked towards the noise and found him standing naked in front of the coffee pot, with a bright red scratch on his upper back near his neck. He turned to face her, his hair a disheveled mess. His eyes frustrated, pain blatantly running through them.

"I'm really, really sorry," she said.

He held his hands up to her. "Give me a bit. I need space."

She walked over to him, poking his chest with her finger. "Don't you dare be mad at me. You're the one who insisted on trying something while I was asleep. You knew I wasn't feeling well."

For a second, she thought he was going to argue, but instead, he hung his head. "You're right. I'm sorry. I was hoping you were feeling better," he said, massaging the back of his neck, "but I guess not."

"Here, sit. Let me take a look at your back."

He sat down on the kitchen chair, and she grabbed the first aid kit from the puke-smelling bathroom. The smell made her instantly nauseous again. She burped, and her mouth filled with an acidic taste. Swallowing hard, she made her way back to the kitchen.

"This might sting a little," she warned him as she cleaned the scratch mark. "Good news is you don't need stitches."

He pulled her onto his lap. "No, but I could definitely use something else," he said, winking at her.

"Baby, you know I wish I could, but I'm still feeling queasy. You don't want me puking all over you, do you?" She pushed against his chest, attempting to extricate herself from his grip.

"It's a chance I'm willing to take," he said, nuzzling her neck.

Her stomach continued to flip and roll. And the mere thought of sex made her go green around the gills. "Sorry, no can do, Wade."

"Come on." He slid a hand up her shirt. "It's been two weeks."

"Wade, I said no," she growled at him.

He set her aside and stood up. His arousal and frustration were plain to see. This was the first time they had gone this long without sex. She loved intimacy as much as he did, and she didn't want to hurt him by saying no.

She reached out and put a hand on his shoulder. "Sorry, I really want to, but I need another day or so to get over this."

"Ya, okay. Sure," he grumbled, disappearing into the bathroom.

She really needed to get her body sorted. It was time to visit the doctor and figure out what the heck was going on. She'd do that first thing in the morning.

Chapter Three

Nerina entered the examining room. Along the back wall sat a blue cushioned bed which was lined with white paper. Hopping up on the bed, she acquainted herself with everything in the small room. There were body part posters along the opposite wall. One was of a spine, and another had a picture of an ear.

It was the first time she had ever been in a doctor's office. She never needed to come before. Reaching out, she squeezed a little rubber ball that was hanging from a holder. A wide belt-looking type thing was attached to it. The belt thickened when she squeezed the ball.

After five minutes, a plump, short, middle-aged gentleman in a white lab coat walked in. She dropped the thingamajig as if it were a hot potato.

"Hi, Mrs. Douglas, I'm Doctor Jericho. How can I help you today?"

She explained about the nausea and her out of whack hormones. "I don't know what's wrong with me."

He grabbed the thing she had been playing with and wrapped it around her arm, squeezing the ball and watching the rectangular display on the wall. "Your blood pressure doesn't look too bad." He put the device in the holder before turning back to her again. "When was your last period?"

She took a moment to think. Her period was never regular, so she couldn't give him a date specifically. "It only happens a couple times a year, so I don't know. Three or four months ago, maybe?" she answered tentatively.

"Let's do a pregnancy test." He took a small cup out of one of the cupboards and handed it to her.

"Um, what do I do with this?"

"Pee into the cup and fill it to here." He pointed to a number on the side. "There is a cupboard on the wall inside the bathroom. Place it in there when you're done." The doctor left the room, heading into what looked like another examining room.

She walked into the bathroom and did as the doctor ordered, trying not to pee on her hand. Once she was done, she returned to the little room again. It was a few more minutes before the doctor came back into the room.

"The test was negative. Why don't you lay back on the table for me?"

He pushed on her stomach, making an odd noise with his tongue. Pulling her shirt down, he told her she could sit up now. She watched as he typed away on the computer.

"What do you think is wrong with me?"

"It's hard to say." He paused while he finished typing. "It feels like your uterus is slightly enlarged, so I'm going to send you for an ultrasound. Considering that you are so nauseous, I want you to take this form to the hospital and get it done as soon as possible. You do have insurance, right?"

"Yes."

"Good." With that, he handed her the ultrasound requisition and left the room.

Why did he feel the need to send her to the hospital? Her chest tightened, and her heart thumped wildly against her rib cage. She tried to take a deep breath, but her airway refused to listen. What if she was dying? What if she had a big tumor and was one leg away from death?

Why else would she be sick now? She had never been sick a day in her life, and now she couldn't keep her head out of the toilet. And this whole sex thing with Wade. She always wanted sex, and now it was like her libido was dead. That made her think something was wrong. Very wrong. Nerina climbed in her car and went directly to the hospital.

When she arrived, she explained her reason for being there. Surprisingly, it didn't take her long to see the doctor and then be directed to the ultrasound area. The nausea overtook her when the tech was taking her to the room,

"Sorry, give me a moment," she said, fleeing to the safety of the bathroom, barely making it in time. Much to her horror, she missed the toilet on the first heave.

A few minutes later, there was a knock on the door. "Are you okay, miss?"

"Just a second," she gasped between heaves.

When her stomach settled, she cleaned up to the best of her ability, with only paper towel to aid her. She stepped out of the bathroom and whispered to the tech, "You may need to get the cleaners in there."

"Let's see if we can get this done before your stomach gets upset again."

The woman dropped some cold gel on her abdomen and picked up a controller. Nerina watched as images appeared on the monitor, but she couldn't make out anything.

After a few minutes of silence, the tech asked, "Is this your first pregnancy?"

Nerina's jaw dropped, and her eyes widened. "Come again?"

"This—here—is the head." The woman pointed to a blob on the screen.

Squinting her eyes, she tried to see a baby. It didn't look like anything more than a blotch on the screen. How could she be pregnant? It wasn't possible. In the past, she'd dreamed of becoming a mother one day, only to have it cruelly ripped away from her. But could it be possible that they were wrong? Excitement swirled in her belly as she reached out and touched the screen. "I'm really pregnant?"

"About eight weeks by the looks of it." The tech frowned and squinted at the screen, moving her face closer to it and then further away. "Excuse me, I'll be right back."

Nerina ran a hand down her face, shock filling her. Between not getting her period every month, and her messed up bicornuate uterus, they had told her she would never be able to get pregnant. Hearing that news when she was eleven years old devastated her. Every girl dreamed of marriage and having kids. Well, almost every girl.

A giggle escaped her as a grin spread across her face. "Me? I'm pregnant? Holy cow!" She poked her stomach.

"Oh crap, bad idea." Covering her mouth with her hand, Nerina searched frantically around the room and spotted a garbage can.

When the tech returned, followed by a doctor, they found her hunched over the garbage can, losing the remains of her stomach.

She glanced up at them sheepishly. "Sorry."

The two of them waved their hands in front of their noses to ward off the putrid smell that filled the room. The man hit some buttons on the keyboard and examined the images on the screen. He made a noise and motioned for the tech to step out of the room with him. The tech handed her a towel to wipe her face.

Nerina sat back up on the bed. "Is everything okay?"

"Sorry, I'll be right back," the woman said.

An uneasy feeling washed over her. She had seen this happen in a movie, and it never ended well. The tech was quiet when she entered the room again, handing her another towel to wipe the goo off her stomach.

"What's going on?" Nerina asked.

"I'm afraid I'm not allowed to say anything. I'll take you back to the room, and the doctor should be in to see you shortly."

She touched the woman's hand as it rested on the doorknob. "But you already told me I was pregnant."

"I thought you already knew that. Come with me," she said as she started to walk out of the room. Nerina scrambled to keep up with her, despite her stomach churning.

"Please, I'm scared. Is something wrong with the baby?"

"I'm sorry. I could get fired if I say anything." The tech pointed to the empty room. "Wait in here. I'll let them know you're back." With that, the woman fled the room.

A lump formed in her throat, and she swallowed hard. "Just my luck."

Pulling out her phone, she tried to distract herself by listening to country music. No bad thoughts were going to drag her under today. Not when she had received the best news of her life.

An overwhelming thirst washed over her, and her tongue scratched against the roof of her mouth. Placing her phone on the bed, she poked her head out the door and asked the closest nurse if she could have a glass of water.

The water didn't quench her thirst. She was on her fifth glass of water when a young doctor walked into the room, looking only slightly older than her. He raked a hand through his thick black hair, and his dark gray eyes focused on the file he had in his hand. Sighing, he placed the file on the table and locked his hands behind his back, rocking on his heels. She bit her lip as she waited for him to speak.

"The tests confirm that you are pregnant, which accounts for the nausea that you've been experiencing," he said, clearing his throat.

"I sense a *but* coming?"

A flash of what looked like pity passed over his features. "There's no easy way for me to say this. According to the ultrasound, it looks as though the baby may suffer from a condition called Sirenomelia."

"Sireno-what?"

"Sirenomelia. It is a condition where the lower half of the body is fused together and can be accompanied by other abnormalities. I'm sorry," he said softly. "We are going to refer you to an obstetrician who has knowledge in this area. He will be able to talk with you about your options." When she sat there dumbfounded, he put a hand on her shoulder. "Are you okay?"

She gave a small nod, struggling internally to keep her composure.

"I'll just go and get your paperwork, then you are free to head home."

As soon as the doctor left the room, the dam inside her burst into tiny shards. Tears streamed down her cheeks faster than she could wipe them away. Nerina pounded the bed harshly with her fists, releasing all the pent-up frustration inside her. How could the universe be so cruel as to bless her and curse her all in one breath?

With the doctor's referral in hand, she stumbled out of the hospital and walked in a daze back to her car. "Damn, why am I so thirsty?" she said, running her tongue over her chapped lips.

As she sat there, preparing to drive home, her legs started itching from the bottoms of her feet up to her crotch. Nerina slipped off her shoe and scratched her foot, slowly working her way up. By the time she stopped, red scratch marks from her nails covered her legs.

"What on earth is going on with me?"

Wade tapped his fingers on the gray and white marble counter, waiting for the coffee pot to finish dripping. What was taking her so long? She said she was just going to stop at the market and pick up some anti-nausea meds.

Grabbing a cup, he poured some coffee before sitting down in the lazy-boy. Nothing made him more uncomfortable than when he was away from her. If he had his way, he'd glue himself to her side. But Kyle and Maggie insisted that he give her some freedom, so she didn't suspect anything. That idea didn't sit well with him, not when he knew the dangers out there. He pulled out his phone to text her.

Fifteen minutes went by, and he still hadn't heard from her. Unable to sit down, he got up and paced back and forth in the living room.

Relax, man.

This wasn't the first time that they'd been apart for an hour or two, so he wasn't sure why there was such a bad feeling lingering in his gut.

An hour later, he heard the lock click and relief filled him when his white and blue haired beauty walked through the door. He rushed over and took her in his arms, letting out a long breath.

"Wade, you're squishing me," she said, her voice muffled against his chest.

"Sorry." He released his hold slightly and studied her face. She was even more pale than usual. Her turquoise-colored eyes didn't have their usual sparkle. "Are you okay? Where were you?"

"I think you better sit down." She took his hand and pulled him to the black suede couch.

The sadness in her voice only intensified the bad feeling he had. Instead of listening, he kissed her and nearly gagged from the vile odor in her mouth.

She blushed and scrunched up her cute little nose. "Sorry, I puked just a few minutes ago and haven't had a chance to freshen up."

Clearing his throat, he said, "It's okay. So, what were you going to tell me?"

"I'm pregnant."

"Pregnant? Well, that explains your date with the toilet. It's having more attention than I am," he said, winking.

She punched him in the shoulder. "Can't you ever be serious for once?"

"It's what you love about me." He was about to joke again, but the look on her face told him he better not. Her eyes were shooting daggers at him. "Sorry."

"The doctors believe—"

"Wait, you went to the doctors today?" He stood up and started pacing again. "Oh man. Oh man. Oh man."

"Sit down. You're making me dizzy." Nerina tried to reach for him, but he took a step back. His face became as pale as hers, and his hands balled into tight fists. He'd never gotten mad at her for going anywhere before. Her stomach flip-flopped at the sound of his voice as he muttered under his breath.

"Why didn't you discuss it with me first?" he gritted through his teeth.

"Why would I have to? It's perfectly normal for a person to visit the doctors when they aren't feeling well." Confused by his reaction, she glanced at him for an explanation.

"Yes, but you're not..." He closed his lips tightly and turned away from her. His back ridged, and his hands still clenched.

She stood up and grabbed his arm to turn him around. "I'm not what, Wade?"

"Normal! You're not normal," he said, his voice cold and harsh. With that, he stormed out of the house, leaving her alone and bewildered.

Chapter Four

"We have a problem," Wade said, as he slouched in the chair across from Maggie and Kyle.

They sat perched on the edge of the couch. They had a gigantic whopper sized dilemma looming over their heads. He didn't relish the idea of breaking the news to them, but he had no other choice. They were the only ones who could convince her not to go through with it. If he asked her to contemplate ending the pregnancy, she'd toss him out on his butt. She had always dreamed of being able to have kids.

"Spill it, kid," Kyle said, folding his arms across his chest.

He slid down the chair even further, stuffing his hands in his pockets. "I...um—we."

Damn!

He was supposed to protect her, not knock her up. The new situation messed everything up. Everything they had worked so hard for would be down the drain, and he would be the one to blame. Why on earth did she have to go to the doctors on her own? But that was their fault really. They had kept the truth from her. She didn't know any better.

Kyle came over to the chair where Wade was sitting and loomed over him. "Sea nymphs got your tongue, boy?"

Wade fiddled with the coins in his pocket to try to buy himself some more time. His throat suddenly dry. "Can I have some water, please?"

How was he supposed to tell them the gig was up? Oh boy, he was toast. Totally and completely burned to a crisp. All because he couldn't control himself. The king of mercenaries ended up being just as bad as the sailors who fell victim to the sirens. If Kyle didn't kill him, the other man in her life certainly would.

And once Nerina found out, she probably wouldn't stop them from throwing him off the deepest abyss with a weight tied to him. Maggie grabbed a glass of water for him. He took a sip. It helped his throat a little but not much.

"I guess there is no other way to say it," he said, his voice squeaking as he spoke. He stopped for a moment and took another mouthful of water, swishing it around before swallowing it, trying to buy another few seconds. He looked up at Kyle, who stood unnervingly close to him, and said, "Could you, by any chance, go and sit with Maggie?" He didn't exactly want to get decked by the man.

"No! I am going to stay right here until you tell us, even if I have to wring it out of you."

Wade stood up and side-stepped by him, moving around to the back of the chair. He needed something in between them before he spilled the news. "Okay. Well, Neri is pregnant," he said, taking a few more steps away. The man looked like he was about to jump over the chair and strangle him.

Kyle's face turned beet red, and his eyes were like flames of fire. "She's what?" he roared.

He felt like he was a teenager who had just told his girlfriend's parents she was pregnant. No worse. He had just told a guardian the only news that could get them all in trouble, especially him. The man's hands started to glow, and Wade backed up until his back bumped into the wall.

Without more water, he had no hopes of diffusing the power that was about to be shot his way. He put his hands out in front of him. "Wait...wait."

Maggie walked up to her husband and put a hand on his arm. "Sweetie, let's sit down and talk. Fighting him won't change anything." They sat back on the couch.

Rescued, he slumped against the wall in relief. One bullet dodged. Now that they knew and hadn't chosen to kill him, they could help him figure out what to do about it.

"He trusted you, you know, to keep her safe." Maggie glared at him. Her hands clenched on her lap as if trying to control herself.

"I know." He hung his head in shame. "I messed up."

"You did more than mess up, kid. She was supposed to be kept in the dark until she was thirty. If anyone even gets a whiff that she's been awakened, we could have a battle on our hands," Kyle said.

"You have to keep her away from the ocean. The baby will awaken her dormant side, but the sea will be the final catalyst that sets everything in motion. We have to wait as long as possible for that to happen," Maggie warned him.

"Can't you convince her to get an abortion?"

"How can you even suggest something like that?" Maggie's voice increased an octave as she shook with rage. "Maybe I should have let my husband have his way with you." She closed her eyes and took a deep breath before opening them again. "That isn't even an option. Her life is too closely intertwined with the baby's life. If one dies, they both die. Do you even understand who she is?"

"Yes."

"Then who is she?" Maggie asked.

"She's the heart of Atlantis."

"Boy, she's the very life of Atlantis. I don't know if you even realize what a grave position you've placed us all in." Kyle's fists glowed again. Bright red-orange embers jumped between them, coming dangerously close to the magazines on the coffee table. "Mark my words. If she dies because of your carelessness, there is nowhere you can go that will be safe from me."

Wade swallowed hard. The future was about to get very interesting for them all. They had opened a can of worms, and there was no going back now. He had to figure out how to keep her out of harm's way so that the man's threats didn't come to pass.

He wasn't sure how he was going to do that. There wasn't going to be an easy way to tell her that they had to move away and leave her beloved mermaid show behind. She wasn't the type to give in willingly, but he'd throw her over his shoulder if he had to.

His loins stirred to life at the idea, and he chuckled. It definitely had some hot and sexy possibilities. Climbing in his car, he decided they would leave within the week, and he wouldn't take no for an answer.

Even if he had to do what he was first commissioned to do. Kidnap her.

Nerina sat on the couch with her legs folded underneath her, holding a cup of coffee with both hands. *You're not normal.* The words kept bouncing around in her head ever since Wade walked out.

Her eyes misted over with tears. Everyone else has said that to her but never him. He was her safe haven. The one place she could be herself and not have to hide or pretend. He had never made her feel ugly until today. Sick or not, she needed some fresh air and needed to be near the ones that made her smile. The ones who made her forget all about being different and loved her for who she was.

Standing up, she grabbed her purse and keys off the table by the door. When Nerina opened the door, someone grabbed her. She shrieked and whacked the intruder in the head with her purse. The person loosened his grip on her and stepped away, giving her a moment to look up at him.

"What the hell, Neri!" Wade groaned, rubbing the red spot on his cheek.

She whacked him again for good measure and said, "That's for telling me I'm not normal." Shoving past him, she continued down the hall to the elevator. The words he spoke previously had been burned into her mind like a cattle brand. How could he have even said something like that? It wasn't like she could help looking the way she does.

When she neared the elevator and pushed the button, she was picked up from behind and gathered into his arms like a baby. Before she knew it, they were going back down the hall towards their door.

"Heck, no. Put me down." She pushed against his chest, but he tightened his grip. When they reached their apartment door, she gripped onto the door frame, refusing to let him take her inside. "Now, Wade!"

"We need to talk," he said, trying to pry her hand off the door frame.

She smacked his hand away. "Right now, I don't want to talk. I'm heading to the aquarium. Put me down!"

He slowly set her feet on the floor but kept a firm grip on her waist. "I'm going with you."

"I don't want you to." She fought back tears as his words came back to repeatedly. Trembling, she said, "Let me go, please."

Wade dropped his hands, and she raced down the hallway. This time she took the stairs, so she didn't have to wait, knowing he would be watching her. She slammed the door open and walked into the dimly lit underground parkade.

After taking a few steps inside, she leaned over and rested her hands on her knees. He couldn't seem to understand the depth of the pain he caused her, and there wasn't even any point in trying to get him to see it. No one else lived in her shoes. No one had to live the life she was forced to be a part of.

As she walked towards the car, a stitch like pain started low in her abdomen. Rubbing the spot, she opened the car door and sat in the driver's seat. If it was not one thing, it was another. The pain made her stomach roll, and she let out a loud burp. *Second hand coffee. Yuck.*

She waited for her stomach to settle and then drove to the aquarium.

Inside a lab, across town, a small team of scientists were gawking at the data in front of them. They'd never seen anything like it before. A human, yet she wasn't.

"How is this even possible?" Jason, the youngest of the group, asked. He had recently graduated from university and was there as part of a post-doctorate program. It was just the boy's luck to be part of the group that may have possibly stumbled upon the greatest discovery in the realms of evolution.

"Gene splicing?" another suggested.

"No, I don't think so," Craig Jenson, the senior scientist, said. He pulled out his glasses and examined the paper again. The information didn't make any sense to him. "Are you sure the DNA wasn't contaminated in any way?"

"Someone has to be pulling our leg," Michael said, pulling his aging face away from the microscope in front of him.

Aside from Jason, the rest of the men had been in the field of genetics for their whole lives. Some even forty-plus years, like Craig. He was on the verge of retiring and to come across something spectacular, like the information in front of them, may have just landed him the famed Nobel Prize.

"We have to get our hands on that girl," Craig announced. "It's the only way we'll know for sure."

"I'll call the hospital and see what information they have on her." Jason jumped up and rushed into the small office off to the side of the lab.

The doctors crowded around each other. All clamoring to get another glimpse of the paper.

"She could very well be the next stage in human evolution," Craig said.

"Or one that predated modern man," Gerry commented. He'd been leaning against the wall, remaining silent through much of the exchange. "We've all heard stories of Atlantis, of when the city sunk into the depths of the ocean."

Usually, myths would be rejected, but no one reprimanded him this time. He'd always been the fanciful one, looking beyond science for answers. There was so much they didn't know about life yet, and just when they thought they were getting a handle on it, something would come and pull the rug out from under them.

If they were going to solve the puzzle of her genetics, they needed her. Craig wanted that prize, and he'd stop at nothing to get it. He wanted his name up there with the big honchos. There was no way he was going to die among the masses as a faceless scientist.

Excitement pumped through his veins. He was so close to fulfilling his dreams. He rubbed his hands together, letting out a deep chuckle. She was his ticket to the science hall of fame, and he was itching to get his hands on her. Yep, the woman was a dying man's dream come true. He limped his way over to the office. Time was of the essence. They needed that information. And he was going to get it, even if he had to break into the hospital himself.

Chapter Five

Nerina wished she could hop in the water and swim with her dolphin friends. Sadly, she was too afraid she'd puke with her upset stomach. Instead, she sat on the edge of the tank, feet dangling in the water. The dolphins swam over and laid their snouts on her thighs.

"Oh, I've missed you guys." She touched them gently on the melon, smiling. One kept clicking at her and motioning for her to jump in. "Sorry, I can't today."

Swimming with them was the highlight of her job. Nothing else even came close to how incredible it was. With being pregnant, she doubted her boss would let her get in the water with them, let alone be in the mermaid show. As much as she hated the idea of being land bound, the new life inside her came first.

This may be the only time she'd ever have a child, and she wasn't going to jeopardize the baby in any way. No matter how much the sparkling water called out to her. One of the dolphins tugged on her shirt playfully, his eyes begging her to jump in.

"I know. It's killing me, too," she said softly. Leaning back, she grabbed a ball and threw it into the water. They all swam after it, tossing it back and forth, chattering away with each other as if they didn't have a care in the world. *Lucky.* Worries of her future were prevalent in her mind at the moment.

She couldn't believe it. Here she was, pregnant, and Wade was being a cold-hearted cretin. The happiest moment of her life had been turned to utter crap by him and the doctors. Why couldn't they let her have one day where she could be on cloud nine? One day to pretend everything was normal. One dolphin appeared to sense her distress and swam over to her.

"I'm scared, Jojo," she said, letting her face rest against his snout, hugging him. She had to visit another doctor to find out exactly how bad the baby's condition was and what they could do about it.

Did the doctor mean surgery when he spoke about options? They were supposed to call her in the next day or two with the appointment time. Waiting sucked. How was she even supposed to sleep tonight?

Her shoulders cramped under the tension, making her head hurt. Nerina tilted her head to the side to stretch the muscle, and Jojo tilted his head, too. She laughed, sticking her tongue out at him, and he did it back.

"Copycat," she said, laughing. They never failed to cheer her up. But she knew she couldn't stay at the aquarium forever. She and Wade needed to talk. He needed to know about the baby's condition.

She pulled her legs out of the water and went to stand up, but her legs flopped over to the side as though she had no strength in them at all. "Help," she tried to yell, but her vocal cords wouldn't work, so it sounded more like a squeak. Her chest constricted, making it hard to breathe.

Looking down at her feet, she noticed a strange, whitish blue tinge on her toes. She reached down and touched them, squishing them like they were pure jelly. With her heart pounding, she started to pull herself to the bench where she'd placed her purse. That was when she heard his voice.

"Neri," Wade yelled.

Nothing scared Wade more than seeing her pull herself along the ground. The change was happening more quickly than he'd anticipated. Thankfully, the dolphin tank wasn't connected to the ocean, so it didn't have the full power behind it. He looked around quickly to make sure no one else was around. When he reached her, tears were flowing down her cheeks.

"What is happening to me?"

"It's all right, sweetheart." He picked her up and carried her inside the building. He grabbed a clean towel out of the cabinet and began to dry her legs.

"I think I need to go to the hospital."

"You'll be fine. Let's get you dried off, and I'll take you home."

"Are you crazy? I need a doctor. My feet are..." She paused a moment as she poked her toes and found them perfectly normal. "But they were—"

"Your feet are as gorgeous as always," he interrupted.

After putting on her sandals, she tentatively stood up, shifting her weight between each leg. "That was totally weird," she said.

"Come on, Neri. We should go." He went to take her hand, but she pulled away from him.

"I'm still mad at you." She picked up her purse and left the room, walking towards the parking lot.

Wade ran a hand through his dark hair and sighed. She wasn't going to make this easy. Not that he could blame her. He knew how insensitive he had been earlier, but her news floored him. That was why it didn't surprise him when she climbed into her car instead of coming with him.

He followed her car closely. Now, more than ever, she needed him, and he needed to convince her that it was time to leave their beloved home behind before something else happened.

"Move?" Nerina gaped at Wade. The tension in the room could have been cut with a knife. They'd barely talked for days, and now he announced they were moving. No ifs, ands or buts about it. "And you were going to discuss this with me when?" she asked with her hands on her hips.

"I'm discussing it with you now."

"No, you're telling me. Besides, I'm not well enough to move at the moment." Even now, her stomach rolled like the waves in the ocean. The fighting didn't help either. They had never fought before, and it was killing her inside. What on earth was happening to them?

Tears pricked the corner of her eyes. He had always been so nice to her. When everyone else poked fingers at her, he accepted her without question. Never even brought up the fact that she looked different in a negative way until the other day. He had torn her heart out of her chest and handed it to her on a silver platter.

"I don't want to go anywhere with you," she said adamantly.

"Why are you being so difficult?"

"Me? I come home and tell you I'm pregnant, and you take off, yelling something about me not being normal. Now, you want me to run off with you to who knows where, and leave everything I know and love behind?" Walking towards the bathroom, she glanced back over her shoulder and said, "You're a dick."

After locking the door, she sat down on the side of the bathtub, holding her queasy stomach. The last thing she wanted to do was puke again. She'd already done it twice today. Once in the morning, and again when Wade cooked hot dogs for lunch. The smell did not agree with her. Being sick was not fun, and all the strange things happening to her made it ten times worse.

She looked down at her toes that were resting on the blue bathmat and wiggled them. Turning sideways, she put one foot in the bathtub and turned on the water. The water cascaded over her foot. She waited for something to happen, but nothing did. She was beginning to wonder if she had imagined her legs turning to jelly at the aquarium. But that made no sense. The experience was far too vivid in her mind.

"Come on, you stupid thing." She shook her foot and suddenly slipped. She landed sprawled out on her back in the bathtub with one leg hanging over the edge. The water soaked through her blue jumpsuit.

Wade heard a loud thump and knocked on the locked door. "Neri, are you okay?" All he could hear was the sound of her laughing and the water running. But not just any laugh, the hysterical one where you end up hiccuping by the end of it.

Grabbing a toothpick, he picked the lock and walked in to find her still sprawled in the tub. His lips curled into a grin, and he burst out laughing. Reaching into his pocket, he grabbed his phone.

"Don't you—hiccup—dare," she said, scrambling to get out of the tub, but it was too late. He'd already snapped the photo and rushed out of the room.

They squared off in the kitchen. Him on one side of the table, and her on the other. "One more step and I click send," he threatened, smirking. The world wide web was just a quick click away.

"Don't..." She tried to speak, but a hiccup got in the way.

He couldn't help but double over in another fit of laughter. "You sound like a mouse."

She picked up a paper towel roll off the table and threw it at him. "You are—hiccup—so mean," she said, sticking her tongue out at him. With a flip of her hair, she turned and walked away from him. Her clothes stuck to her butt in a very alluring manner as her hips swung from side to side.

He tilted his head, watching her as she crossed the living room. Desire shot through his body, lighting a fire inside him that had not been quenched in far too long. What would she do if he went over there and peeled each layer of clothing off her wet, sexy body?

No.

There were far more important matters to discuss than his wacko Neri-crazy hormones. The topics of discussion were nowhere near as much fun as making love to his incredibly hot wife, but it needed to be done. So, he sat there at the table, waiting for her to come out.

When she didn't come out, he went into the bedroom and found her bent over, searching the bottom drawer for something to wear. He swallowed hard as his gaze drifted down to her bare behind. His friend hardened at the sight of her. He reached down and adjusted himself.

Focus, man, focus.

And he focused all right. Focused on the wrong thing or maybe the right one, depending on how one looked at it. Walking up behind her, he slid his hands around her waist. "This has possibilities, you know," he said, slowly rubbing up against her delectable body.

"Wade, we..." She stopped talking and moaned softly when he reached down between her legs, rubbing her with his thumb.

"Later," he said, nuzzling her neck.

Her legs buckled under his touch. He picked her up, carrying her to the bed. This was more like it. No arguing or fighting. Just the two of them together in every way that counts.

He brushed her hair away from her breasts and kissed them, caressing them gently with his tongue. Nothing else mattered. Not his mission. Nothing. Just her beneath him, responding to his touch. She arched her back as he drew circles on her belly with his tongue, making his way down to the spot that was his and his alone. His hand reached there first. She was wet and ready, causing him to harden even more.

"You're such a siren," he murmured, burying his face between her thighs.

Her thigh muscles tensed, and she pulled away from him. Knowing he somehow messed everything up, Wade covered his head with the sheets and groaned. His body needed release, but that definitely wasn't happening now.

"We need to talk," she said, sitting on the edge of the bed.

"Fine," he muttered. "Just let me have a cold shower first."

When he stood up and turned away from her, she grabbed his arm. "No, we'll talk now."

Spinning around to face her, his erection bounced dangerously close to her mouth. "Unless you wanna finish me off, I need a few minutes to refocus."

Desire flared in her eyes, and she licked her lips. It almost looked like she was contemplating it. Sadly, the look quickly disappeared, and she glared up at him, pushing him away from her. "Don't be long."

Damn, he was so close!

Chapter Six

Long after the sun went down, three dark-clothed men hid in the shadows outside of SeaWorld. They watched as the security guard walked by the entrance, shining his flashlight through the gate. They had scoped the place out carefully over the last few weeks. And with the help of their inside man, they knew where to go to get the information they were looking for.

"All clear," a deep voice boomed into their earpiece. "Go."

That meant their buddy in the Security Room had temporarily disabled the cameras, giving them the freedom to finish their task. There were three other guards patrolling, who were none the wiser. They had twenty minutes before those guards made it back to the Security Room for the switch.

The smallest of the three intruders tossed their grappling hook and scaled to the top of the wall, motioning his friends to follow. Landing quietly inside, they rushed across the courtyard and around the side of a building to the employee entrance.

The largest man of the group whispered into his lapel, "We're here." His dark turtle-neck sweater looked ready to pop as his biceps flexed in anticipation.

The other two scanned the area, keeping a lookout while they waited. Soon, the door cracked open, and light lit up the area where they were standing. The guard stepped to the side to let them in.

"Hurry up." The big guy shoved his buddies inside and quickly followed behind them.

"You have fifteen minutes to get in and get out. Once you're finished, I want you to leave me and my family alone. I'm done," the guard, Sean, said, running a hand through his dark brown hair. He was tired of getting caught in their tangled mercenary web.

But they kept threatening to turn the rest of his family into outcasts if he didn't go along with their schemes. His parents were getting old now, and he didn't want them to have to face a whole new world.

When the news got out that the Spirit Daughter of the Albions, the life givers, worked at the aquarium, they came at him with their ultimatums all over again. The leader of the Outcasts had attended the park a few months back with his daughter and saw her. That was when the caca hit the fan.

He hung back and watched as the hooded men ransacked the Human Resource office, searching for her personal information. Glancing at his watch, he said, "Five minutes left. You guys have to get going."

"Not till we get what we came for," Moose said.

"You're going to get caught if you don't go now." He tapped his foot on the ground, his heart racing.

"So what?" Moose lifted his black sweater, revealing a gun sitting in the waistband of his pants.

Oh crap!

What on god's green earth had he gotten himself into? He should have known they wouldn't care if someone ended up getting hurt. And if by some chance he made it out alive, they would pin whatever they did on him anyway. He didn't think this job through thoroughly.

"Come on, Moose. You said no one would get hurt," he complained.

"Well, then"—he pointed to a cabinet on the wall—"help us."

"Eureka," the third guy said, waving a folder over his head. He was the tall beanpole of the group, standing a head taller than the rest of them.

Moose snatched the folder out of his hand and stuffed it in the waistband of his pants next to the gun before turning to Sean. "Last chance to come with us?"

"No, thank you."

"Suit yourself," Moose responded.

Sean watched the men walk down the hall to the employee entrance. When they opened it, there was a guard on the other side about to swipe his access card. The guard's eyes widened, and he reached for his gun, but it was too late.

Moose had already fired, hitting him between the eyes.

The radio was playing quietly in the background as they sat across the kitchen table from each other, neither saying a word. Wade sat slouched in his seat, strumming his fingers on the table. Nerina had her hands wrapped around another glass of water, staring at the fruit basket sitting in the middle.

"When I went to the doctors, he said that the baby..." She closed her mouth when he cringed upon hearing the word, her eyes narrowing. "What's up with you?"

Staring at the ground, he said, "Nothing."

She banged the table, making him jump. "Don't lie to me." They've never had secrets before, and she wasn't going to let him start now.

He sat up a little straighter and looked at her. His expression was blank of emotion, like a veil had been placed over his eyes. She couldn't tell what was going inside that head of his. In a way, she was afraid to find out. What if he didn't want the baby?

A shiver rippled down her spine, and her stomach twisted in

knots. "The baby has a condition called Sirenomelia," she said carefully, gauging his reaction.

His shoulders stiffened, his hand clenched into a fist and then nothing. She thought she saw fear in his eyes, but he quickly masked it, and she was stone-walled again. It was like he was becoming a guy she didn't know anymore.

"We have an appointment to visit another doctor to discuss what our options are." She picked at a thread on her pink unicorn t-shirt, not wanting to look at him anymore.

The chair fell over as he scrambled away from the table. "No, you can't."

He paced the room, muttering away to himself. Suddenly, the current song on the radio stopped for an important news bulletin.

"A security guard was shot during a break-in attempt at SeaWorld. The police and paramedics are on site. We will provide you with more information as it becomes available."

Wade frantically looked around the room, pulling at his hair. "We have to go. We have to go now." Grabbing her by the arm, he pulled her into the bedroom and took their suitcases out of the closet.

"Hold on. What are you talking about?" Nerina grabbed his shirt, pulling him down on the bed. There was no way she was going anywhere until he explained what was going on.

"We don't have time for this. They could be here any second," he said, standing back up and returning to the task at hand. "Go and pack our travel bag."

"Why? What's going on?"

Her mouth went dry when he looked at her. Darkness emanated from his eyes, as though a thunder cloud had converged inside them. She wasn't sure if she imagined it or if another soul was looking at her in that moment. The temperature in the room suddenly dipped, causing her to wrap her arms around herself. She shivered violently, and the hair on her arms stood on end.

He quickly turned away. "I don't have time to explain. Just go pack."

"No! I'm not going anywhere with you." She rushed out of the room, grabbed her keys, and took off down the hall in her bare feet.

Wade heard the front door slam. "Oh hell! Not again." He was about to take off after her when the phone rang. "What?" he snapped.

"You need to go now," Kyle ordered.

"Tell me something I don't know," he said breathlessly, running down the hallway after his run-away wife. Wasn't this supposed to happen at the wedding and not after?

"Tell me you have everything under control."

"I would if I could, but I can't," he mumbled. "I gotta go." He let out a long noisy breath as he reached the door to the parkade, shoving it open. Nerina was already on the other side of the parking lot, almost at her car.

"Neri, wait!" he shouted, his voice echoing all around him. The last thing he needed was to spend the night looking for her when everyone else was, too. The shooting at the aquarium could have been random or the work of an environmental extremist group, but he didn't think so. The timing was too coincidental.

He had allowed himself to get too close to her, and even helped her when she wanted to start up the mermaid show at the aquarium. He'd been so stupid. If anyone had him wrapped around their little finger, it was her. Her bright, turquoise-colored eyes had ways of making him do things just by looking at him. He loved her smile, her sensuous side, everything. It made him want to have his wicked way with her whenever they were together.

He smacked his forehead and shook his head as he ran towards the car. No time for those thoughts now. "Nerina, stop!"

She turned and looked at him. "Just leave me alone," she said, and with that she climbed in the car and shut the door.

He reached for the handle and tried to open it, but she quickly pressed the automatic lock. Leaning his head against the window, he groaned, "Come on, let me in."

She rolled the window down half an inch. "You might want to move. I'm about to back up."

"Please don't do this. We need to stay together."

"When you get *yourself* together, you know where to find me." The car engine revved, and she put the car in reverse.

The vehicle jerked backwards, and he jumped away from the exterior to avoid having his toes crunched by the tires. "Stubborn, pigheaded woman."

Rubbing the tension out of his neck, he made his way back inside to finish packing. He'd wasted enough time. It wouldn't be much longer before the assailants found their way to the apartment. Hopefully, Nerina would be smart enough to go to her parents' place.

"Don't let him in," Nerina begged, placing herself between her parents and the door.

"He's involved now whether you like it or not," Kyle said, opening the door, much to her displeasure.

"Daddy," she whined.

"Don't take that tone with me, young lady. This is my house. I decide who to let in that door, not you," he said sternly.

She flopped down on the couch, pouting. When she arrived, she told them all about his bizarre behavior, and they didn't bat an eyelash, which puzzled her even more. In fact, they seemed surprised by her arrival completely and wondered where Wade was.

"Darling, would you be able to go into the other room? Your dad and I need to speak with Wade alone."

She eyed them curiously. There were quick unspoken glances between the three of them. "Why are you guys acting so weird?"

"Do what your mother says," her dad said.

Every muscle in her body tensed, and heat rushed to her face. "Stop talking to me like I'm a child."

"If you were a child, we wouldn't be in this mess to start with because you'd still be living in my house. Now, do what your mother says and go to the other room," her dad repeated.

Stomping her feet, she made her way into her old bedroom. Everything was still the same as it was the day she left. Posters of world-famous mermaids, like Hannah Fraser and Mermaid Melissa, were all over the wall, as well as dolphins and other marine life. Some kids loved rock bands. She loved any mythology related to the ocean.

On her headboard sat every single mermaid movie ever made. She may have been a little obsessed with it all. Smiling, she flopped back onto the bed, and her head sunk into the body sized pillow, as she reminisced over her teenage years. Those were simpler days, and yet complicated all at the same time. Simple in the fact that she didn't have to worry about adult things, but she'd never forget the trouble that the kids gave her.

"It's a Walker. Don't let her bite you."

"It's a ghost, run!"

"I thought vampires only came out at night."

All the taunting and teasing made her hide in the far corner of the library during lunch, which happened to be where the mythology section was, along with books about the ocean. She had devoured everything she could on the two topics and loved every second of it.

After school, she'd go home and tell her mom all about it. Now that she thought about it, her mother had never said anything more than 'oh ya' or 'really.' They never had any deep discussions about it.

Returning to the present moment, she could hear their hushed voices beyond the walls of the bedroom. Getting up, she tiptoed to the door and opened it slightly. They were too engrossed in the conversation to hear the slight click of the handle. She sighed in relief and then slapped a hand over her mouth.

"Take her to the safe house," Kyle said to Wade.

"Are you guys coming?" he asked.

Kyle handed what looked like a key to her husband. "We'll follow behind you shortly. First, we have to make sure that her father is apprised of the situation."

Her father? Nerina backed away from the door, shaking like a leaf. Her throat constricted, making it hard to breathe. No. It wasn't possible. It couldn't be. Her stomach jumped into her chest, and she flung the door open, racing to the bathroom.

Making a beeline for the toilet, she fell to her knees in front of it. Tears flowed down her cheeks in endless rivers as she retched into the bowl. She couldn't believe it. How could they have lied to her all these years? Who was she? Who were they?

There was only one thing she knew for certain. The man sitting in the other room was not her dad.

Chapter Seven

Nerina heard them coming down the hall and slammed the door shut, turning the lock. She didn't want to see them, didn't want to hear any of the lies they would inevitably come up with.

Sliding down the door, she pulled her knees close to her chest and wrapped her arms around them. A loud cry ripped from her mouth, her shoulders shaking. It wasn't fair. They had all lied to her, even Wade. He knew and didn't tell her.

"Honey, please open the door," her mom said softly.

"Go away," she cried, hugging her knees even harder. Looking up, she saw the window above the toilet shining like a halo. She needed to go somewhere to think, to be anywhere but here.

"Open the door, Nerina," Kyle, her *fake* father, said. He was a fraud. A phony. Standing up, she used her sleeve to wipe the tears away. The window wasn't overly big, but she could squeeze her small frame through it.

Flipping the latch, she pushed open the window. She was on the first floor, so it was only five feet above the ground. Slipping through, she gently lowered herself to the ground and rushed along the side of the house to the gate. When she rounded the corner, something snagged her arm. Before she knew it, she was pulled against a warm, hard body.

"Somehow I knew you'd try something like this," Wade said, giving her his all-knowing, annoying smirk.

"Let me go." She squirmed to break free of his grasp, but to no avail. He started to direct her back towards the house. Digging her feet into the ground, she pleaded, "No, you can't make me go back in there. Please."

"Sorry, you need to talk with them." He continued to maneuver her towards the front door.

With all the strength she could muster, she turned and kicked him in the shin. Violence seemed to be taking root inside her, and she hated it with a passion, but she was her own person and would make her own decisions. If she didn't want to go back in the house, she wasn't going to go.

He let go of her arm and grabbed his shin, jumping up and down on his other leg. "You little..."

She didn't stick around to find out what the last word was going to be. She was already out on the sidewalk, hightailing it down the block. A sharp pain in her lower abdomen brought her to a halt, making her duck around the side of the nearest house.

She leaned against the building and held her stomach, waiting for the pain to subside. Was it supposed to hurt like that? She knew next to nothing about being pregnant, but she knew that worrying and stressing wasn't too healthy for the baby. There had to be a place she could go to lay low for a while, so she could sort out the thoughts that were running through her mind like a freight train. Pulling out her phone, she dialed Jenny's number.

"Hey, girl! What's up?" Jenny answered.

"I need you to pick me up," she whispered into the phone, acutely aware that Wade was limping down the street looking for her. Ducking behind a large green shrub next to her, she watched as he looked around.

"Where are you?" her friend asked.

"I'm at the blue house just a couple doors down from my parents." Nerina peeked out from behind the bush and found Wade staring at her hiding spot. "Crap. Hurry, please!" she begged, pressing her back against the side of the house.

"Be there as soon as I can."

She hung up the phone and stuffed it back in her pocket, wiping her sweaty palms on her pants. Her friend's house was at least twenty minutes away, and the odds of her remaining hidden until she arrived decreased significantly with each passing second.

"Nerina, I know you're still here. I can feel you."

"I can still feel you, too, Mr. Nincompoop," she mumbled under her breath. It was like their own personal radar. Something she'd never been able to understand. There was no playing hide and seek with a man who could sense her. If she stayed there much longer, he'd find her. She knew all he had to do was close his eyes and concentrate. Some type of psychic mumbo jumbo. If only she knew how to turn it off, then she'd be able to hide from him indefinitely.

Wade ran a hand through his jet-black hair and glanced around him. He could only begin to imagine what was going through her mind right now. Fear, anger and uncertainty were all rolled into one no doubt. Her eyes had displayed each one when he held her briefly, just before she decorated his shin with a deep shade of purple and blue. His leg still throbbed from the unwanted attention.

There was no protecting her from the pain that would follow in the days ahead, but he could at least protect her physically. He let out a hard laugh. It might be him that needed protecting by the end of all this if he couldn't keep his flighty wife by his side.

If anything happened to her, he'd have not only the Outcasts after him, but the entire royal forces of Atlantis, too. He'd wind up having to live out his days hiding in a cave, like a hermit, only coming out for food and water. His life would be like that reality show, Mountain Men. He shuddered.

Closing his eyes, he slowly took a deep breath in and held it for five seconds before letting it back out. Repeating the steps again and again until her image began to take shape in his mind. Well, not an image really, more like energy—her life force. Their souls were entwined together forever. Humans had no clue what it meant to be a true soulmate, to become one with another beyond the physical plane.

Most people believed that sex was the most intimate way to connect with someone else. For the two of them, they connected on a deeper more spiritual level. Their souls were joined in ways that he hadn't ever imagined before.

He'd had sex with others, and it was nice, but nothing had ever enveloped him so completely as her spirit did when they were together. Sex was just the icing on the cake and damn addicting.

Shaking his head, he returned to the task at hand. Turning around slowly, he waited until her image grew brighter. When he opened his eyes, he was facing the blue two-story house again. There weren't too many places to hide, except a few green privacy shrubs on each side of the house.

On one side, there were two shrubs, separated by a gate which led into the backyard. On the other side sat a lonely green shrub. He didn't think she'd actually enter another person's yard, especially one with a beware of dog sign on the gate, so he limped towards the large green shrub on the west side of the house.

Sighing, Nerina blew a tuft of hair out of her face. The gig was up, and she knew it. When she chose to hide behind the bush, it was a spur of the moment decision. Now she was cornered. The only thing left to do would be to hop over the fence, but where could she go from there?

Her body tensed when he approached the other side of the shrub. She'd give anything to be able to go invisible right about now. That was the one superpower she itched to have in moments like these, to not be found unless she wanted to be.

"Come out, Neri. I know you're back there."

Crouching behind the bush, she held her position, bringing her hands up to her face, palms out. He came around the bush, stopping right in front of her. His eyes narrowed, and his lips curled down into a frown.

Scratching his head, his eyes scanned the immediate area. What was he waiting for? Why wasn't he hauling her up and taking her back to the house? She was right there.

"Damn. I could have sworn..." He stopped talking when her foot hit a twig, snapping it in two. "Oh, don't tell me..." Reaching down, his hand landed on her head. Suddenly she appeared in front of him, kneeling. "I knew it! You learn fast, kid."

"I'm not a kid." Dropping her hands, she lifted her chin and rose to her full height of five feet four inches. The top of her head reached to just below his nose.

"No, you are all woman!" he said, as his gaze traveled down the length of her body.

She took a step away from him, her back pressing against the house. He took a step towards her and rested his right hand against the wall, cupping her chin with the other. Placing a leg between hers, she was firmly wedged between him and the building. His thumb caressed her jaw line. Finding herself leaning into his touch, she placed her hands on his chest. His heart raced beneath her touch with a tempo that matched her own.

"Wade, I..." Their eyes met, and Nerina lost track of what she was going to say. His desire laced eyes made her heart skip a beat. He gave her a crooked grin before brushing his lips against hers. She wanted to stay mad at him, but his warm, moist lips against hers felt so much better than being angry.

Desire pooled in her belly. Her hands, through no volition of her own, slid up behind his neck, pulling him closer. Her body went into overdrive as his tongue traced her lips, encouraging her to open.

She wanted this, needed this. The feel of his hands against her skin awoke every nerve in her body. There was an unbridled passion that always burned beneath the surface whenever they were together, and it consumed every part of her.

His hands slid beneath her shirt. She moaned softly when they made contact with her bare skin. He buried his face against her neck. The heady scent of his sea breeze aftershave made her smile. He was the man she had always dreamed about before they met, literally. But the strange part was that he was a man without a face. Everyone else in her dreams had a face, except him. And his scent had always lingered in her room long after she awoke.

Despite never seeing his face, she knew it was him the moment they had met. The sweet salty smell had engulfed her senses. She could remember thinking he must have just gone for a swim because they'd met on Coronado Beach.

Even now, his wonderful smell wrapped around her, like a cocoon. She breathed in deeply and sighed. His hands caressed her breasts, her nipples hardening under his touch. All her frustrations melted away until they were nothing more than a whisper in the wind.

Reaching down, she let her hand brush the bulge in his pants. He groaned as she gently squeezed him. "Careful, girl. You're playing with fire."

"Got anymore matches," she asked slyly, slowly undoing his belt.

"You're going to be the end of me." Wade said, leaning his forehead against hers. He wanted to do this as they hadn't been able to do it for so long. However, they were right in front of a window, and he wasn't an exhibitionist. She wasn't either. "We have to stop."

For the last couple weeks, she was the one to halt sexual intimacy between them with all her visits to the porcelain god. Now, she was all over him, and he was the one stopping it. He wanted to kick himself in the ass, but there was a time and a place for everything. Once he got her to the safe house, they could have their fun.

"I don't want to stop," she said, pressing her lips against his collarbone. His arousal throbbed with such intensity he had no choice but to take a step away from her. The wanton look in her eyes almost made him lose what was remaining of his control.

Taking a deep breath, he tried to think of everything but her, which was kind of hard to do with her standing right there. He closed his eyes and thought of mathematical questions. When he opened them, she was still staring at him intently, biting her bottom lip. Where was a cold shower when you needed one?

Chapter Eight

"Neri," a female voice called.

If there ever was an ice-bucket challenge, this was it. Wade leaned his head forward and pinched the bridge of his nose.

"You had to go and call her, didn't you?" he grumbled.

Standing on the sidewalk was the woman from work who hated him with a passion. Jenny's red hair was as fiery as her temper, which she'd directed at him more times than he could count. Dressed in an emerald-green jogging suit and white sneakers, she ran over to them.

"What did the dolt do now?" Jenny asked, completely ignoring him.

He never understood what her issue was with him. Waving at her, he said, "The dolt is standing right here."

Without even an acknowledgement, she took his wife's hand and proceeded to walk with her to the car. The lady had some nerve ignoring him.

"Sorry, but I don't think so." He grabbed Nerina's arm and pulled them both to a halt. "She's coming with me."

Jenny glared at him. "She called me to come get her, and that's exactly what I'm doing."

"Over my dead body," he snapped, pulling her towards the house, while her friend tried to pull her towards the car.

"I'm not a wishbone, people." Nerina yanked her arms away from them, swaying slightly. "Excuse me." Clamping a hand over her mouth, she frantically looked around and then ducked behind the shrub.

Jenny rushed to Nerina's side and pulled her hair back out of her face, rubbing her back. "Now look what you've done," Jenny said, her eyes shooting flaming darts in his direction.

"Me." Wade bumped the woman to the side and held his wife's hair while she continued to retch. "We were doing fine until you showed up."

"Would you"—Nerina was interrupted by yet another gut-wrenching heave—"both shut up."

She didn't want them to fight. In fact, all she wanted right now was to be left alone. When Jenny arrived and Wade pulled away from her, all the issues and struggles of the day came flooding back. Only one memory remained. Her dad wasn't her dad. Did that mean that her mom...

No!

She didn't even want to consider the possibility she didn't belong to either of them. Resting one arm against the blue wood-paneled house, she took a few deep breaths. Her stomach finally appeared to be calming down again. Standing up, she turned and looked at them. They looked like they were in a Mexican stand-off, ready to draw their guns.

She placed her hands on her hips. "If anyone has a right to be angry here, it's me." Turning to Jenny, she said, "I'll meet you at the car."

With a fragrant flip of her long, dark red hair, Jenny threw Wade a smirk before strolling back to the car. He stepped in between them, blocking Nerina's exit.

"Please move," she begged. The last thing she needed was for him to fight her on this. She needed a single night away to sort out the thoughts in her mind and couldn't do that around him or her family.

"I can't do that."

She approached him and laid a hand on his chest. "Look, I know I can't avoid the situation forever, but I need some time to think."

"Time is something we don't have."

"It's not like someone is gonna jump out of the bushes and grab me, geez. I'm just going to her house and stay there for the night."

Begrudgingly, with his fists clenched at his sides, he stepped out of her way. As she went to walk by, he grabbed her arm again. "Stay inside the house. Don't go anywhere. Do you understand?"

"Yes, master!" she said, bowing.

He took her by the shoulders, his gaze intensely burrowing into hers. "Nerina Douglas, I'm not joking. You are in danger. Promise me you will stay inside," he said, his grip tightening on her shoulders.

She swallowed hard. "Okay, I promise."

Ducking, she slipped out of his grasp and rushed towards the car. By the time she reached the car door, her body was shaking uncontrollably. She didn't understand what was going on, but something was definitely in the air. A deep, dark sense of foreboding wrapped itself around her spirit as they drove away. She could only hope Wade was overreacting, but she had a feeling he wasn't.

When Craig's group finally managed to get Nerina's address, he immediately sent the guys down to her place. The research was at a standstill without her. He was sitting in the lounge with a newspaper when they returned, empty-handed. "No luck?" he asked, frowning.

"Nope," Jason replied, plopping himself down on the couch. "We waited outside for hours, but they never came home."

Tom paced the length of the room, chewing on his nails. "There were some other weird people there, too."

The new information made him sit up and take notice. "Other

people are looking for her?" That wasn't a good sign. There was no way he was going to let another group swoop in and scoop his discovery. "Jason, go back to the house. Take Tom with you. Stay there until they come back."

"Awesome! surveillance duties." The youngster grinned. "This is just like the movies."

"Well, boy, if you find her, you can bet Hollywood will want full dips on the movie rights. You can be their star," he said as his stomach rumbled, reminding him he hadn't eaten all day. "I'm closing up for the night. Let me know if you find anything."

"Will do, boss," the two men said in unison. They sauntered off towards the parking lot, eager to return to the house.

"How could you let her go?" Kyle's eyes glowed red with anger, literally.

Wade had returned to the house to let them know what was going on, and now he found himself backed into the corner again with the man's volcanic like temper. He held his hands up in surrender. "Don't worry. I plan to camp outside of the house. All night if I have to."

"Honey, we don't have time to battle him over this. We have to go," Maggie said, walking into the room.

"Keep her safe. Or so help me, I will hunt you down, and no one will be able to find a single body part of yours by the time I'm done with you."

Frustration coursed through him, and he walked right up to Kyle, looking him square in the face. "Regardless of what you guys think, I would die for her and not because of some lame-ass command from the king, either. I love her. She means everything to me."

Maggie stepped between them, wagging her index fingers at them. "If you boys dare mess up my house, you two will be the ones that go missing."

Kyle smirked, giving his wife a kiss on the forehead. His gaze was still on Wade. "Go, watch over your wife. We'll meet you at the cabin in three days."

He was more than happy to oblige and quickly left the house. Jenny had a small one-story house in a quiet cul-de-sac, not too far away from their apartment. That was one of the reasons he wasn't too fond of the idea of her going there. They needed to be as far away from the area as they could get, but no, he'd been a pushover as usual.

His soft spot for Neri was going to be a huge problem if he didn't reel it in somehow. There was something electrifying and captivating about her eyes and her smile. It roped him in every time. Not anymore, though. They couldn't afford it. Her life was in danger. He could feel it in his bones.

Screeching his tires, he pulled away from the curb and high tailed it to his house and packed a suitcase. Once he was done, he got back in his car and started the drive to Jenny's place. The sooner he was there, the better.

Twenty minutes later, he parked near the opening of the cul-de-sac, so he could see everything, but they couldn't see him. His bold little spitfire would give him an earful if she knew where he was. Looking over, he saw Jenny's white Nissan parked in the driveway. Everything looked quiet in the neighborhood, and he hoped it would stay that way.

No one from his old life knew about Jenny that he was aware of, but there was something about her that rubbed him the wrong way. When the girl became the make-up artist and hair stylist for the mermaid show, she stuck to Neri like glue from the very beginning. When he tried to talk to his wife about it, she shut him down completely and called him paranoid.

There were times Jenny would stop everything she was doing just to cater to her, and his wife lapped it up like a thirsty kitten. She could be so naïve about people that it drove him insane. How could Jenny, who was only twenty-one years old, own her own house already and not even be married? It wasn't like she made a hundred grand a year being a stylist for the show.

His eyes glanced up at the horizon. The sun was setting, decorating the sky in an assortment of red and orange hues, reminding him to pay even more attention as the light faded around him.

He cracked his window down a shade and heard a siren go whizzing by on the street behind him. A whiff of smoke filled his nostrils. Coughing, he pressed his nose against his sleeve and rolled up the window, not that it helped. The bittersweet rubbery smell lingered inside the car.

Staying awake to monitor the neighborhood was going to be a challenge. Nerina's little escapade the night before left him with little sleep. His bones ached, and his eyes, well, needless to say, he could do with some toothpicks to keep them open. If he got worse, he would have to pop into the twenty-four-hour convenience store on the corner and grab an energy drink.

For now, the tall cup of joe sitting in his drink holder should keep him going for a little while. He had no intention of falling asleep. But you know what they say, the road to hell is paved with good intentions.

A few hours later, his eyelids started to droop until a light in the rear-view mirror caught his attention. He looked over his shoulder and watched as a dark-colored van turned into the cul-de-sac, pulling to a stop a few car lengths behind him.

Three men climbed out of the vehicle and walked towards the house under his watch. They were dressed in t-shirts and jeans, so it didn't look like they had any malicious intentions. When they walked by his car, the gait of the well-built guy looked familiar.

Squinting his eyes, he tried to get a look at the man's face, but it was too dark to see anything more than a faint outline of his profile. The two burned-out lights on the street didn't help the situation any. Granted, it worked in his favor too. They didn't notice him sitting there. He heard a door slam, and the lights of a car in the driveway in front of him came on, illuminating the three men as they continued to approach the house.

"Oh, hell no!"

Regardless of whether Nerina would hate him for spying on her, he pulled out his phone and called her.

"Geez, Wade. Can't you give me just one night?"

"Three guys are coming to the door. Don't answer it!"

"What? How do you..." She stopped talking when the doorbell rang in the background. Her voice rose an octave when she said, "Are you spying on me?"

He cringed and pulled the phone away from his ear. "Be mad at me later. Whatever you do, don't answer the door. I want you to listen to me very carefully. You both need to go out the back door right now."

"Give me the loser." He heard Jenny say.

"Look, she doesn't want to talk to you. Now leave her alone," her friend hissed into the phone. "We have guests coming,"

"Don't let them in!" When she didn't respond, the sinking feeling in his gut grew into a black hole, threatening to swallow him whole. "Jenny? Jenny? Do you hear me?"

There was a click, followed by dead air.

Chapter Nine

Back at Nerina's apartment, smoke pummeled into the dark sky. The sparks from the flames lit up the surrounding area like a massive fireworks display. Flames had engulfed the entire third floor of the building. Firefighters struggled to get control of the fire, trying to prevent it from jumping to the next building. A few of the men dedicated themselves to dousing the surrounding buildings with water.

Crowds of people stood on the opposite side of the street. Some were in their pajamas and wearing housecoats. Others were in their street clothes. There was a young woman who had a child perched on each hip and another hugging her legs. All three of the children were wailing loud enough to wake the neighborhood.

Jason watched as a firefighter scaled a ladder to reach a man that was waving his arms from his third story balcony, flames dancing dangerously behind him. A spark landed on his sleeve, and the man panicked, causing him to crash into the balcony railing and tumbling headfirst over it.

The crowd gasped as the man fell to the ground, landing awkwardly in the bushy shrubs that lined the front of the building. Two firefighters ran over to him and pulled him to safety just as a portion of the roof collapsed, landing in the exact same spot. News crews arrived on site and were setting up their cameras to film the action.

"We should go," Tom said, sitting on his hands.

"Just hang tight. I'm going to see if she's here." He climbed out of the car and started walking towards the solemn crowd. The smoke-filled air clogged his airway. He brought his hand up, covering the lower half of his face. His eyes stung as he wandered closer to the group.

There was a plump, gray-haired woman sitting on the seat of a walker, talking on her cellphone. "Yes, dear. I'm fine." She paused a moment, apparently listening to what the speaker was saying. "Thank you. I'll see you soon."

"Excuse me, ma'am."

She looked up at him, giving him a lopsided smile that didn't reach her eyes—one of which had a cloudy look. "It's sad. I've lived here for thirty years."

"So, you'd know everyone who lives in the building then?"

"I was the first tenant that ever moved in." She pointed a crooked finger to the corner unit on the first floor. "That's mine. The nicest gentleman used to live across from me. Mark...Mike...Matthew." She went silent for a moment before clapping her wrinkle-skinned hands together. "No—Martin. That's it. I remember now. Oh, he had a gentle soul. Very sweet.

"Cool. I was wondering if you know a girl named Nerina?"

The elderly woman pulled at the hairs on her chin and then shook her head. "No, can't say that I do. If you are looking for a girl, the one with the three kids is single. She could use a strapping young lad like yourself to make a good, honest woman out of her."

"Thanks, but no, thank you," he responded politely. "I'm looking for a specific girl. She might be a little out of the ordinary."

"A strange, sweet kid moved in upstairs a while back, but she's taken I'm afraid."

That perked his interest. "Can you tell me what was so strange about her?"

"You know, I could never understand why young people want to dye their hair white. It goes gray soon enough," she said, shaking her head.

"Her hair's white?"

"White and blue last I saw. She's a tiny wisp of a thing, too, and always so pale. I..." The woman hunched over, hacking up a storm. "Sorry, dear. My lungs and smoke don't mix."

He nodded at her, scanning the crowd for anyone who had that description. The closest person to fit that description was the woman crazy enough to have three kids. But even then, her hair was blond, not white. The old woman gripped his arm as she started wheezing. Her face pale.

"Hey, sir." He waved over a firefighter. "She needs oxygen."

The firefighter nodded his head and hurried towards an ambulance attendant. Jason looked around and noticed that the block had filled with even more people, but none of them fit her profile. *That would be too easy.* He rolled his eyes. After climbing back into the car, he grabbed a towel from his bag and wiped his burning, watery eyes.

"Any luck?" Tom asked.

That depended on how you defined lucky. He had found out a few unique details about her, but they still didn't know where she was. Craig wanted them to wait around until she came back, but even his chest had tightened from all the smoke, and his partner didn't seem too eager to stick around.

"She's not here, but a lady told me that the girl we are looking for has pale skin and white-blue hair," Jason said.

"Albino?"

"That's what I thought at first, but her blood work doesn't fit the profile."

"Does anything though?"

The man was right. Her DNA had left them completely baffled.

Not just because of the extra strand, but because it was changing before their very eyes, intertwining itself with the other two strands. The hostile strand was quite marine-like in nature, making the increasing oxygen-processing gene count all the more intriguing.

She was a walking universal wonder—a superhuman. She could even be an alien for all they knew. The possibilities were endless, and each one more exciting than the last. He couldn't wait to meet her. Hopefully, she wouldn't turn him into a frog.

"Jenny, hold up," Nerina said, finding herself—yet again—between someone and a door. This was becoming a habit.

"Not you, too! Your husband has made you paranoid," she said, rolling her eyes.

That part was true. The look in Wade's eyes earlier triggered her fight and flight response. She'd spent the last few hours jumping at almost every sound, from the fridge turning on to the clink of a glass being put down on the table.

Darn him.

"You need some fun tonight, and I intend to make sure you get it." With that, her friend stepped by her and pulled open the door. "Hi, Ash..." Jenny started to say, turning to greet the visitors, but her voice trailed off as soon as she came face to face with them. "Wait, you aren't Asher."

"Nope."

Nerina swallowed hard as she stared at the man filling the doorway. His biceps flexed slightly, veins popping out everywhere. His t-shirt left little to the imagination as his six-pack made it look like a chain-link fence was hidden beneath his attire.

There was a tall, skinny guy behind him, who was looking down at the ground, and another person who looked like a shrimp in comparison. Her stomach churned at the thought of seafood. Or maybe it was because of the men standing in front of them.

"You aren't selling anything, are you?" Jenny asked.

"No, our van broke down. We were wondering if we could use your phone?" the burly guy asked. "Nimrod here stepped on the only cellphone we had." He pointed to the smallest guy in their group.

The short guy's jaw dropped open. "What on earth are you talking—"

The big guy elbowed him in the chest, silencing him. The murderous look he gave him made a chill rip through Nerina. Maybe Wade was right, and they should have ducked out the back. Or, at the very least, they shouldn't have answered the door. If these men tried anything, they wouldn't be able to defend themselves.

But now, with the door open, it was rude to not help someone in need. She turned to look at Jenny to see what she wanted to do with the visitors and found her eyeing the tall guy in the back.

"Wait! Aren't you the guy that bought me that drink earlier?"

His cheeks reddened when the other two men looked at him. "I, uh—ya," he stammered, shrugging his shoulders.

"I knew it." She smacked her leg, laughing. "What a small world. Come in, come in."

"Hang on a second," Nerina said to the men, pulling her friend to the side. "I'm not sure that's a good idea. Can't you just hand them your phone, and they can call from outside?" The warning her husband gave her a few moments ago weighed heavily on her chest.

"Oh, come on, girl. Live a little. Besides, he's harmless." She motioned for the men to come inside.

Where was her husband? She stuck her head outside to see if she could spot him, but it was too dark to see anything beyond the driveway. If he was so worried, why wasn't he rushing in to save the day? It didn't make any sense. Had they already hurt him?

She pushed away the thought immediately. He had called her as they rang the doorbell, which meant he was fine. He must have just been jealous watching the guys walk to the door and thought he could trick her into leaving the house. Comical really, wasn't he the one who commanded her to stay inside?

Jenny had taken the taller guy's arm and was guiding him to the white leather loveseat, while the others sat down on the matching couch. Nerina sat in a wicker basket chair off to the side, staring at the dark violet carpet beneath her feet.

"What's your name?" Jenny asked the man beside her.

"The man who looks like a dinosaur is Tony. The mini sardine beside him is Glenn, and I'm Andy."

Glenn flicked a pen at him from off the coffee table. "Cool it with the small man jokes."

She understood the man's irritation. Being the butt end of a joke never felt very good. A person could pretend they didn't hear it, but it was like a knife being pushed into your heart.

"What happened to the van?" Nerina asked.

"Not sure. Something started knocking around in the engine and then it died," Tony said, shrugging his shoulders.

Jenny grabbed her cellphone off the coffee table and handed it to Andy. "You can use this to call a tow truck."

He got up and disappeared into the kitchen to make the call, coming back a few minutes later. "All done. They should be here in an hour, hopefully."

"Did you guys want a drink or anything?" her friend asked. "I have beer and soda."

Everyone put in their drink order, and Andy followed her into the kitchen to help. The other two guys turned and looked at Nerina. She squirmed under their scrutiny, feeling very much like a piece of jewelry on display.

"You're that mermaid, right?" Glenn asked, rubbing his almost bald head.

Tony elbowed him again. This time, the smaller guy punched him in the shoulder and said, "Stop doing that."

"You guys have seen the show?" she asked, her eyes widening.

She didn't peg them as marine lovers. In fact, she didn't know what to think about them, and she wasn't comfortable being alone with them. Not with how the big guy was staring at her like she was a tasty appetizer.

"Are you guys almost done in there?" Nerina yelled into the kitchen.

"We'll be out in a minute."

Not soon enough for me. "I'll come help." She went to get up, but by then, the two of them had returned to the living room with a few beers for the guys, a margarita for Jenny, and a juice for her because she couldn't drink alcohol. Not that a long island iced tea wouldn't come in handy right about now to calm her nerves.

Sipping away on her juice, she watched Jenny entertain the boys while they waited for the repair guy. Her anxiety slowly floated away on a huge fluffy cloud and disappeared right through the ceiling, leaving her lighthearted and giddy. A warm fuzzy feeling washed over her, like a bubbly waterfall. *Who would have thought that cloud nine was a real place?* Giggling, she poked a fluff ball forming in front of her.

"Wow," she murmured, as it burst into all the colors of the rainbow, like a coral reef. "I wanna to go for a swim. Anyone else wanna to go?"

Yes, the water. It was her home, and where she belonged. She grabbed the bottom of her sweater and tried to pull it over her head but didn't succeed. It got stuck, blocking out the pretty lights that were dancing around the room.

"Uh, hello?" She waved her arms in front of her, feeling much like a banana waiting to be peeled. *Do bananas have feelings?*

Unseen arms pulled the clothing the rest of the way over her head. She tried to focus on the two headed person in front of her, but everything kept moving at super speed. This must be the Matrix. They could do so many cool things there. Would she get to see Neo? He had neat black glasses. Why couldn't she have cool glasses like that?

"Can you fly, too?" she asked the two-headed person.

"Let's go for that boat ride, princess," a distance voice said.

"I want my tail. Can we go get my tail?" she asked.

"It's all covered, darling," another far-away voice answered.

She tried to stand up and ended up falling back into the chair. The force knocked it over backwards, and she landed on the ground with a thud, along with the chair.

"Help, help. I've fallen and I can't get up," she said, laughing as her arms and legs flailed in the air. "Turtles, turtles, rah rah rah. Turtles, turtles, ha ha ha. I love turtles." She snorted and giggled, sounding very much like a pig on laughing gas.

"How much did you give her?" the little shrimp asked the beanpole.

Why did it suddenly feel like it was time for Veggie Tales? Where was Bob the Tomato and Larry the Cucumber? "I'm hungry. Can we get somethin' to eat?" she asked.

"Obviously I didn't give her enough."

"Up we go, princess." The hulk-man picked her up in his arms, throwing her over his shoulder.

"Moose. That's what I'll call you," Nerina said, yawning. Her heavy-lidded eyes refused to stay open, and she found herself drawn into the world of dreams as the sandman came to claim her.

Chapter Ten

Wade needed to find some way to distract them so that he could get to her without being seen. If they saw him, it would be game over. However, not running in there with guns blazing was the hardest thing he'd ever done. He needed a plan.

Think, man, think.

Their number one mission would be to take her back to their headquarters on a private island off the coast. There was no way he could let them run off with her. Pulling out his Swiss army knife, he flicked out the blade.

He looked around to make sure the coast was clear before heading over to the passenger side of the van. The smell of smoke still permeated the air, stinging his eyes. With the knife in hand, he bent down and slashed the tire, listening to the satisfying hiss of the air escaping.

Opening the door of the unlocked vehicle, he dug around in the glove box for matches. The neighborhood was going to be in for a light show tonight. The intruders wouldn't be able to sneak his wife out of the house unseen. Hopefully, they'd run outside without her, and he'd be able to get in the back door before they realized what was happening.

Climbing over the seat and into the back of the van, he untied the half full gas container stored on the shelf and dumped it all over the floor. The fumes burned his throat as he scrambled out the back, hoping like heck that no had seen him. He glanced around quickly and saw that the area was still void of people.

He lit a match, tossed it into the vehicle and rushed to the side of Jenny's house to watch the action unfold. When he reached the living room window, a loud bang resonated behind him. One by one, porch lights came on, and people stepped outside to see what all the fuss was about.

Standing on his tiptoes, he looked inside the window, only to see his wife hanging over Moose's shoulder, motionless, and Jenny was sprawled out on the love seat. His knuckles turned white as he gripped the window frame. Baring his teeth, a low growl originated from deep inside his throat. No one messed with his wife and survived!

The fire hydrant at the edge of the yard began to rattle and shake, increasing in vibration with his anger. The valve cover popped off, bouncing across the street. Water sprayed out the side with such force that it sounded like Niagara Falls.

Moose laid Nerina down on the couch and motioned for the others to investigate. Wade crouched down near the corner of the house and watched as Glenn and Andy made their way down the walkway. They looked at the fire hydrant, the flaming wreckage and all the people milling about on the sidewalk. Sirens were audible in the distance.

"We are so totally hooped," Glenn said.

"You can say that again." Andy shoved his hands in the pockets of his jacket and slowly walked towards to the house, shuffling his feet against the concrete.

"Psst...over here," Wade called.

Their heads whipped in the direction of his voice. Quietly, Wade moved towards the backyard before they even knew where he was. He spotted a hose on the ground. If he could only get them out of the public eye, then he could have some fun with them. They would never want to see another popsicle for as long as they lived.

Following the hose, he found the faucet near the back door and turned it on. He put a kink in the hose and then jumped off the other side of the porch, waiting for the men to come around the corner.

Looking beneath the porch, he watched as their feet rounded the corner and approached the wooden deck. He had to do this at just the right moment before they had a chance to react.

"Are we hearing things?" Andy asked.

He popped up from his hiding spot, grinning. "Nope."

They jumped, bumping into each other as they turned to face him. Releasing the kink in the hose, he doused them with water. With a flick of his wrist, the water turned white as it turned to ice, leaving them looking like Frosty the Snowman. They tried to talk, but the ice muffled their voices. It didn't take much of an imagination to guess what they were saying.

He was sure it didn't feel very good, but he had no sympathy for them. They deserved this and a whole lot more. Hopping up onto the porch, he looked through the kitchen window. Moose was pacing in the living room, walking by the kitchen entrance every ten seconds.

That should give him enough time to get inside and duck behind the dark gray and blue island. He reached for the handle and turned it.

Locked. *Crap.*

Now what? Looking back at the two guys, he figured he still had a good ten minutes before they found their way out. Could he lure her captor out somehow? Rushing back to the front of the house, he peeked around the corner and saw Moose peek his head out the door.

"Hey, Moose, there's a guy in the back," Wade said, giving his best Andy impression.

"Deal with him," was the reply he got back. Standing on his tiptoes, he glanced in the window and saw that the man had moved into the kitchen. Slipping inside, Wade scooped his wife up off the couch as he heard the guy growl. The back door slammed open, shaking the floor.

"What the hell?" Moose bellowed.

He must have found his boys. When Wade took a step towards the bathroom, he banged his knee on the end table. As his knee cap was pushed backwards, red-hot pain seared through him. He bit his tongue to keep from crying out, but the bang was loud enough to be heard out back. Moose stormed into the house.

"Shit." Wade mumbled.

He had enough time to duck behind the couch with his wife, holding his hand up and palms out, fading invisibly into his surroundings. The big guy cursed up a blue streak when he noticed that only Jenny remained, and his prized catch wasn't where he had left her.

If only he could have moved both women before the guy came back, but as it was, his body shook with exertion at having one other person wrapped in his arms while invisible. The other two quickly joined Moose in the living room.

"It was him, boss!" Glenn rubbed his hands up and down his arms, lips still blue from the cold.

"Wade?"

The two men nodded their heads. So much for surprises. Moose pulled out a gun from the back of his pants and walked over to their unconscious host, running the barrel across her cheek.

"We can do this the hard way or the easy way." He clicked the safety off.

Wade swore silently. If he didn't try to save Jenny, Nerina would never forgive him. Yet, if he uncloaked them, he could very well be the one looking down the barrel of the gun, and they wouldn't stand a chance.

Moose wouldn't think twice about shooting him. He knew that for a fact, considering his leg sported a scar from their last meeting. Nothing deadly, but that didn't mean the guy hadn't improved his shooting skills since then.

His wife groaned, but he couldn't slap a hand over her mouth without revealing their position. He should have just pulled a Moose move earlier and thrown his wife over his shoulders when she tried to leave with Jenny.

"You have till the count of three, and then I'll blow the head off her pretty little friend," Moose threatened.

Out the front window, Wade could see the flashing lights from the fire trucks and police cars. Not that they were much help. The man had a silencer on his weapon, and no one would be the wiser if he made good on his promise. There was too much going on outside.

"Hey, by the way, did you hear about the calling card we left at your place?" Moose moved about the room, kicking his foot out slightly as he walked, apparently hoping to find them.

"Ya, it was a pretty hot message," Andy said, joining in on the taunting.

His eyes widened, and every muscle in his body tensed. The smoke in the air and the burning rubber smell weren't just from some stranger's building. It was his home. Everything they had built together as a couple. Rage boiled inside him, like a dam waiting to burst.

They would pay. He would see to that. Moose stopped right beside him. Wade held his breath, and he hoped Nerina wouldn't make a peep. The man was so close that if he kicked his foot out, it would connect with the limp legs of his wife.

"You might as well come out before I start counting."

Sorry, Neri, I can't risk your life to save hers. Frustration filled him. There was too much at stake to try to help Jenny. He couldn't give away their position, no matter what. The thought made his stomach roll. His wife would never look at him the same way again.

She wouldn't see him as her knight in shining armor anymore, and it would be even worse when the entire truth came out. He wouldn't simply be placed in the doghouse. He'd be totally and completely kicked to the curb. It was a lousy deck of cards that fate had dealt him. Whoever came up with this stuff needed a severe talking to.

"One."

He felt like a man standing in front of a firing squad, getting ready to face his death sentence. Images of his past popped in front of his eyes. Back to the time when he'd been the one pointing a spear at an innocent person. Cringing, he could still feel their blood on his fingers.

"Two."

Letting out a quiet breath, he braced himself for the quiet pop of the gun, indicating that the deed had been done. He sent out a silent prayer to whoever might be listening.

Moose placed his finger on the trigger.

"Three."

Chapter Eleven

"Should we wake Craig?" Tom asked, as they stared at the blazing inferno. The firefighters were still fighting to get it under control.

"Nah, let's just wait to see if she comes back," Jason said, staring at the activity in front of him. The blaze had no intention of making the firefighters job any easier. The oxygen in the air fed the fire as quickly as their hoses could pump.

There had to be some type of accelerant causing it to be such a monster to deal with. He heard more sirens and thought they were coming their way, but they passed right on by. Was the world falling apart tonight?

Jason listened as the sirens appeared to just stop, instead of fading slowly into silence as they moved further away. "You don't think that could be related, do you?"

"We could always take a quick drive around the neighborhood and see if we can spot the other incident." Tom watched as another emergency vehicle sped past them. "I could do with a little fresh air."

Turning the vehicle around, they went in the direction of all the activity. About three blocks away, they saw flashing lights halfway down a side street. It looked like something big was going down.

Roadblocks had been set up, and the police were refusing to let anyone through.

He pulled into the twenty-four-hour convenience store and parked the car. "Looks like we walk from here."

"What are the odds that we have two unrelated fires this close together?" Tim asked.

"Probably as likely as finding someone else with her DNA." Jason waved his hand in front of his nose. "I should have brought nose plugs."

They walked towards the bustling activity. On the other side of the barricade, he could see a bomb squad van, an ambulance, fire trucks and unending cop cars. The flashing lights lit up a charcoaled-colored van off to the side that was still smoldering away. Across the street, the firefighters were fighting to turn off the hydrant that had made a huge puddle in the street.

"It's off as far as it can go," one firefighter yelled over the rushing water.

"Then it shouldn't still be spraying. Let me try," another shouted, grabbing the wrench.

A female cop walked up to Jason and Tom. "Sorry, guys. You can't come any closer."

"Do you mind if we ask what happened?"

"Sorry, I'm not at liberty to discuss it." She reached up to re-position her hat, revealing her long brown hair pulled back into a bun.

"We're looking for a young woman with white hair. Have you seen her?" he asked, taking a shot in the dark.

She rolled her eyes. "A missing girlfriend is the least of my concerns right now."

"No. She's not my girlfriend. She's..." What could Jason say? It wasn't like he could come out and say what they discovered. The lady would probably roll her eyes again. In the end, he just let the lady walk over to a car that had approached the barricade.

"I'm afraid we can't let anyone in or out until the team is done investigating."

The man behind the wheel scowled at the cop and sent a few choice words in her direction.

"Sorry, sir. I understand that you're tired. We're moving as quickly as possible to resolve the situation."

Jason didn't envy her job in the slightest. That was why he became a geneticist. Genes didn't grumble at you or threaten you. Well, not in the *punch-you-in-the-face* sense anyway. He'd had enough of that in school.

Turning back to the charcoaled van, he watched as the investigators slowly approached it, taking pictures. He had a gut feeling that both incidents were connected—the apartment fire and this one.

If the bomb squad was here, they must be thinking someone placed a bomb in the car. Jason pulled out his phone and took a picture of the vehicle. "I think we should stick around here for now."

"But what about the apartment?" Tom asked.

"Why don't you take the car back there? I'll stay here." Jason knew it was the only logical thing to do. That way, they could keep an eye on both places. She was bound to show up sooner or later. It was the law of averages.

He watched Tom disappear into the parking lot of the convenience store before returning his attention to the cops on site, who had started knocking on the doors of nearby houses. The ones that didn't have people standing outside. Other officers were questioning people on the sidewalks.

News vans pulled in beside him and started filming, even questioning him about what was going on. There was nothing he could say to clarify the situation any, so he just pointed to the female cop who was monitoring the barricade.

The news crews hounded the cop with various questions, to which she answered, "All we know at this point is that we responded to a call about a vehicle fire. That's all I can say at this present time."

"Do you suspect that it was a bomb?"

The cop's lips pressed into a thin line. "The chief will speak with you as information becomes available."

Jason plunked his butt down on the sidewalk and continued to watch the mayhem. Hopefully, something turned up before the end of the night to make breathing in all this smoke worthwhile.

~

"Wait." Andy stepped between Moose and the girl. "Is that really necessary?"

"Move." Moose motioned with the gun.

"Look. We know he's here somewhere. He can't stay hidden forever. Let's wait him out."

Dissension in the ranks saved the day, for the moment anyway. Sweat poured down Wade's face. His hands shook with exertion, and his thigh muscle seized up, cramping intensely. He bit down on his cheeks to keep from crying out in pain.

His strength was quickly fading, and he couldn't keep it up much longer. The thought of failing her shot daggers into his heart. The ache in his chest intensified as his energy dipped dangerously low.

Struggling to keep his eyes open, his hand slipped. He caught it just in time before he revealed their location. He had to do this. Giving up was not an option. Too many lives depended on him.

The two men continued to argue, and Moose walloped the other guy on the head with the butt end of the gun, knocking him to the ground. "I told you to move."

With his head in his hands, Andy rolled on the ground, groaning. "Asshole."

"Let's do this again, shall we? Should I count back from three? Nah." the man said, shaking his head. "I'll just shoot."

But his injured partner wouldn't have it and kicked the guy's legs out from under him. The man fell, smacking his head on the coffee table, shattering the glass. Wade wanted to yell, 'timber,' but decided against it.

The gun went off when it hit the ground and the bullet hit the arm of the loveseat, narrowly missing Jenny's head. Glenn dove for cover behind the couch as the gun bounced again, pointing in his direction.

His shoulder clipped Wade's jaw, and all three of them landed in a clump on the floor in a tangled mess of limbs. The man's eyes widened at the sight of them. "Hey, guys—"

Wade silenced him with a punch to the face, Glenn's eyes rolled into the back of his head. He scrambled to his feet, picked up his wife and rushed towards the door. The sound of a bullet striking the floor beside him made him freeze. He hung his head and groaned.

"Not another step," Andy said.

Why couldn't he catch a break? Wade turned back around to face them and grinned. "So, how'd it feel to be a human popsicle?"

The man's face reddened to the color of a tomato. "You should be nicer to a man with a gun."

"I don't think he has any plans to be," Wade said as Moose clamped a hand down on Andy's leg.

He was glad to see they didn't get along any better than they used to. While the two continued their power struggle, Wade tiptoed towards the door. Shifting his wife in his arms, he reached for the handle when a gun shot rang out, breaking the glass window beside him. He dropped to the ground, covering Nerina's body with his.

Looking back, he found Moose on his feet, his forehead sporting a lump the size of a gulf ball, already turning black and blue.

"I was wondering when you'd start growing antlers," Wade quipped. He shouldn't goad the bull, but he couldn't help it.

"You always thought you were such hot stuff, but not so smart today, are ya?" Moose sneered. "Hand her over, and I might just spare your life."

He looked down at his wife, who was totally unaware of everything that was happening. She was out like a light. Jenny hadn't even budged an inch since all the action began, but at least they were both alive.

Off to the side, Glenn and Andy groaned, slowly pulling themselves to a kneeling position.

"You really should get yourself better help, Moose," Wade said, nodding his head towards the two men. "Maybe, men who won't mutiny."

Moose's face reddened. "Shut up and give me the girl." He raised his gun, and another shot rang out, shattering the glass on the other side of the door.

If the first gunshot didn't alert the police out in the street, the second one certainly would. All he had to do was bide his time, keep the man talking and avoid the gun, if at all possible. He stood up, carefully watching Moose's trigger finger.

"You probably have about two minutes before the cops surround the house. I'd suggest ducking out the back if you don't want to get caught," he said to them, hoping they'd take his suggestion.

"Or we could just tell them that you were trying to kidnap my woman, and I shot you." Moose kept the gun trained on him.

"There's that." Wade swallowed hard, his heart racing. If he wasn't holding Nerina, he'd be a corpse setting sail for the underworld. He looked down and readjusted his grip. She looked so serene in his arms. He hated how the life she knew was about to go up in a puff of smoke. Nothing would ever be the same again.

They wouldn't have their quiet little suburban life anymore, and he quite liked the normality of it all— getting up every morning, going to work, coming home and then making sweet love to his now unconscious mate. Her skin looked more pale than normal against his black t-shirt.

"What did you give her?" he asked, narrowing his eyes at their assailant. "It better not have hurt the baby, or I swear to god—"

Moose raised his head towards the ceiling and let out a deep roar of laughter. "You knocked her up? That's priceless."

A growl rose from Wade's throat, and his fists clenched. He wanted to punch the man senseless. His muscles shook and arms ached under the strain of carrying his wife. Her normal feather-like weight suddenly tripled. He wanted to put her down, but nothing would stop Moose from taking that shot if he did. Unable to stay standing, he dropped to one knee, cradling Nerina on his thigh. Wind whistled by Wade's head as a bullet shot past him, knocking the gun out of their assailant's hand.

"Police. Freeze."

Four policemen filed out of the kitchen surrounding them, guns trained on every single person in the living room, except the unconscious women.

"Get down on the ground now! Keep your hands where I can see them."

"It was self-defense. He was running off with my woman," Moose snarled at them, making a run for Wade. The closest officer—equal in muscle mass—tackled him to the ground, sitting on him.

Wade lowered his head to hide a smirk. "Officers, if you check the wallet in my back pocket, and my wife's wallet, you'll see he's lying."

One of the cops clicked the button on his radio. "Delta twenty-one. We have a double ten-fifty-three at 10434 Wellborne Drive."

Another cop checked his wallet and confirmed that he was who he said he was. Placing his wife gently on the couch, he brushed the hair from her face as he kissed her forehead.

"They don't need an ambulance," he told them. "I think they'll be okay once they sleep it off."

The only female cop in the room quirked an eyebrow at him, giving him a strange look. "We'll decide that, sir."

Wade smacked his forehead at the turn of events. They may have just jumped from the frying pan into the fire.

Chapter Twelve

Wade returned to the hospital room with a cup of coffee and found a straggly gray-haired man slouching in the chair, massaging his foot; his coffee-stained white t-shirt barely containing his pot belly.

He glared at the intruder. "Who are you? And how'd you get in here?"

"Easy there, boy. The name is Jenson. Doctor Craig Jenson." Craig extended his hand. When he made no move to shake it, the man dropped it on in his lap.

Wade's eyes swept over the man, taking in every single detail. The front edge of the guy's shoes had started to come apart. His blue jeans were tattered and fading in color, and last, but not least, he lacked a lab coat and name tag. "You don't look like a doctor."

"I'm off duty at the moment, actually."

Wade placed his coffee on the table at the end of the bed and crossed his arms. "Then what are you doing in my wife's room in the middle of the night?" The last thing he wanted was to talk to some strange person after he'd spent three hours in the emergency ward with his sleeping beauty, having the police grill him over what happened.

"Your wife is a remarkable woman, Mr. Douglas."

His shoulders tensed, causing a shooting pain up the back of his neck. Massaging the growing knot in his shoulder, he glanced over at Nerina, who was all cozy under the covers. Ever since they arrived, he'd been trying to plan a way out, scoping out the emergency exits before anyone discovered her. Sadly, the place had been too busy for him to try anything.

With her being unconscious, it wasn't likely he'd get very far without someone noticing them. And apparently, she wasn't going to be waking up anytime soon either. The doctors told him that the buffoons gave her a drug called Ambien, and that she'd be out till sometime in the morning.

He'd asked about the baby, and they told him not to worry, saying it was a class B pregnancy drug, nothing to be concerned about. The baby's heartbeat was strong and clear, and all Nerina's vitals appeared to be okay.

His heart wasn't, though. It was pounding a million miles a minute. He could smell the danger as he stepped between Craig and his wife. Widening his stance, he let his arms rest loosely by his sides, preparing to fight if he had to.

"What are you doing here?"

"All my life I've waited for blood like hers. Unique. Different."

His breath caught in his throat as a tremor rippled through him, and his blood rushed from his head to his feet. Leaning over, he rested his hands on his knees, trying to breathe.

Calm down, Wade.

If he ended up on the floor, he'd be no good to her. It was possible that the doctor was thinking about something completely different, right? Standing back up, his eyes blacked out momentarily. He squeezed them closed for a second and re-opened them, only to find the man staring at him curiously.

"How did you get her blood?"

"A colleague from the hospital here sent it to me when your wife came in the other day, saying he'd never seen anything like it." The corner of the man's mouth curled into a creepy grin. "I'm inclined to agree, especially after seeing it again today."

Wade shrugged his shoulders. "What? Do you guys think she's some type of alien or something?" He tried to grin and chuckle, but it came out more like a snarl than anything else.

"Yes, actually."

He swore under his breath. This was going so far south it wasn't funny. "I'm calling security."

"I think you'll find that won't help, Mr. Douglas. They've been instructed not to interfere unless you try something."

"You forgot to ask yourself one question, Doctor Jenson," he said, imitating the doctor's formal speech before moving to the center of the room. Above him, in the pipes, he could feel the water coursing through the fire system.

"What's that?"

"Is she the only one?"

The man's eyes widened, and fear passed through them. The pipes overhead groaned and creaked under the pressure of the water gathering inside them. As the pressure increased, the fire alarm sounded. Wade heard shouts from outside the room, as nurses rushed around trying to find out what was going on.

With a twist of his hand, the sprinkler above him burst open, showering them with water. Craig gasped and sputtered as the water clipped him in the face under Wade's guidance.

Before the doctor recovered, Wade picked up his wife and rushed across the room, stopping only when he reached the door. When his hand touched the wall, every drop of water in the room froze.

The doctor sat there. His mouth opening and closing like a fish, his eyes bugging out. He likely would have sprinted towards them if his feet weren't frozen to the ground.

A crowd of people were gathered down the hall to his right, so Wade went in the opposite direction, aiming for the emergency exit down at the end. The last thing he wanted to do was cause problems for the nurses on the floor, but drastic times call for drastic measures.

"Hey, you, stop!" a female voice yelled when he reached the door.

"Not on your life, lady," he mumbled, hitting the push bar on the door with his hip. Man, he wished she'd wake up already. His arms were taking a triple beating carrying her around so much. Carrying her to bed was one thing, but right now she was a limp noodle, complete deadweight. But he'd carry her to the moon and back if it meant she was safe, even if it almost killed him.

He made it down two floors when he heard a door open from below, radios squawking. There was no time for him to hide because he knew the police would be all over the building in minutes, especially with the fire crews, who were no doubt just pulling into the parking lot.

Whispering into her ear, Wade said, "Neri, if you're gonna wake up, now would be a good time."

She didn't stir, not even a groan. The men's boots echoed on the stairs, getting closer with each step. He stood on the landing with nowhere to go but up. When he turned to go back up the stairs, the door above him opened as well.

Now he knew what a caged animal felt like. Pulling Neri as close to his body as he could, he backed into the corner and faded from sight. Hopefully, the people in the stairwell would be none the wiser.

He held his breath as they approached the landing, converging on his location. Two security guards, a nurse, and an orderly stopped right in front of him. The male orderly stood only inches away.

"I could have sworn he was right here," the orderly said, swinging his arm dangerously close to Wade's head.

"They could be anywhere by now," the nurse said, pulling her black hair back and securing it in place with a butterfly clip.

"We'll do our best to find them, ma'am," one of the security guards said, proceeding to click the button on his radio. "Fox-2-Alpha to Fox-2-Charlie, monitor and secure all exits."

The orderly and the nurse ascended the stairs back up to their floor, and one of the guards followed them, commenting about wanting to check the next floor up. The last member of the group went down the stairs.

When the second door clicked shut, he let out the breath he had forgotten he was holding and allowed himself to become visible again. "That was too close for comfort."

He still had another few floors to go before they reached the basement. By the time he reached the door leading to the underground parkade, his arms ached, and his shirt was soaked. This was not the day to forget to wear deodorant, not that he had time to remember hygiene etiquette these days.

As he reached for the doorknob, his burning muscles protested, and his fingers refused to grip it. Using two hands, he finally twisted it far enough to swing the door open.

"Crap."

He spotted his car on the far side of the parking lot and quickly glimpsed at the camera above him. He remembered seeing it when he drove by the door earlier. He knew he only had a matter of minutes to get to his car before the police and the security team stormed in on him. His disappearing act came in handy, but it had its limits. If he was too tired, his body wouldn't listen to his demands.

He hurried across the parking lot. If he made it through this, he doubted lifting a cup of coffee would even be possible. His feet dragged across the concrete. Each step made his calf muscle twitch, reminding him that he needed to work out more. He'd grown slack in that area in recent years.

Leaning up against the passenger door, he fought to get it open. He placed Nerina in the front seat and laid it back slightly, fastening her seatbelt. When he reached his side of the car, the building door closest to him burst open, and the same two guards barreled through it.

They approached his car, guns drawn. That was his cue to hightail it out of there. He wasn't superman and taking a bullet did not appeal to him. Starting the vehicle, he put it in drive. The tires squealed as he sped out of the parkade.

Thankfully, the cops were too busy paying attention to the fire-fighters to even see him exit. At least one thing went his way tonight, but he knew that once the security guards shared the description of his car and the plate number, he'd be back on their radar again. And he knew it wouldn't be so easy to get away from the police, not with their helicopters and other contraptions that could pinpoint your location.

He missed being under the ocean. Humans had far less tech-nology down there, although even that was being invaded more and more as time went on. Once he was far enough away from the hospi-tal, he pulled over to the side of the road to use his phone.

"Andre, I need a huge favor."

Nerina groaned as the slightest movement made a hundred BB gun pellets ricochet around her brain. The foundation beneath her jerked every now and then, knocking her head against something solid. Sharp pains coursed through her. Flashes of white light flickered in the darkness, spreading out like a spider's web, disappearing only when the pain settled.

Her heavy eyelids refused to budge. With much reluctance, she rubbed them with the palms of her hands, regretting it almost imme-diately. The weight against her eyes caused knife-like pains inside her temples.

She moaned. Someone needed to get the license plate of the truck that had hit her. If she didn't know any better, it felt like some-body put her body through a meat grinder and taped her back together like Humpty Dumpty.

Attempting to open her eyes again, a sliver of light appeared, sending a shockwave of pain through her skull. A coppery metallic taste filled her mouth, and her stomach bubbled with nausea.

"Wow, hold...don't puke...Andre's..."

She plugged her ears, catching only the odd word. The voice

sounded like a huge chorus singing through a stadium's loudspeaker. When she could finally open her eyes, everything was blurry. Squinting, she looked around. They were traveling in a car, but the route looked unfamiliar to her. Not that she could see anything. Everything had a white haze to it. Nausea overtook her and bile rose in her throat.

"Please pull over," she said, throwing her hands over her mouth.

Instead of pulling over, Wade reached behind her seat and produced a four-liter ice cream container and plopped it on her lap.

"You can't be serious?"

He pointed to the bucket, giving her no other option. Not that she could have waited for him to find a safe place to pull over anyway. It was coming whether she liked it or not. Her husband tried to help by pulling her hair back as he drove down the road. It only partially worked. Only a bit of puke found its way into her hair. The rest made it into the bucket.

"I don't suppose you have a lid, do ya?" she asked.

Wade shook his head.

The migraine kept every muscle in her body ridged and tight which made the pain worse. She leaned her head back against the seat and closed her eyes, trying to imagine anything but the scenery flying by them.

What were they doing in a car? The last thing she could remember was sitting with Jenny in her living room, waiting for her friends to come. She placed her head in her hands. All the thinking made her brain hurt.

"Easy does it. Just sleep it off. We have quite the drive ahead of us," he said in a much quieter voice than before.

"How'd I get here?"

That was a loaded question, and Wade wasn't sure exactly how much to tell her. It's not like he could say she got so drunk and blacked out. She'd know he was lying, considering she was pregnant.

"And why do I feel so horrible?"

"Rest for now. We'll talk later when you're feeling better," he said, keeping his eyes on the road. He didn't want to let the cat out of the bag until Kyle and Maggie were with them, but continuing to keep it a secret wouldn't help their relationship either. Not that she'd want to have one with him when the whole truth came out. That was one thing he was almost certain of.

Her eyes closed, and her breathing evened out as she drifted off to sleep again. He watched her out of the corner of his eye, wishing he could take them back in time and stop all this from happening. He was off the hook for now, but he knew that wouldn't happen a second time. Once her fighting spirit came back, the battle of secrets would be worse than before.

Chapter Thirteen

The loud blare of an air horn caught his attention, and Wade's head snapped up. A semi-truck was set on a collision course with his friend's car. His heart skipped a beat. He cranked the steering wheel and swerved to the right. Nerina's head hit the bony part of his shoulder as she fell sideways.

Groaning, she pulled herself up to a sitting position, rubbing the side of her head. "What the heck just happened?"

Oh, nothing major, just a near-miss because of his stupid, idiotic sleep-deprived brain. Pulling over to the side of the road, he reached behind the chair and pulled out his thermos of coffee. "Sorry, babe. I must have dozed off."

"If you tell me where we're going, I could drive."

With the drugs she had been given, she wasn't safe to drive until they had cleared out of her system. That meant he was in control for now and could keep them on the right track. "No, that's okay. I'm just going to pull into the next hotel we see."

She let out a puff of air, blowing the hair out of her face. "Why do you have to be so stubborn?"

"Knowing you, you'd probably turn the car around and go back."

She stuck her tongue out at him.

"There are better uses for that tongue, yah?" he said, winking. That earned him not only a heated glare but also a swat on the shoulder. She must be feeling a little better. "How's the head?"

"It hurts, but I'll live."

"There's some water in the back if you need something to drink."

"Thanks."

"Your color is coming back a little now." He reached out and gently caressed her pale cheek with his thumb.

"What happened last night?" She ran her hand along the vehicle's unfamiliar dashboard. "Whose car is this?"

Wade pulled his hand away and placed it back on the steering wheel. "I'm too tired to talk about it now."

Nerina tilted her head and studied him. His mouth opened wide as he yawned for the fifth time in a row. The dark bags under his blood-shot watery eyes made him look like a raccoon.

A cool draft slightly ruffled the clothes she had on, making her shiver as cool air from the vent drifted across the skin of her leg. When she glanced down, a blue hospital gown came into view. She ran her hand over the material, trying to remember what had happened the night before. Nothing good, by the looks of it.

"Have you developed some sorta weird fetish?" she asked, trying to squelch her rising panic.

"If I do, you'll be the first to know." One corner of his mouth curled into a slight grin. But the other appeared to have no energy to join it, and the humor never reached his droopy eyes.

Their vehicle approached a sign that told them they were nearing a Super 8 in a town called Fruita. Her stomach could definitely do with a break from all the bumping around on the road, and Wade needed to sleep before he crashed the car. She didn't exactly want her brains splattered all over the road.

After they parked the car in front of the motel, she opened the door to step outside but quickly closed it. "Smells like poop."

"Wasn't me."

Nerina rolled her eyes. "Always the comedian."

He hadn't her a sundress and instructed her to change her clothes. Once she was ready, she plugged her nose and got out of the car, rushing into the motel. Thankfully, they had parked close to the entrance. Once inside, she dropped her hand. The aroma of waffles from the continental breakfast filled the foyer. Despite being nauseous, her stomach growled.

After they registered, the hotel receptionist handed them access cards and Wade's credit card. "Your room number is 202. It is on the second floor—to the left of the elevator. Enjoy your stay, Mr. and Mrs. Carlton."

"But we're not—"

Wade pulled her away from the desk before she could finish her sentence. "Don't say anything," he warned.

She bit her bottom lip as she grabbed the handle of her luggage, following him to the elevator. As they stepped inside, she asked, "Did you steal someone's reservation?"

"No."

Opening his wallet, he slipped in the credit card, but not before Nerina saw the name on it.

"Adam Carlton?"

"Stop asking questions." Wade smacked the second-floor button with the side of his fist.

A lump lodged in her throat, tears pooling in her eyes. Turning her back to him, she quickly cleared her throat and wiped the tears away before they had a chance to fall.

His hand came to rest on her shoulder, and his forehead leaned against the back of her head. "Sorry, sweetheart."

Quickly turning, she buried her face in his chest and wept.

"Please, baby. Don't cry." Wade wrapped his strong arms around her small frame and held her close. When the doors open, he picked up the suitcase, and with his arm supporting her, they made their way to their room.

Once inside, she collapsed on the bed, shaking. "We just

committed fraud. Oh my god. I can't go to jail. I can't," she cried, her teeth clattering. "We have to go back down there. Tell them the truth. I can't lose the baby."

He kneeled down in front of her, rubbing his hands up and down her arms. "It's okay. Take a deep breath."

"We have to. I can't—" A hiccup-filled cry burst from her mouth. They were criminals. No better than the people on those stupid police television shows. Her baby would be born in jail. The thought made her cry even harder. "Damn you, Wade." She pounded her fists against his chest.

He grabbed her hands and brought them down to her lap. Cupping her chin, he said, "Nothing is going to happen to you or our baby. I promise."

In his eyes, she knew he meant every word, but no one could foretell the future. Not even him.

Nerina sat in surreal disbelief in front of the television, unable to take her eyes off the images being shown on the six o'clock news. She watched as a man who looked like her husband carried a body out of her friend's house, placing it on a stretcher. The person in his arms looked like her.

"Three men are in custody after an attempted abduction of two women in the San Diego area late last night. The police thwarted the abduction after two gunshots rang out of the home and alerted them to their presence. The police were in the area investigating a possible car bombing in the same cul-de-sac. Sadly, one of the women, Nerina Douglas, has since disappeared from the hospital." Her picture appeared on the screen—one that had been taken at SeaWorld in her tail.

"The woman was removed involuntarily by her husband, Wade Douglas, during a sprinkler system malfunction. In other related news, it has been revealed that the apartment fire just down the road from the attempted abduction was also the home of Mr. and Mrs. Douglas. If you see them, you are to call the police immediately. Wade Douglas is wanted for questioning and possible arson charges. He is considered armed and dangerous. Do not approach him."

Clicking the off button, she sat staring at the blank screen. The images of the fire burned into her retinas. Her home. Everything was gone. The ground opened up and swallowed her stomach, her body following quickly behind it. As invisible hands squeezed her throat, Nerina gasped for air. *This wasn't happening.*

Her mind spun in circles, making her dizzy. Nausea settled deep in her stomach, making itself known by a toxic-flavored burp. She shuddered, scrunching her nose in response. The subway sandwich she'd eaten when they had reached the motel tasted a lot better than it did now. Pickles didn't taste as good coming up as they did going down.

Blech.

She sat perched on the edge of the bed, trying to process everything the reporter had said and match it with what she could remember. Her mind was blank. Totally blank. Nada. Nothing. The last memory she could recall was sitting with Jenny in her house.

Crap. Jenny!

Trembling, she rooted through their suitcase, searching for her cellphone. "Where is the cotton-pickin' thing?" She dumped out all the contents on the table in the corner. No phone.

Stomping her foot on the carpet in frustration, Nerina looked over at Wade. The big doofus was sleeping like a rock, spread out sideways on the bed, flat on his stomach and gloriously naked—his one arm under the pillow, the other by his side. The sheets had been pushed off the end of the bed, so she had a complete full view of his gorgeous body.

She licked her lips appreciatively, heat pooling in her belly. The all too familiar ache arose between her thighs, dampening her underwear. Groaning, she turned away, determined to stay on task. His pants were on the floor beside the bed. Walking over, she reached down and checked the pockets for his phone. Maybe he had Jenny's number in his phone as they all worked at SeaWorld.

Pockets were empty, except for the car keys and his wallet. She searched his jacket, which hung on the back of a chair, and his suitcase. Where could his phone be? That was when she saw the corner of something black sticking out from under his pillow. He must have hidden it there when she jumped in the shower.

Lifting the pillow slightly, she saw her phone there as well. She looked at him, her lips pressing into a firm line. His mouth hung open, and his eyes twitched. The prick was probably dreaming of how many more ways he could get them into trouble. Grabbing her phone, she turned on the screen and went to call Jenny. She scrolled through the contact list and then her phone log. Jenny's number was nowhere to be found.

Her infuriatingly 'wanted' husband must have deleted her number. Nerina picked up her pillow and clocked him on the head with it. He groaned and rolled over, his eyes blinking. What right did he have to invade her privacy? When she raised the pillow into the air again, he grabbed it, pulling it away from her.

"Don't even think about it," Wade warned, his voice still husky from sleeping. Not quite the wake-up call he was hoping for, but there she was. Her face flush wish anger as she kneeled beside him. How had he managed to get himself into trouble while he was sleeping? "Did I say another woman's name or something?"

"You know, I have half a mind to call the police on you, you jerk." Her hands gripped the fitted sheet on the bed, her nostrils flaring.

Yep, her fighting spirit had returned. He only wished it could have waited until he woke up on his own. "I told you we wouldn't get in trouble over the card."

"I'm not talking about that." She got up from the bed and grabbed her hair with both hands, pulling it. If she pulled any harder, she'd yank it right off her head. "How could you not tell me about our home? Or about the men who tried to kidnap me? How could you take my phone and delete Jenny's number? How is it that you knew about Kyle not being my dad? I didn't even know."

The questions were fired one right after the other, like a machine gun firing off round after round relentlessly. "Wow. Slow down, darling."

"Don't *darling* me. Our faces were plastered all over the evening news."

"Shit." He should have expected that. They should have just pulled into a rest stop instead of coming to a motel. "Get your things. We're leaving."

She walked over to the door, flipped the latch, and leaned against it. Her arms crossed. "I'm not going anywhere until you tell me what's going on."

He raised his head towards the ceiling and let out an exasperated groan. "Once we get to where we're going and you're safe, you can ask me questions until your heart's content. Okay?"

"No! First off, where's Jenny?"

"She's fine. She's safe. Can we go, please?" Moving the curtain, he looked outside and saw three cop cars in the parking lot. Instead of waiting for her to get their stuff together, he rushed around and threw everything back into their suitcase. He pulled her away from the door and flipped back the latch, ready to head into the hallway.

"I'm pretty certain you aren't going to want to go out there dressed like that," she said, a glimmer of humor briefly flitting across her eyes—an interesting contrast to the frown etched on her face.

Looking down, he realized he was naked and grinned. "What's one more charge to my name?" He reached for the handle of the door jokingly, and she swatted his hand away.

"Just get dressed." She pushed him towards his pants.

He was slipping. Who in their right mind forgets to get dressed? Shaking his head, he hurried over and put on his clothes. He grabbed two baseball caps out of his suitcase and handed one to her. "Hide your hair under it."

She twisted her hair into a high bun and placed the hat on top. "I feel like Marge Simpson."

"Just as long as that doesn't make me Homer." He walked over to the window and looked outside. All the cops still appeared to be outside by their cars, talking with one of the desk clerks. The lady pointed towards Andre's blue Mazda and then up to the window of their room.

Stepping away quickly, he said, "It's time to leave. Now!"

Chapter Fourteen

Déjà vu. The last time he said that she had told him no. The only thing that got Nerina moving this time around was the look on his face. It was the one you made when you were up the creek without a paddle, and that scared her. Everything about the last few days made absolutely no sense.

How had she gone from having the perfect life to being on the run? And why was it she had no idea what she was running from? The direction they were going didn't feel right to her. They were about eleven hours away from home.

Or at least, where home used to be. Her eyes began to water again. *Talk about being a water fountain, sheesh.* She quickly wiped the tears away as she followed Wade down the stairs and out the back of the motel.

When they reached the corner of the building, he put his hand across her chest, pressing her against the wall as he looked around the corner. He swore under his breath, but she still heard it. With his hand resting on her breast, her nipples hardened, straining against her bra. His hand slightly squeezed her sensitive breast, letting her know he was fully aware of the awakening desire within her.

What a strange day. Nothing could get more bizarre, could it? Wade slid his hand across her body and took her hand, pulling her towards the trees they saw across the lot.

"Don't we need the car?" she asked.

"It's swarming with cops. We'll have to find another way."

They ducked behind the clump of trees just off the property, hidden by the shadows of the night. As she crouched in the darkness, a twinge of pain jabbed her low in the abdomen. Cringing, she decided to kneel instead.

She stared at Wade. His chiseled jaw was set. His fists tight. He narrowed his eyes as he stared at the action in the parking lot of the motel. She wished she could read his mind and find out what was going on inside that head of his. Here they were, in the middle of nowhere, and she had no idea what any of this was about.

"Give me one good reason why I shouldn't go over there and turn myself in?" Nerina whispered.

When he turned to look at her, the darkness in his eyes reminded her of a storm rolling in, and she bit her lip.

"How do you do that?" she asked.

"Do what?"

"Your eyes, they change. One minute they're normal and the next, I swear..." She shook her head. "Never mind." It had to be her imagination running wild again, just like it did when her feet turned to mush as SeaWorld. His eyes were a sexy, smoky blue color that drove her insane.

They had captivated her from the moment they met, or rather, they mesmerized her. The depth inside them sucked her right in, or it could have just been that weird thing where they could sense each other that drew her to him.

Now his ability to change his eye color made her want to go running straight towards the cops. Turning her attention back towards the motel, she watched some of the cops stroll inside the building, while a couple of them remained outside.

"We need to go," He grabbed her arm, pulling her towards the

Colorado Welcome Center. Only a few semi-trucks remained in the parking lot. They ducked behind one as they made their way over to the building.

"Do you know how to say anything else?" She pulled out of his grip, continuing to walk beside him. He was being so closed lipped it wasn't funny.

"I don't know what you want me to say."

"How about the truth? Don't I deserve that?"

He shivered. He'd spent the last few years trying to forget the truth. It was ugly. How could he tell her that he's known all about her since the very beginning? As well as the fact that he'd been tailing her for months, working up the courage to do what was asked of him before she knew who he was.

When he saw her on the beach and pretended to bump into her, he was going to follow through with the plan. But when he looked into her eyes, he was lost. The moment he touched her, they connected, and that was the end of the plan. He couldn't bring himself to kidnap her, couldn't put her in harm's way.

The leader of the Outcasts, Russ, occasionally hired Wade to do the odd job for them because of his ruthless mercenary reputation in their world. The man wanted Nerina and asked him to bring her in.

They even gave him three of their men to help him. That was how he'd met Tony—also known as Moose—along with Andy and Glenn. They were not the brightest men on the block but generally efficient at getting things done.

Refusing to do the job after he'd already agreed to it was a death sentence. One he'd managed to escape from but just barely. You don't say no to them and get away with it. Russ sent the guys after him. They took great pleasure in trying to use him as target practice, like a pop can sitting on a fence.

Once he escaped, he had returned to Atlantis for the first time in years and informed the king of the man's plans. He'd asked for the permission to marry his daughter to keep her safe. His royal highness was happy to oblige under the guise of being grateful to him for saving the life of his people.

Little did Wade know, the King of Atlantis had his own plan from the moment he laid eyes on the young lad.

~

August 1993

Off the coast of California, a white motor cruiser, "The Triton," drifted to a stop, water rippling behind them. Two people were on-board. One was at the helm, and the other, a young woman, was on the lower deck near the stern of the boat.

The young woman looked into the water. The moon's reflection stared back at her serenely. Not a single cloud interrupted the endless expanse of the stars above, allowing one to see the Milky Way. But she didn't care about the heavens above or the bright shooting star that passed overhead.

Star light, Star bright
First star I see tonight
I wish I may
I wish I might
Have the wish I wish tonight.

She had no need for the silly nursery rhyme any longer, her life-long wish was about to be granted. In mere moments, she wouldn't just be Maggie, the wife of Kyle Winters anymore. She'd be more than that. Her life was about to take on new meaning. Something she had longed for, but never thought she would ever have.

The moon's reflection shattered as two pure white heads broached the surface. She watched as a man placed his hands on the swim platform, hauling himself out of the water, his biceps bulging under the weight of his body. He scooted backwards on the platform, giving Maggie her first full glimpse of him, his silver tail glimmering in the moonlight.

She gasped, her mouth hanging open. Her husband told her about them, but seeing one in person blew her mind. The legends she had read about were true. Mermaids did exist. And she was about to hold the most precious one in her arms. She wanted to jump up and down, but she decided to let her spirit jump instead. If she appeared to be a giddy schoolgirl, they might change their mind.

"Talise, it's time," the man said to the other white head still half submerged in the water. He motioned for her to come up. "We don't have much time."

Slowly, the woman swam up to the boat and handed a bundle of kelp to the merman. Maggie couldn't believe this was happening. The other creature disappeared beneath the surface. A moment later, she appeared again and partially jumped out of the water to gain the leverage needed to pull herself up onto the platform.

The mermaid pulled her long white hair out from under her silver tail. Their skin was so pale and clear, looking like it had never seen the light of day. The woman locked eyes with Maggie. Sadness rang through the depths of her gaze.

Maggie gave her a small smile, nodding her head. The pain of letting go was something she could understand, having lost her uterus to cancer before she met Kyle. The procedure saved her own life, but on the other hand, it took away the life she had hoped to create.

A small cry emerged from the bundle of kelp, tiny arms poking through the seaweed.

"Shhh, darling. It's okay." The young woman leaned over and took the young infant from her husband.

They removed the kelp, and Maggie caught her first glimpse of the child. She didn't look any different than her parents. Holy crap. Strong genes. "Do you all look like that?" As soon as she asked, she slapped her hands over her mouth, blood rushing to her face. "That was rude, I'm sorry."

The man smiled. "Only the royal family." The smile soon left his face as he continued, "We are all that is left of the original Atlantians."

"Maggie, I want you to meet King Dathan and Queen Talise," Kyle said.

Unsure of their customs, she quickly did a half bow. This was the closest she'd ever been to any type of royalty. A nervous shiver ran through her at the thought of caring for a royal. She was certain to mess up and do something wrong.

"You don't cut off people's heads, do you?"

King Dathan chuckled. "We left that barbaric act behind when we came to this planet eons ago."

She wiped away the sweat forming on her brow as everyone laughed at her expense. They talked for a bit longer before it was time for the baby's parents to return to the water. Queen Talise took her husband's hand, and they placed their other hand on the baby's bare chest.

A glowing white light surrounded them. Maggie covered her eyes and looked away. When she looked back, only two mer-people were left. The infant no longer had a tail, only two cute little legs.

She reached down and pulled a soft pink blanket out of a diaper bag and handed it to them. Queen Talise gave her a bitter-sweet smile. One that she understood all too well. Saying good-bye was never easy, even if it wasn't forever.

The queen held the baby girl up to her chest and rested her forehead against hers, tears flowing down her cheeks. She whispered to the infant in a language unknown to Maggie.

King Dathan placed an arm around his wife's shoulders, pulling her close. "Despair not, my dear, she is in good hands." He sat up straight and motioned for Kyle to come forward. "Remember our discussion, she is not to know who she is until it is time."

The two shook hands in agreement, and the young woman handed the child to Maggie. Upon relinquishing her baby girl, Queen Talise let out a loud, high-pitched cry. Clouds appeared from out of nowhere, darkening the sky until not a star was left to light the way.

A loud clasp of thunder caused the infant to start crying. Maggie gently rocked the baby in her arms and watched as the king tried to calm his wife before the storm grew to proportions that even she couldn't stop.

"Do we have to do this?" she asked, pleading with him to change his mind.

"It must be done."

The king slid back into the water, holding out a hand to his distraught queen. She gave her child one last look before quickly disappearing under the water, refusing to take his hand.

"Not a word of this to anyone," King Dathan commanded. The two of them nodded their heads and watched as he disappeared beneath the rolling waves.

A second later, he re-appeared beside their boat, giving it a gentle knock. As they looked over the edge, he said sheepishly, "Her name is Nerina Anastasia Albion. Protect her with your life."

With that, he slid into the depths of the ocean, leaving the two of them alone with his child, praying that one day they would be united again.

Chapter Fifteen

Present day...

"Where ya folks headin'?" the semi-truck driver asked, pulling out of the parking lot.

Wade looked around the sleeper cab. Scattered across the floor were discarded candy wrappers and socks up the yin-yang, smelling a bit like rotten eggs.

"Just north-east really." He didn't want to say too much, given their situation. The less the man knew the better.

"I can take ya as far as Lake Granby. I'm afraid that's the last stop on my schedule."

"Thanks for your help."

They had lucked out. The guy was getting ready to pull out when they walked by his truck, an early morning delivery he'd said. Wade was certain the man never saw the evening news because he didn't bat an eyelash when they approached him. They gave him a cockamamie story about their vehicle dying, leaving them stranded.

"It's the least I can do. Having your engine crap out totally sucks balls."

Nerina bit the corner of her lip. Wade knew she hated lying, so he took the reins instead. Not that he liked being dishonest, but he didn't know what else he could do under the circumstances. She was too innocent to spin a web of deceit.

"The name's Marty." The man stuck out his hand.

Wade shook the callous covered hand. "Casey and April. We're on our honeymoon," he said, winking at her. She rolled her eyes and looked out the window.

"Holy hell, what a lousy start! You guys first-timers?" Marty asked.

"Pretty much."

His response didn't go unnoticed by his wife whose forehead creased in confusion. *Crap.* He had put his foot in his mouth again and dug a deeper grave than the one he was in already.

There was so much about his past she didn't know, and he wasn't sure how much longer he could hide it from her, even he almost forgot about his past transgressions from before their time together.

He should have just said *yes* to the damn question. Nerina was staying quiet for now, but he knew that wouldn't last very long once they were alone. The longer they drove, the more her expression made him worry. It was unlike her to be so quiet.

Wade reached around and touched her knee, but she pulled away from him, moving to an area of the cab he couldn't reach. He sighed. They still had another three hours before they reached Lake Granby. He hated the idea of her having so much time to stew away in her frustration. He was sure that by the time they reached the safe house, she'd have thought of a million different ways to maim him.

Marty turned on the radio, and they sat listening to the country music station in silence. The driver would occasionally belt out a line or two, tapping his fingers on the wheel to the beat of the music. Why couldn't the man have had a pair of earplugs on the floor with all the rest of his stuff?

"Don't worry, pretty lady," the truck driver said, glancing over his shoulder at Nerina who was still sulking. "Things will get better."

She produced a weak smile before turning to stare out the window, resting her chin in the palm of her hand. What did Wade mean by *pretty much*? Why couldn't the bone-headed guy ever give a straight answer? It's not like she would have cared if he was involved with someone before they met. Everyone had a past, even her.

What rubbed her raw was the fact she could barely recognize the man sitting in the passenger seat. Each time he opened his mouth, a new crack appeared in the image of the man she knew.

Pretty soon that image would shatter, and all she'd be left with was a mystery man whose ring she wore on her left hand. The man who was comfortable with lying and hiding the truth from her. She leaned back, wrapping her arms around her waist, her stomach cramping again.

Squeezing her eyes shut, she willed herself not to cry. Her emotions reminded her of a roller coaster ride. They were all over the place. She wasn't sure if it was because of the pregnancy or because of how crappy her life was at the moment.

"Is there a place we can stop?" she asked. "I need to pee."

Marty looked at the time and checked out a green sign as they drove by. "We should be coming up to a truck stop soon."

"Thanks," she said. More than anything she needed a breather from the both of them. They were driving her insane. The truck driver couldn't sing even if his life depended on it, and Wade wouldn't stop his incessant staring.

She needed a few minutes alone to regain her sanity or find what was left of it. Her mind was teetering dangerously close to the edge of a cliff. One more step and she was sure to fall off it.

They slowly pulled into a truck stop. As soon as the man stopped the semi truck, Nerina bolted out the door. She didn't stop running until she rounded the corner of the building, not even when she heard Wade call her name.

"If you can't find her soon, man, I gotta go." Marty said, checking the ratchet straps on his load to make sure they were still secure. Satisfied, he pulled off his gloves and stuffed them into his back pocket.

Wade nodded his head as he walked towards the store. Once inside, the bell above the door alerted the employee, who was half asleep, that he had a customer. The gentleman stood up from his seat behind the counter and looked at him with half-closed eyelids.

"Have you seen a girl wearing a black baseball cap and a blue windbreaker?" he asked the man.

The guy placed his hands on his back and stretched, mouth opening as wide as it could go in the world's largest yawn. "She came in like"—he paused to check his watch—"twenty minutes ago, asking for the bathroom."

"I've already checked it. She's not there."

"Sorry, dude. I have no idea." The employee sat back down in his chair, shrugging his shoulders.

Wade smacked his hands down on the counter and leaned over slightly, looking at the ground. *Women!* Raising his head, he asked, "You don't have any rope, do you?"

"By the door, bottom shelf."

After he purchased the rope, he went to walk out the door when the employee called out to him. "Check behind the shed. There is a table there."

That sounded like the perfect hiding place for his wayward princess. As the bag dangled from his hand, he envisioned her tied to the bed, and desire raced through him, making his jeans tighten too much for his liking. *Jeepers Creepers, where the hell did that come from?* He'd never been one for fetishes or bondage games.

He stuffed his hand in his pocket, attempting to re-adjust himself before the jeans cut off his much-needed blood supply. The rope was merely to stop her from running off again, nothing more.

"Go back to sleep," he mumbled to his pulsating body part. "Do you hear me?"

Stupid things have a mind of their own. Whoever decided to give them brains was probably having a laugh at his expense? He was lost in thought when he rounded the shed, smacking his knee on the edge of the picnic table. Grunting in pain, he swallowed a curse word when he saw her sitting there. Her elbows were on her knees, and her face was buried in the palms of her hands, her shoulders shaking.

Knowing she was crying hit him like a cold shower. He placed the bag on the bench, moved around to her side of the table, and sat down behind her, straddling the bench. Wade pulled her against his chest and rested his head on her shoulder, wrapping his arms around her.

He felt like a heel. "I know things are rough right now, but we'll get through this," he said softly, giving her a gentle squeeze.

"Who am I, Wade?" She tried to sniffle but snorted instead.

"You are, and always will be, my beautiful, sexy wife." He reached into his pocket and pulled out a hanky. "Even with that snot bubble coming out your nose."

With a wobbly smile, she gave him a weak tap on the shoulder as she took the hanky. "What did you mean when you said, *pretty much?*"

He wished he would have just said yes to the truck driver's question, and then maybe she wouldn't have tried to hide again. Poor girl didn't need any more doubt in her life than what had been placed there already.

"Sweetheart, we have to go. The truck driver is ready to leave without us."

"First, tell me what you meant."

How could he tell her the truth when it had to do with a world she wasn't even aware of yet, and during a time of his life that was better left forgotten? His chest tightened as an image passed before his mind's eye—one of despair and agony. He would never forget the blood or the weight of the gun in his hand.

"I was married once before. Can we go now?"

He moved away so quickly that her butt cheek slid off the bench, and the rest of her body went with it, landing in a heap on the ground.

Nerina winced as her hand scraped the concrete beneath the picnic table. "Gee, thanks. You're such a gentleman."

She looked up at her husband, who appeared to be frozen in his spot. Standing up, she waved a hand in front of his face. No response. His watery eyes darted back and forth at some unseen foe.

"Wade?"

When she touched his chest, his hand shot out, grabbing her neck. As soon as his hand closed around her throat and blocked her airway, he appeared to snap back to reality.

He gasped, his eyes widening. All color drained from his face as he pulled his hand away. "I'm sorry. I'm so, so sorry."

Rubbing her burning throat, she stepped away from him, tears spilling from her eyes. Her only consolation was the utter look of horror on his face as he stared at his traitorous limb.

"I'm sorry, I didn't..." He looked at his palms and shook his head, his own tears falling. "I didn't know it was you."

She figured as much. "It's okay. Don't sweat it."

"It's not okay. I hurt you."

Taking his face in her hands, she gave him a quick peck on the cheek and said, "And I kicked your shin earlier. We're even."

Leaning his forehead against hers, he closed his eyes. "What did I ever do to deserve a woman like you?"

"Good question." There was a moment of silence, as she sucked in a breath and walked her fingers up his chest, lazily linking them behind his neck. "Kiss me."

In the dim light that shone down from the side of the shed, she watched as his eyes darkened, and a wicked sexy smile spread across his face. "With pleasure."

Nerina licked her lips, shivering with anticipation. She knew that smile—the one that promised to bring all her erotic sexual fantasies to life. He was not selfish lover and loved to take his time. He pulled her flush against his hardened manhood, which sent a spark of desire between her thighs.

Wade lowered his head and brushed his lips against her, gently nipping at her bottom lip to encourage her to open to him. She gladly obliged, deepening the kiss. His tongue swept inside, mating with hers. Her fingers knotted in his hair, desperately trying to pull him closer.

His hands slid down her back and came to rest on her ass, squeezing her cheeks gently. He rhythmically pulled her against himself, groaning at the divide of clothes between them. Picking her up, he laid her on the picnic table and quickly joined her, one leg splaying across hers.

He leaned down to kiss her, but even before their lips met, they were blinded by a bright light that lit up their cozy, little darkened nook like the fourth of July.

"Freeze."

Chapter Sixteen

"I see you kids found my old make out spot?" the voice said.

Wade shielded his eyes, making out the blob of a shadow behind the light. "Marty, is that you?"

"By George, you should have seen your faces." Marty lowered the light to the ground and smacked his other hand on his knee repeatedly, roaring with laughter. The guy thought he was such a hoot. All that time alone must be frying his brain.

Wade really needed to get Nerina to the safe house. The interruptions were beginning to drive him crazy. They didn't have any quality time alone anymore. When they got off the picnic table and stood up, the man pointed the light at them again. Wade looked over at Nerina. Her long, white-blue hair was being blown around by a light breeze. It was no longer hidden under her baseball cap.

The guy gasped in surprise. "Hey, you're that girl. I had my suspicions, but holy hell."

Wade's heart rate increased, and he placed himself in the empty space between them, blocking the man from being able to see her. He widened his stance, his hands forming tight fights by his sides.

Marty raised his hands in surrender, turning off the light. "Wow, cool your jets, kid. It's fine. I ain't gonna turn you in."

He eyed the guy warily, not sure whether to trust him. Now that he knew who they were, it was risky getting back into his truck, but there was much more at risk if they didn't. In this day and age of the World Wide Web, their faces were probably plastered everywhere, which meant the guy in the store probably recognized him, too.

"How do you know about us?" he asked.

"You're like the top trending story."

Stupid technology. How was he supposed to keep her safe if everyone in the world knew about her? That meant even people here would be able to recognize them if they didn't do something about it soon.

He pulled Nerina off to the side and asked, "Honey, what do you want to do?"

She raised an eyebrow, giving him the 'you know what I want' look. Didn't she already know going back home was off the table? There was nothing left for them back in San Diego.

Leaning over, he grabbed the bag off the bench. "We aren't going back."

Biting her bottom lip, Nerina tilted her head and looked at the slightly overweight man. His cab was filthy, and it looked like he'd been wearing the same clothes for days, but his eyes were gentle which spoke volumes of his character. Despite his weird sense of humor, she felt they could trust him.

Although, if she had her way, she'd hitch a ride back to San Diego. She wanted to see Jenny for herself and know she was okay, but she knew they had no choice but to get back in that truck again— an idea she didn't exactly relish.

Jenny must be beside herself with worry. And now, Nerina had no way to contact her. All because *someone* took it upon himself to mess with her phone. Glaring at Wade, she turned and started walking towards the cab.

"She has a quick temper, doesn't she?" Marty said, slapping Wade on the back. "Ya got your work cut out for ya, man."

She heard that but missed her husband's reply because his words were carried away by the wind. That was probably a good thing for him. She was ready to slug him again. If it wasn't for him and whoever was chasing them, she would be back in her own apartment, cuddling under the covers. Not out here in the middle of nowhere, having to make a less than desirable choice of getting back in that stinking truck.

When she neared the truck, she turned around to see where they were. They were both still standing in the place she'd left them, watching her. "What are you boys staring at? Let's get this over with."

"That's my sexy spitfire," Wade said, grinning.

"Now what?" Nerina asked.

They were standing on the side of the road near Lake Granby, watching Marty's truck lights disappear into the darkness. She rubbed her hands up and down her arms, trying to break the chill of the night air. It might not be winter yet, but it certainly felt like it.

Wade glanced down at the map on his phone. "We walk. It's only five hours away."

"Walk? You're kidding, right?" Dawn wouldn't break for another four hours or so, which meant they'd be walking in the dark.

"We do have legs last I checked." He picked up their luggage and started off down the road.

"I'm pregnant, and I'm nauseous. You can't truly expect me to walk that far." She plopped down on a nearby rock, ready to cry. They'd been awake all night. She hadn't slept a wink in the guy's truck.

Wade placed the suitcase on the ground and hung his head. Walking back to where she was sitting, he kneeled in front of her and placed his hands on her knees. "Neri, we have no other choice."

"I'm tired. I haven't slept since yesterday morning."

He placed his head on her knees. "I'm sorry, babe, but we have to keep moving."

"It's too cold to walk. We don't even have any gloves."

Taking his jacket off, he placed it around her shoulders and gave her a big hug. "We are almost there. Only another fifteen miles."

Usually, she wouldn't baulk at fifteen miles. She had to stay in good shape to swim in her silicone mermaid tail, but lately, her body felt blah. Being sick all the time ate whatever energy she had left.

"Can't we rent a car?" she asked.

He shook his head. "We can't risk anyone seeing us."

"Well, won't every car driving down the road see us if we're walking?" Nerina asked, pointing at a car that was coming their way.

"It's still dark, so that works in our favor. When it gets light, we should be close to the north side of Lake Granby. I'll get us a motel there so you can rest for a bit." Wade stood up and held a hand out to her.

She shook her head, rejecting his help. "So, we're becoming creatures of the night now?"

"For now, yes."

The one thing about walking was it kept the blood circulating, and a person could stay warm, but she wasn't crazy about the idea. Zipping up Wade's jacket, she pulled her hands into the sleeves and stood up. "Fine. I'll walk," she said, taking a few steps in the direction he took earlier before looking over her shoulder at him. "I'll let you carry the luggage."

"Already acting like a queen," he mumbled.

She scowled at him. "I heard that."

Before they reached their destination, Wade was going to regret making her walk the whole way. He was the reason they were in this mess. His decision to remove her from the hospital made him a wanted man and left them stranded in the middle of the night, in the middle of nowhere, out in the freezing cold.

As they approached a corner, Wade looked down at his phone.

He was grateful to have something else to focus his attention on instead of the glare she was giving him. "Looks like this is the street we need to take."

He took her north through the town to reach the highway that was highlighted in yellow on google maps. The streets were deserted, which meant they could pass through undetected, much to his relief.

Hopefully, the media attention would blow over once the next big news story hit the stage. He had enough to worry about between the stupid doctor and the outcasts. The last thing they needed was the entire United States watching out for them.

They walked in silence for nearly an hour and had reached the highway about thirty minutes ago. The odd car passed by them, but no one paid them any mind, despite them carting luggage down the roadside.

"Wade?"

He made a hum of acknowledgement.

"What happened at the hospital?"

He stopped walking, and she bumped into his back. Closing his eyes, he took a deep breath, letting it out slowly. The muscles in his shoulders and upper back totally seized, causing an ache between his shoulder blades. Why couldn't she have waited? He still wasn't sure how to answer the questions he knew were coming?

"You were in danger. I had no choice," he replied, rolling his shoulders to ease the tension.

"Why? What happened?"

"I really don't want to get into it while we're out in the open like this."

"Who do you think is going to hear us, the boogeyman?"

He could almost hear her rolling her eyes behind his back as he started walking again. "Let's just focus on getting to the house."

"We have four more hours to go, don't we? Might as well do something to pass the time," she said, walking beside him for the first time since they left. "I deserve to know why I'm walking outside in the freezing cold."

When she placed his hand on her arm, he covered her hand with his and sighed. She never made things easy for him, but he loved her more than anything else in the world. He wanted to tell her. Yet, he didn't want to at the same time. If he opened his mouth, he'd end up having to lie about something, and he didn't want to dig his grave any deeper. He was already up to his neck in dirty secrets.

"Well?" she prodded again, squeezing his arm.

Wade looked around at everything but Nerina. Her eyes could entrance him to answer just about any question. Thankfully, in the dark, he couldn't see much. The flashlight he held only lit a few feet in front of them. Darkness surrounded them on every side.

She stepped in front of him, putting her hands on his chest. "Wade, look at me."

Oh boy, here we go.

Sliding her hands up his chest, she linked them around his neck, pulling his head down to look at her. He closed his eyes, not wanting to look at her. It wasn't that he was a chicken, but he'd rather not get into a fight in the middle of the street.

She brushed her lips against his, murmuring, "Wade, please talk to me."

His hand dropped the handle of their luggage, and he pulled her close, eagerly returning the kiss. A second later, she stepped back, causing him to open his eyes to see where she went. *Doh!* She knew the game all too well.

"What happened at the hospital?" she asked again.

He glanced at the ground, pressing his lips together tightly as he fought over what to say to get them moving again. Standing on the side of the road was getting them nowhere.

"I saved you. That's all you need to know."

"Saved me from what?"

"From those men at the house, from the doctors, from the whole damn world." Wade grabbed their luggage and stormed off.

"Why do I need saving?" she asked quietly, her voice trembling.

With hunched shoulders and his back facing her, he said, "Because you're different."

"I've been different my entire life. What's the big deal now?"

"Others know." Too many people knew about them, and that made it unsafe for them to stand outside in the open. They had to get moving again. He took her by the arm and tried to make her walk.

She pulled away and wrapped her arms around herself. "Well, it is kind of hard to hide. I have white hair and pale skin. It's not exactly a secret." Her voice broke as she spoke.

He knew that if it wasn't dark, he'd see tears falling down her face. In the stillness of the night, the confident façade that she usually displayed shattered in a million pieces on the ground.

"You know, everyone has told me how different I am, but I never expected it from you," she whispered. "I don't need you telling me I'm a freak."

Groaning, he dropped the suitcase on the ground and sat down on a large boulder on the side of the road, pulling her into his arms. She resisted, but that didn't stop him from gathering her onto his lap. The pain in her voice cut him deeper than the chill in the air ever could.

"You aren't a freak, sweetie." He held her close, taking a moment to breathe in her lilac scent.

"Then what am I?"

For years he'd kept this secret from her, and now on a highway, still hours away from the safe house, he whispered the truth in her ear.

Chapter Seventeen

"I'm sorry, sir." Andy cowered on the ground, his hands covering the back of his head as a gun cocked behind him. The barrel inches away from him.

"She was in your grasp, and you let her slip right through it." Russ pressed the barrel between Andy's fingers and up against his skull. He'd waited years for this moment, only to have his men screw it up.

"It wasn't our fault," Glenn said, ducking behind Moose when the gun swung in his direction.

"Did I ask you to speak?" Russ snapped.

Moose shoved Glenn, knocking him on his side. "If you wouldn't have put me with these two idiots again, I would have had her."

Russ crouched down in front of him, digging the gun into the soft area right under his chin. Moose barely flinched and didn't even blink. "Don't blame the man with the gun. It won't end well for you," Russ said, clocking him on the side of the head with the butt end of the weapon, knocking him out cold. "Take him to the pit."

Two of his men dragged Moose out by his feet, disappearing down a long tunnel. Glenn and Andy looked at each other with wide eyes, sweat beading on their foreheads. They were at the private entrance in the underground caverns of the island. Russ was already waiting for them when they arrived.

"I expected better from you guys. Maybe I should just toss you all into the pit."

"No, no. Please." Glenn hunched his shoulders, staying as close to the cave ground as possible.

His lips curled into a grin, showing more teeth than necessary. That was what he liked to see. Submission. If he wanted something done, he refused to let anyone walk all over him. He had to make them cower in fear and be the big bad boss. His father taught him that.

Rest in peace, bastard.

"Why not? It's not like you guys are any good to me." He motioned for his other men to grab them.

"Wait, wait," Andy said, leaning away from the men who came over to him. "There's a way for us to fix this."

Motioning for the guys to stop, he pressed his gun into Andy's forehead. "If I like what you have to say, maybe I won't blow your head off."

He swallowed hard, going cross-eyed as he stared at Russ' finger on the trigger. "I know where her best-friend lives."

Russ pulled the gun back, resting it up on his shoulders, slapping Andy on the back. "Best news I've heard all day. Maybe you're still useful after all."

He laughed when the two men sighed in relief. "I just want the girl. Is that too hard to ask?"

"No, sir," Andy and Glenn said in unison.

"Good. Now get out of my sight."

When the two men left, Russ turned to Charlie, his right-hand man. "Go with them. Make sure they don't screw up."

His man nodded, following the two men up the stairs. Soon, Russ would be restored to his former glory, and he'd make the king pay for taking his life away. And the man's daughter was just the way to do it.

If they wouldn't give him his life back, then he'd take away theirs as well.

Maybe he'd even have his way with the girl before all this was over. She was a delectable little thing with curves in all the right places, so perfectly scrumptious. It shocked him when he saw her at the aquarium in an almost perfect replica of her family's tail color.

He knew, without a doubt, that she was the king's daughter, but he had no idea what she was doing on the surface. That didn't matter, though. It worked out better for him anyway. He didn't need to coerce anyone into sneaking into the court of the king and snatching her from there.

Maybe he would take her as his wife and flaunt it in the king's face when he stripped his title away from him, taking his place on the throne. Slowly, Russ made his way up to the house in search of his little treasure.

"Lauren, where are you?"

"Daddy," the little girl yelled, running into his arms, bubbling with excitement. "Did you find her?"

"Not yet, dear, but soon." He picked her up, swinging her around.

"Can she really make me a mermaid?"

"Yep, and she can make you all better, too."

They didn't have much time to track her down as his daughter's time was running short. She deserved to see where she came from, and the man who took her mother from her. If they had been in Atlantis, his wife would have survived. His body trembled with anger. The king would pay for what he did to them, and he would pay in every way possible. Russ would make sure of that.

His daughter wrapped her arms around him, giving him a kiss on the cheek. "It's okay, Daddy."

He gave her a small smile before putting her down. "You're right, sweetheart. Everything will be okay."

That was a promise he intended to keep, even if he had to take matters into his own hands.

Jason sat watching the news in his apartment, bummed that they hadn't manage to speak with her. He was parking the car when Craig went up to the hospital room. Even before he had a chance to see her, the fire alarm went off, and everyone was evacuated.

When he had finally caught up with Craig, he was raving about a man who could turn water into ice. He'd thought the doctor had finally lost his marbles. People couldn't do that sort of thing. No human anyway. Who would have expected there to be two of them? Two finds of the century, according to his boss.

Apparently, the girl's husband got her out of the building without anyone seeing them, and Craig wasn't able to follow them because his feet had been frozen to the floor. The only time he'd seen that happen was in a fantasy story. Now it seemed like Jason had found himself right in the middle of one.

He felt like he was on candid camera, and someone was pulling a prank on him. Aliens and people with powers weren't real. They couldn't be. But then again, here they were.

Jason shook his head as he got up to go to the fridge. Pulling out another beer, he popped off the cap and turned back to the television set. Right in the center of the television screen was a picture of Nerina and Wade. He rushed to turn up the sound.

"Police are asking the residents of Colorado to keep their eyes open for Nerina and Wade Douglas. They were last seen at a truck stop in Villa Grove."

He clicked off the television and grabbed his phone. Before he even dialed Craig's number, his phone started ringing.

"We're taking a trip," Craig said, even before Jason said hello.

"I take it you saw the news?"

"Yes, pack your bags. We're swinging by to pick you up in thirty minutes."

"As much as I understand your excitement, sir, how do you expect to find her? Colorado has a population of about five million,"

Jason said. Not that Craig would listen to the voice of reason. His heart was set on finding the girl.

"Luck, my dear boy."

"Why don't we just stay near her friend's place? She's bound to be back for her."

The doctor stayed silent for a moment. "Okay, you're about her age. Why don't you go be-friend the girl and see what you can find out?"

Well, that took a weird turn. How was he supposed to approach her? "What if she's one of them?"

"She's not. I checked her blood. Let me know what you find out."

With that, his boss hung up the phone, leaving him staring at it. He wasn't a people person, let alone a ladies' man. What was he supposed to do now? Just walk up to her and say, 'Hey, where's your friend'?

That would definitely go over well. She'd probably view him as some freak if he showed up at her house and likely wouldn't give him the time of day. He had a genius IQ, but if his ability to socialize with the opposite sex was graded, he'd probably get a D minus or an F.

He was twenty-seven years old, and he still didn't know how to talk to women. That was pretty pathetic, but you couldn't avoid women forever, right? He had to do it sometime, and what better way than to practice on her? It wasn't like they were going to become a thing. That eased some of the pressure he was feeling. But then he remembered if he failed, they may never have another chance to find the other girl.

"Great! Thanks, doc." He grabbed his jacket and decided to stop by the hospital first to see if she had checked out yet. She'd probably have a police escort for a few days, so he'd have to be careful that no one became suspicious of him. He didn't think Craig would be too impressed if he had to come and bail him out of jail. It was time to play it cool, like a cucumber, and act like James Bond. James always seemed to get the girl.

Why couldn't he have been like a line-backer or something? They didn't even have to try. Girls just hung on their every word. Jason was the nerd in the corner. Women never even looked in his direction. Frankly, he was okay with that. It gave him a chance to concentrate on his studies. Of course, with no prospective girlfriends, he went to his own prom dateless, hanging out along the wall with the other single, dateless guys.

He placed his palm on his forehead, shaking his head. Man! He was boring! Surely, as an educated man, he could figure out how to charm a lady.

Stop being a wuss.

If his professor buddies could do it, so could he. He pulled into the parking lot of the hospital and parked the car. All he had to do was walk inside and ask if Jenny was still a patient. Nothing to it, right?

Chapter Eighteen

Nerina stared straight ahead, refusing to acknowledge that he had even spoken. If he wanted to play games with her, then so could she. A mermaid? What a load of crock. Why couldn't he be serious for once? Even while they were running for their lives, he was still joking about her looks.

"I have to pop into the store when we reach the town center," he said. She grunted a response back, not caring at this point.

When they finally arrived on the north side of Lake Granby, they'd seen their faces all over the newspapers and decided to keep going to the safe house instead of getting a hotel. But first, he stepped into a drugstore with his hat and sunglasses on to purchase hair dye. Apparently, she wasn't allowed to look like herself anymore, either.

They started walking again, and soon they were walking down a trail on the east side of Shadow Mountain Lake—a water reservoir attached to Grand Lake. Daylight made the trail easier to see, but she didn't want to walk anymore. Her feet were sore. A blister had formed on the back of her heel, and another one was forming on the ball of her foot. Each step made her cringe in pain. She sat down on a nearby rock and gently removed her shoe, peeling off her damp sock.

Wade placed his pack on the ground and pulled out the first aid kit. He crouched down and placed her foot on his lap, tending to her blisters. "There. You're good to go."

Internally, she struggled. One part of her wanted to say thank you, and the other didn't want to speak to him at all. Did he think she was still a child living in a fantasy world? All this time she thought he supported her job as a mermaid performer, and here he was, making fun of it.

If only she was a mermaid, then she could dive into the ocean and disappear into its depths, never to be stared at ever again. She'd never have to worry about what people think or put up with jokes being made at her expense.

Not wanting to be rude, she mumbled, "Thank you."

"So, you can speak."

Nerina glared at him as she put her sock and shoe back on. Getting up from the rock, she continued down the trail in silence until they came to a fork. Wade pointed to her left, and she started walking in that direction. In the distance, she heard a howl and shivered.

"Please, talk to me," he said, putting his hand on her shoulder.

"Why don't you talk to me first, then?"

"I thought I just did that," he said jokingly.

"That." She shook her finger at him. "That right there ticks me off so much."

He spread out his arms, palms facing the sky. "What'd I do?"

"I give up." She wanted to smack him, but what good would it do? He was like every other typical guy. How could he be so cute, yet so cotton-pickin' annoying at the same time?

They lapsed back into silence for the remainder of the walk. The trail came to an end, and they exited the forest. Any other time in her life, she may have enjoyed the scenic walk. The lake beside them was gorgeous, but today, her mind was too far gone to enjoy anything.

She was a walking zombie, ready to collapse. He better not expect her to walk very much farther. She had exhausted all her energy. Her muscles ached, and all she wanted to do was cry. She did that a lot lately. Sometimes for no reason at all.

The twinges in her side progressively got worse, but she refused to let him see how bad it was. "Are we almost there?" she asked.

"Just another block or two."

She sighed. The area didn't look too well developed. Hopefully, they would have power. Some houses lined the lake on one side of the road, while the other side remained covered in trees. The unpaved road crunched beneath the soles of her shoes.

Why on earth did Wade bring her all the way out to the middle of nowhere? There weren't even any stores on this side of the lake or anything that looked remotely like entertainment.

"Where are we?" she asked, kicking a rock across the dirt road. Thankfully, the sun was shining overhead, warming the cool air.

"Grand Lake."

She'd never heard of the place. But from what she'd seen of it so far, it would be a nice place to visit in the summer, but visiting a beach house in the winter made no sense to her. The two didn't exactly go together very well. She pulled her hands inside her sleeves and hugged her chest. With how cold it was already, she could imagine the pristine lake freezing over soon.

She continued to follow Wade until he stopped in front of a pine log cabin. Pulling a key out of his pocket, he walked up to the light blue door and shoved the key in the lock. Nerina didn't follow him. She just stood there, staring at the building.

"Whose place is this?"

"It belongs to Kyle and Maggie."

How come they never told her about this place or even brought her here while growing up? Off to the side of the cabin sat a sky-blue Range Rover which was all set for driving in the harsh winter climate that Grand Lake was known for. The vehicle sat under a wooden garage to protect it from the elements.

Turns out it even had valid insurance. A huge stack of firewood lined the back wall of the garage. Did someone know they were coming? She shivered at the thought. As she went to go up the stairs, her legs were far too tired to cooperate. Wrapping her hands around her knee, she tried to put her foot on the first step and almost fell over.

Wade came back down the stairs and scooped her up in his arms. He didn't put her down until they entered a bedroom. The bed in the room looked rather inviting, with its thick flowery duvet. He gently laid her on the bed, and she crawled under the covers. She fell asleep as soon as her head hit the pillow, entering a dream world that was as strange, if not stranger, than real life.

Her vision was hazy, and she couldn't see much more than a few inches in front of her. She was unable to move, wrapped up like a burrito. She tried to speak, but all that emerged was a loud, high-pitched cry.

"Shush, my darling. Everything will be okay." Cool, moist lips pressed against her forehead. A soft and gentle voice began to sing as a woman's image swirled in her vision. Her turquoise eyes captivated her, and the woman's long white hair enveloped her like a cocoon. The melody of the song soothed her, even though she didn't understand the words.

It was unlike any language she'd ever heard before, but it pulled at her heart strings. She felt like she'd heard the song a thousand times before. It kind of reminded her of a nursery rhyme that parents would sing to a young child.

"Mommy loves you," the woman murmured in her ear, cuddling her close.

The image faded and Nerina's eyes snapped open, her heart thumping erratically in her chest. It wasn't possible. It couldn't be. She pulled her hair away from her face, wiping the sweat off her forehead.

Had her entire life been a lie? Or was this just her imagination running wild? She rolled over and looked on the nightstand but didn't see her clock. Did she knock it down while she was sleeping?

She looked over the side of the bed and didn't notice it on the ground. Reaching over, she turned on the lamp and an unfamiliar room stared back at her. That was when all the events of the last few days filled her mind.

"Wade, get your butt in here!" she yelled.

Wade cringed when he heard his name. When she sounded like that, nothing good ever came from their conversations. He procrastinated by leaning down and throwing another log on the fire.

His wife had been asleep for about five hours, and he'd hoped she would forget about wanting to talk to him, but that was only wishful thinking. He wished Kyle and Maggie were here already because he had a feeling Nerina wouldn't let him off lightly, not if her tone had anything to say about it.

When she called for him again, her voice was higher pitched than the last time, and he figured he better listen. He walked over to the bedroom door that was slightly ajar, and he saw her with her back propped up against a pillow, her hair all tousled from sleep. The epitome of sexy, but he doubted she had sex on her mind.

His friend down below did, though, perking up at the sight of her. "I highly doubt you're going to get lucky right now," he said under his breath, adjusting his pants. He pushed open the bedroom door.

"What's wrong, sweetheart?"

She pulled her legs up to her chest and wrapped her arms around them, giving him a guarded look, effectively closing him out of any type of embrace. He figured as much. Sitting down on the side of the bed, he waited patiently for her to talk.

"I don't know which hurts more, learning that Kyle isn't my father or that you knew and didn't tell me."

Wade looked down at the brown multi-colored carpet which had seen better days. His heart squeezed in his chest as her pained voice took hold of it in a vice-like grip. He'd hurt her. Something which he had never intended to do.

But it was inevitable, wasn't it? The truth was going to come out, eventually. He turned to look at her. "I'm sorry."

"How could you not tell me?"

"It wasn't my place." That was a lousy excuse, but it was the only one he had. Truthfully, he could have told her and warned her of all that was to come.

"Don't give me that bull crap. You could have told me."

"Then what? What good would it have done? Here's the truth. He loves you as much as any father could love a child. For all intents and purposes, he was your father."

"But he isn't my father."

He sat cross-legged in front of her, taking her hands in his. "What is a dad, Neri?"

She knew the answer to that. He knew she did. A dad wasn't necessarily the sperm donor. It was the man who stepped up and took care of you, raising you as his own. The one who was there for you through the hard times. Family was so much deeper than just whose blood runs through your veins.

"But—"

Wade put his finger against her lips. "No buts. He was your dad in every sense of the word."

"That's fine and dandy, but who is my real dad?"

"I think we need to wait for Kyle and Maggie. They can give you more details than I can." He looked away from her as she spoke, hoping she wouldn't see that he had told another lie. He knew as much as they did.

At the mention of Maggie's name, Nerina got up, wrapped her arms tightly around herself, and moved to the bedroom window. She looked so vulnerable, and it tore him apart inside.

"What about Maggie?" she asked.

"What about her?" he asked, knowing full well what she meant.

"Is she my mother?"

He swallowed hard. This was not a conversation he wanted to be having with her alone. The more he revealed, the angrier she would be with him for knowing more than her. Inevitably, she would ask him more questions about himself, and he knew he'd have a big fight on his hands once it all came out. She would fight him physically or run away again.

"Why do you ask?"

She whipped around suddenly and shoved her hands in her hair, plugging her ears. "Stop answering my questions with a question. It pisses me off." Dropping her hands, she placed them on her hips. "Is she my mother?"

Oh boy. He ran his hand through his hair. "I think I better go stoke the fire," he said, standing up and moving towards the door.

"Halt, buster."

He paused in mid-step, chuckling nervously. She had the mother-tone down pat, and she wasn't even in her second trimester yet.

"Yes, Mother."

"Don't mock me right now."

He had to bite his cheeks to keep from laughing at her stern expression. "I'm sorry."

"Well?"

"No, she isn't," he said, sighing.

Chapter Nineteen

Nerina crumpled to the floor. When he rushed to her side, she pushed him away. "Go away!" she cried.

Never in her entire life had she ever felt so alone. She had no parents. No one who cared enough about her to tell her the truth, not even Wade. How did he fit into this whole picture?

He tried to pick her up from the floor, but her fist shot out, connecting with his face. He rubbed his jaw which was already turning red. "Geez, I don't know why anyone thought you needed protecting." Standing up, he marched out of the room, slamming the door behind him. The tears fell unceasingly. If she didn't belong to them, who did she belong? It was bad enough she was different, but to have no one to belong to? No family?

"Wake up, Neri. Wake up," she cried, sobbing into her hands. This couldn't be real. "Please, let me be dreaming."

She wanted in her own bedroom at home, but that was gone. Everything she'd ever known was gone. Caput. Over. And all Wade could do was make jokes. A mermaid... Seriously? Really?

It was bad enough that her baby had Sirenomelia, and that was what he chose to joke about? How much lower could he go? She should have punched him harder or kicked him in the groin, making him wish he'd been truthful.

Gone was the sweet girl who wouldn't hurt a fly. She wanted to boot him all around the room for keeping something like this a secret from her. Shaking her head, she wiped the tears from her eyes. "I refuse to sink that low."

She'd hit him more times than she could remember over the last few days, and that wasn't who she wanted to be. It wasn't right. No matter what circumstances she was facing. Being mad was justified. He knew all about her, while she knew nothing. But did he know who her parents were, and how she wound up with Kyle and Maggie?

Running her tongue over her dry lips, she hadn't realized how thirsty all her crying had made her. Getting up from the floor, she made her way to the bedroom door and opened it.

Standing in the doorway, she listened for Wade. The house was eerily silent. Her stomach dropped through the floor, and her scratchy throat constricted. Had he left her? In truth, she wouldn't be surprised if he did. She'd certainly given him enough reason to.

Her emotions were a tad hard to control these days, even her appendages had a mind of their own. She had never have hit him before, never wanted to. There were other things she'd rather do with him. She had never allowed anything to get in the way of their relationship before.

But he didn't seem to think the same way. She would never have kept that type of secret from him. What was it about men that made them think they could? The way that they compartmentalized everything in their life drove her insane. It's one of the things she learned about him early on in their relationship.

Men had this uncanny ability to create boxes for every part of their life, and they believed no two boxes should ever cross paths. Even if the contents somewhat overlapped, they still didn't think it should affect the other.

If you were upset over something they didn't think should matter, they would look at you as if your head was spinning, like you were some creature from the black lagoon. Now here he was telling her she was actually a *creature.*

A hard chuckle rumbled deep in her throat. Her? A mermaid? Really, seriously? He knew how much she loved mermaids, and the whole myth behind them. Couldn't he have found something else to joke about?

After pouring herself a glass of water, she saw a baguette in a bag on the table and decided to cut herself a slice. Wade walked in as she finished slicing a piece off. Picking up the rest of the bread, she chucked it at his head.

"How could you make fun of me?" she asked, placing her hands on her hips.

He picked up the bread and put it on the counter before resting his hands on the countertop on either side of her, boxing her in. "We really have to make better use of those hands of yours."

"Don't even try it." She put her hands on his chest to push him away, but the warmth of his skin beneath the shirt seeped through her palms, sending a tingling sensation up her arm. Momentarily distracted, she allowed her fingers to wander across his chest, roaming over his nipples.

She heard a sharp intake of breath as Wade's muscles twitched under her touch, letting her know he could feel the connection as much as she did. Tilting her head, she looked up at him, and their eyes locked.

"I promised to give you the moon when we got married, Neri. That hasn't changed for me."

His eyes sparkled with desire and the promises of what was waiting for her if she gave herself to him. She knew he wouldn't force it and was waiting for her to make a decision. He cupped her cheek with the palm of his hand, brushing his thumb along her cheek bone. She rested her hand on the back of his, leaning into his touch.

"You are so beautiful." Wade leaned forward, kissing her forehead.

"Will you still think I'm beautiful when my stomach is as big as a house?" she asked.

"Even then."

He leaned forward, stopping just before his lips reached hers. His warm, moist breath teased her senses as he waited for her to take the next step. And it didn't take her long to make up her mind. She closed the gap between them in seconds. All the conflict over the last few days disappeared beneath the passion rising between them.

She gripped his t-shirt in her hands, pressing herself up against him. His erection stretched his pants taunt against his crotch. Poor guy hadn't seen much action lately, but she'd make sure that today made up for it all. Save him from all his frustration and sorrows before he had a wet dream.

Continuing to hold on to his shirt, she walked backwards towards the bedroom, refusing to break eye contact. Her body was already preparing for him, her center aching to be touched.

Sure, he'd kept secrets from her, but nothing ever felt as right as his touch did on her body. That was what she wanted. Right here. Right now. As she walked backwards, her hands slid down to the waist of his pants, undoing his belt.

She needed the distraction something fierce. She needed to remember that she was all woman, and not some strange crazy freak. His pants fell to the floor, and he stepped out of them.

"My turn." He took hold of her shirt, pulling it over her head before tossing his own shirt to the floor.

She ran her fingers along his define abdomen, following the waist band of his boxers, currently stretched out in front of him. Licking her lips, she slid her hand down even further, cupping him through the material.

He raised his head toward the ceiling and groaned. "You're going to kill me, girl."

"You ain't seen nothing yet." She grinned, pulling his boxers down in one swift motion, his erection bouncing free.

Nerina kneeled down in front of him, running her index finger along the roughened scar on his right thigh muscle. "You never told me about what happened."

His leg stiffened, and he pulled away from her touch, but then quickly scooped her up in his arms. He fell back onto the bed, taking her with him. "Less talk, more play," he murmured, brushing his lips against her neck.

She giggled as his whiskers ticked her skin. They hadn't had much time for regular hygiene, and he'd grown a five o'clock shadow. She kind of liked the ruggedly handsome look. He looked dashing in his birthday suit, sporting his whiskery shadow.

The thoughts quickly vacated her mind when his hand came to rest between her legs, flicking her sensitized nub. She arched her back and closed her eyes, losing herself to the sensation.

Her body cried out, reminding her they needed to do this more often. "Hmm, just like that," she groaned.

"You like that, do you? What about this?" As his palm cupped her, he slid two fingers inside her, paying extra careful attention to the spot she liked. It skyrocketed her to the moon and back.

The ache inside her building, like a volcano ready to blow. Heck, he was good with his fingers. She gripped the bed sheets, rocking her hips in rhythm with his fingers.

"That's it, darling. Let yourself feel everything."

She bit her cheeks to stop from crying out, not that anyone could hear them. He moved his fingers faster and faster inside her until she couldn't help but cry out his name. White lights sparkled behind her eyelids as tremors rocked her body.

Before her body calmed, he was already inside her, quickly taking her to the second peak. She climaxed almost instantly, her whole body on fire. He cried out in ecstasy as her muscles clamped around him, bringing him his own release.

Wade's arms shook with the intensity of their lovemaking, almost ready to collapse on top of her. He pulled out and dropped to the bed beside her, pulling her into his arms. "Man, that was good."

"You can say that again," she said, resting her head on his chest.

His heart thumped erratically, and sweat dripped off his forehead. Her body heat increased his internal body temperature, but he didn't want to let her go. It the first time he'd actually managed to get her in his arms since the morning sickness began.

"Honey?" she said softly.

"Ya?"

"Will you ever tell me about what happened to your leg?"

He took in a sharp breath, letting it out slowly. "I'd rather not go to a dark place after what we just did."

She looked up at him, jutting her bottom lip out. He nipped her lip playfully, before covering her lips with his in a sweet, tender kiss. Revealing the truth would open too many doors—ones he wasn't quite ready to open up yet. He'd rather have this playful time with her while they could before the cat was out of the bag, and he found himself in the doghouse.

Instead, he let his fingers do the talking, tracing her areola and watching her nipple pucker. He closed his mouth around her nipple, sucking gently. She groaned, but it wasn't a 'that feels good' groan.

"Stop." She scrambled out of bed, rushing towards the bathroom with her mouth covered.

Damn. Well, at least they managed to have one quickie, and he couldn't wait until their next rendezvous. He lifted his arms and linked his hands behind his head, leaning back on the pillow.

She might not feel very good, but he felt awesome. He was no longer desperate, nor did he have to jump into a cold shower to cool off. And it stopped her line of questioning, of which he was super grateful.

Hasn't she ever heard of the phrase, 'curiosity killed the cat'? In this case, he'd likely be the cat. If he didn't watch himself, he'd be roadkill, and she'd be the one driving the car.

Of that, he was certain!

Chapter Twenty

"Wow, I look so different." Nerina turned her head to the left, then to the right. Wade had dyed her hair red—a fiery red which almost glittered under the bathroom light.

"I figured it would match your temper," he said, winking at her through the mirror.

She dug her elbow into his stomach. He burst out laughing, rubbing the targeted area.

"You look amazing."

"Now I'm a ghost with red hair. I thought the idea was to make me less noticeable?"

She couldn't take her eyes off the color. The hair stuck out like a sore thumb, even worse than before. But then again, that might be because the two hair colors were as far apart as the east was from the west.

He picked up the scissors that were on the bathroom counter and took her hand, leading her to a chair in the kitchen.

"Do we have to cut it?" she asked.

"A new look, remember?"

She heard the swish of him opening and closing the scissors

dangerously close to her head. Nerina cringed. "Isn't the dye job enough?" Her long hair had been her pride and joy, except for the color. She'd rarely ever cut her hair, except for the trims that Maggie gave her every now and then.

Before he even gave her another chance to think about it, he took a fistful of hair and cut it off. Butterflies rattled around in her stomach. Too much was changing and way too fast for her liking.

He cut it to just above her shoulders, and as she stared at herself in the mirror, she had to admit he did a good job. "Where did you learn how to cut hair?"

"My mom." He shrugged his shoulders nonchalantly.

"What was she like?"

"She..." Wade paused, scratching his head as a sad smile played on his face. After he got kicked out of Atlantis, they had been estranged. More by his choice than hers. His mother understood what had happened and still wanted to see him, but he'd refused to see her.

The guilt had eaten him up inside over what happened, and he couldn't understand why she still loved him and would even risk associating with him. When he regained his place in Atlantis, he went to see his mother at her request. During their visit, he'd asked her why she even wanted to see him. Her reply was, "The love of a mother is unconditional, my dear."

How could he explain his mother to Nerina? "She lives each day to the fullest. Never lets anything get her down. And she bloody cares more than she should."

"Where does she live?"

He stopped brushing her hair, floundering for a response. Should he elaborate on his answer from earlier when he told Nerina that she was a mermaid? The answer hadn't gone over very well. What if he told her that his mom was one, too? And himself as well? He backed away from her as he contemplated his answer. "She's out at sea."

"With the Navy?" she asked, running a hand through her newly shortened hair.

"Not exactly."

Boy, this was harder than he thought. He kind of preferred the silent treatment over the curiosity. He didn't want to tell a lie, and there were already too many secrets he had kept from her.

"On a cruise?"

"No."

His palms began to sweat. If he lifted his arms, the sweat rings on his shirt would give away his nervousness. Why had he brought up the topic of his mother? He pinched the bridge of his nose and groaned.

"Oh, Wade, she isn't dead, is she?"

Despite them having been together for so long, he always avoided the subject of family, even when it came to the wedding invitations. She knew next to nothing about his past, only that he was there with her, right here, right now.

He seriously needed a drink. Walking over to the fridge, he pulled out a beer. He downed it in one swig and reached for another. She snuck up behind him and grabbed it from his hand.

He went to grab it back, but she put it behind her back and said, "Not until you stop evading me. I know you're keeping more secrets from me."

"It's not like you want to hear it," he grumbled, reaching into the fridge for another beer and holding it high out of her reach as he made his way to the floral-patterned couch.

He heard the distinct puncture of the other beer can, causing him to glance her way. Nerina never drank beer. She hated the smell, wouldn't even kiss him after he had a drink. But there she was, taking a large swig while pinching her nose.

A tremor rocked her body after she was done, and her face scrunched up, like she'd just finished sucking a lemon. "I don't know how you can drink this stuff," she said, tossing the can in the sink after remembering she wasn't supposed to be drinking while pregnant.

"It's an acquired taste." He lifted his can in a toast to her.

Nerina came over and sat beside him, massaging the tense muscle in his shoulders. "You can't keep shutting me out, Wade."

Lifting her hand, he gently kissed her palm. "Do you remember what I told you earlier?"

"Yes," she answered, uncertainty filling her soul again.

"I wasn't lying, you know."

She pulled her hands away and scooted further away from him on the couch, drawing her arms around herself again. "I hate when you make fun of my profession."

He moved closer to her and took her face in his hands, staring into her eyes. "It is the truth. You are a mermaid. So is my mother, and so am I. Well, merman."

Tears spilled down her cheeks as she pushed him away. "Don't do this."

"Haven't you ever wondered why you can stay underwater for so long?"

"Fine, if you're just going to joke about my looks again, I'm not even going to bother."

Getting up from the couch, Nerina started walking towards the bedroom. As she neared the door, she turned around to look at him. He was *gone*. She hadn't even heard him move from his spot on the couch.

She glanced around the room, biting her bottom lip. Her stomach flipped and churned. She swallowed hard. Her chest a bundle of nerves. "Wade?"

Then, as she was looking at the couch, a light mist swirled in the exact spot that Wade was previously sitting. A second later, there he was, sitting on the couch as though he had never left, with a gigantic grin on his face.

"What the heck? How—you were..." She plunked herself down on the recliner across from the couch. "I'm going crazy."

She watched him lift his hand, disappearing from view. He reappeared a second later.

"I'm dreaming. I must be dreaming." Leaning over, she put her head in her hands. When he approached her, she shoved him, and he landed on his butt on the ground. "Don't touch me. Don't you dare touch me!"

She ran into the bedroom and slammed the door, locking it behind her.

The Triton, with its chipped paint and aging parts, coasted to a stop at their usual meeting spot. Kyle hadn't had any reason to perform regular maintenance on the boat as they didn't use it as much as they used to. Prior to their departure, he did a quick check to make sure it would function properly. Thankfully, anything that needed fixing looked to be purely cosmetic.

His merman messenger swam on ahead to contact the king to let them know of their arrival. Why the man thought it was a good idea to let his daughter be in the hands of another Atlantian, he would never know. Didn't he know that she'd get pregnant ahead of time? What was going on in that kingly brain of his?

Kyle was the guardian, not some half-assed youth. His family had been the sworn land protectors of the royal family for as long as history had been recorded. They followed them to earth when their own world turned against them. Very few males survived the plague that had almost eradicated them. A plague that was brought to their world by a star. The people named it wormwood as it poisoned the water in which they lived.

They never discovered why only the males of the Atlantians were affected. They'd had no time to figure it out as it spread so quickly. The royal family spent so much of their energy trying to save the people that they almost died themselves. Finally, they had decided to leave their world behind, journeying to the closest planet that was like theirs.

At least that was the story that had been passed down, along with the stories about how the remaining mermaids lured human men to their apparent deaths. The surviving sailors would return to land with their tall tales of how these mysterious half woman/half fish creatures killed half their crew. The truth, however, was slightly different. They hadn't been killed but rather were turned into mermen to further their race.

That practice stopped ages ago, but they still sang songs about it in the deep, so that the sirens who saved their people would never be forgotten. Not that he had ever heard their song himself, but the land people claimed it was the most beautiful thing they'd ever heard. All this happened long before he was born, so all he had were the tales that the guardians had passed down to him.

Meh! Enough reminiscing. Kyle had more important matters at hand. "Maggie, do you see anything?"

"Not yet," came her reply from the deck below.

They were under the cover of darkness. The moon was shining high in the sky. No land to be seen. He wondered if the clear skies would disappear once he told the royal family the news. He could only hope they'd spare him for failing to do his job properly.

Although if he had any say in the matter, the king had to be partly to blame for what happened. Kyle would have sent Wade packing, given his history. But no, he was ordered to work together with him. The young, idiotic whippersnapper knew nothing anything about being a guardian. He was a rebellious, inexperienced fish boy. If one of their own had been with her, Kyle wouldn't have to fix the stupid mess they were in now.

"Kyle, he's here," Maggie yelled.

He descended the ladder, his knees cracking as he went down each rung. The king sat on the landing once again. Something he hadn't done since they made the decision about Wade.

"What is this urgent matter we must discuss?" The king wasted no time with pleasantries and cut right to the chase.

"Wade neglected his duties to protect your daughter." He gripped the edge of the boat, waiting for the man's response.

The king raised his eyebrow at Kyle and motioned for him to

continue. Didn't the messenger fill him in? He'd told the errand boy exactly what to say. Guess the kid chickened out.

"He impregnated your daughter."

A grin broke out across the king's face, the wrinkles around his eyes growing more prominent. "Well, it's about damn time."

"Say what?" Kyle asked, scratching his head.

"They've been married a few years already. I thought it was never going to happen in my lifetime." The king's tail slapped the deck as he clapped his hands, apparently thrilled.

"I thought you didn't want her to know anything till she was thirty?"

King Dathan waved away his previous pronouncement. "I changed my mind."

Kyle's eyes narrowed. "You wanted this?"

"A king deserves a grandchild before he dies, doesn't he?"

Kyle never had a chance to reply. A loud beeping sound emanated from his sonar equipment, distracting him. He rushed over to check what it was, but a hard port-side impact knocked the boat onto its side. Shards of the hull flew into the air. He was thrown against the outer wall of the cabin and banged his head on the light, crumpling to the ground as the boat came crashing back down.

The object tore right into the hull and hit the engine, igniting it into a fiery inferno. The explosion was loud enough to be heard for miles. The sky lit up, and a mushroom cloud filled the air above the boat.

None of them knew that in the shadow of the night, a boat had silently approached them, waiting to strike at just the right moment. And when it did, the man at the helm smiled. His boss would be so happy to know that he had taken out the protectors of the princess and the King of Atlantis, leaving the throne ripe for his master's taking.

Chapter Twenty-One

"Come on, Nerina! Talk to me." He pounded his fist on the door. For five days straight, she hadn't uttered a single word, refused to even be in the same room with him. "Grow up and get your hot butt out here!"

Hot damn!

He sounded just like his father. Wade raked a hand through his hair, his body involuntarily shivering at the thought. The last thing he wanted was to become was a man like him. His father had left his mom shortly after the incident. They were supposed mated for life, but his father couldn't accept the fact that his mom wanted to keep in contact with her criminal son. In the end, the man even left Atlantis because they wouldn't let him marry someone else.

He refused to become a man like him. "Please, Neri?"

"Go away!"

"I can't do that," he said, forcing his voice to remain calm and steady, despite the fact he wanted to beat the door down. "We really need to talk."

"I don't know you. Leave me alone."

He placed his forehead against the door, resting his hands on the wooden surface. "Babe, you don't know you either." When she remained silent, he knew he hit the right chord. "Look, I know it's hard, but I promise I'll help you work through it."

"How do I know I can trust you?"

"I saved your butt at the house and the hospital, didn't I?"

"What if you're working for them?"

He clenched his fists. Hopefully, she would never find that part out. If she found out he used to work with the Outcasts, then all hell would break loose. There was no doubt in his mind.

"If I was, don't you think I'd have handed you over already?"

"How do I know that you aren't waiting for the right moment?"

"Damn it, Neri." He thumped on the door with the side of his fist. "Don't make me break the door down."

He walked over to the kitchen and riffled through the cupboards. When he found what he was looking for, he returned to the door and shoved a toothpick into the little hole in the handle, popping the lock.

She gasped and pressed up against the door, but she was no match for his strength. Wade dug his shoulder into the door and continued to push it open. The resistance from her side disappeared suddenly, and the door flung open, sending him tumbling into the room. He did a face plant on the carpet, with his lips kissing her feet.

Rolling over onto his back, he looked up at her. She sucked her cheeks in and bit down on the sweet flesh inside to prevent herself from laughing, looking much like a goldfish. Her turquoise-colored eyes sparkling.

"You find this amusing, do you?"

"I—" When Nerina opened her mouth to speak, a half laugh and half snort broke free. She quickly clamped a hand over her mouth. She didn't want to laugh, not when so much frustration was coursing through her, but it was there whether she liked it or not.

Laughter bubbled inside her like soapsuds in a sink, itching to overflow. And that was exactly what happened. Another round of laughter found its way out between her pale-colored lips.

She fell backwards on the bed, rolling in laughter. Whether it was because of him flailing his arms and falling face first at her feet, or whether it was just everything catching up to her, she didn't know. But she laughed until her sides hurt and tears slid down her cheeks. *Holy heck!* It felt good to laugh, despite the hiccups that always followed, and the incessant ache in her muscles from contracting so much.

Wade had finally picked himself up off the floor and was staring at her, an odd expression on his face. Something between amusement and desire. It looked like he wanted to join her but was hesitant to do so after the way things had been between them. She held a hand out to him, letting him know it was okay. He laid himself down beside her on his back, Nerina on her side.

She snuggled up next to him and sighed. "Life is so funky."

"I'm sorry that it's been so crazy for you lately." He brushed her hair away from her face, kissing her forehead.

"Did you really mean what you said?"

"About you being a mermaid?"

She nodded her head. The idea was absolutely and totally ludicrous, but think of how awesome that would be? It was something she'd always dreamed about, ever since the day she met the dolphins at SeaWorld. They reacted to her so strangely, and it was something that she stuck with her forever.

And then there was the fact that she could set the world record for how long she could stay underwater. She never understood why, but if what he was saying was true, then it made so much more sense.

"Yes," he said, gripping her a little more tightly, almost like he was afraid that she'd pull away.

"Where's my tail? I thought mermaids changed as soon as they touched water."

"Yes and no. It's somewhat complicated."

She propped herself up on her elbow, looking at him. "We touch water, and pop"—she put her legs together, feet spread apart, mimicking a tail—"out comes the tail."

"This isn't like the movies. It is much slower, and you need to be in the ocean as it harnesses the full power of the moon. Not just any good ole water."

Brushing a lock of hair away from his forehead, she asked, "Is that why you took me as far away from the ocean as possible?"

"Something like that."

"Why not let me change?"

He rolled over onto his side, tracing circles on her stomach. "Because I like you just as you are." Leaning in, he brushed her hair away from her neck, kissing the newly exposed skin. "Sexy, beautiful and intoxicating."

Nerina tilted her head to give him better access, sighing pleasurably, despite a pout forming on her face. "Are you saying I'm not sexy in a tail?"

Giving her leg a light squeeze, he said, "I happen to like your legs." His fingers dance a little higher until they reached the apex of her thighs, resting where the fire inside her was quickly gathering. "I even like what's in between."

"Wade." She wanted to talk desperately, but the sexual need within her was overpowering the desire to know everything. It was his way of distracting her, and as much as she hated getting distracted, she certainly loved the method he had adopted.

Torn, she pulled away from him to break the intense connection between them. He tried to grab her again, but she rolled off the bed and said, "As much as I love your touch, we need to talk."

He buried his face in the sheets and groaned. "What's with you and talking lately?"

"I won't be so easily distracted this time."

"You haven't been easy for weeks," he grumbled as he sat up on the bed, shoving his hand inside his pants to adjust himself.

Her eyes dropped to where his hand had just been, as she bit the corner of her lip. Shaking her head, she ripped her eyes away from the bulge in his pants and stared at a tiny crack in the wall.

Stay focused, Neri!

"Why did we come out here?" she asked.

"To keep you safe."

"From who?"

"If we're going to do this, I need a beer." He left the room, with her hot on his heels.

As they walked towards the kitchen, she noticed a calendar on the wall next to the fridge. She counted the days from when they left and frowned. "Aren't my parents supposed to be here by now?"

He popped open the beer. "They probably got delayed. I'm sure everything is okay."

That was not like her parents. They never allowed themselves to be late for anything. If they attended any functions, her dad always insisted they arrived fifteen minutes early. Even if that meant sitting in the car doing nothing until the doors opened.

"This isn't like them. I mean, they haven't even called." A chill slithered through her body as she imagined them laying in a heap somewhere, dead. "Wade, we have to go back." She gripped the edge of the countertop, her knuckles turning white.

He walked behind her and wrapped his arms around her waist, pulling her close. "Sweetie, it's okay. They know how to take care of themselves."

All she could hear was the sound of rushing water in her ears, her vision blurring behind the tears. Wade pried her hands off the edge of the counter and picked her up, carrying her to the couch.

"Breathe, Neri," he whispered, gently stroking her back.

She buried her face in his chest and allowed herself this moment of comfort. Where could they be? They promised to be here. "What about those men? Do they know where my parents live?"

His body stiffened, and his hand stilled, giving her the answer without him even saying a word. She jumped off his lap and spun around to face him. "Why didn't you bring them with us?"

"Your dad had to go and talk to the k..." He closed his mouth abruptly and looked away.

She placed her hands on her sides, elbows jutting out. "Damn it! Finish your sentences."

"Went to talk to the k..." he mumbled the last word so quietly that she couldn't make it out any better than the first time.

"When I overheard you guys talking, he said that he needed to go speak to my father." She sat down next to him on the couch, resting her hand on his knee. "Who is my real father, Wade?"

He laid his head back on the couch and closed his eyes. "Can't you give a guy a break from the inquisition? Geez."

"This is my life. I deserve to know."

He'd kept all this from her for long enough. Come hell or high water, Nerina would get the rest of the information out of him. All she'd found out so far was that her parents weren't really her parents, and both she and Wade were mermaids, or so he said. Also, he had some crazy, whacked out abilities.

She felt like someone had pulled her into a crazy fantasy-thriller television show, and she was the main character who didn't have a clue as to what was going on. She didn't like being clueless. That made it more dangerous for her and everyone around her.

"Who is my real father?"

Running his hands down his face, he let them drop to his lap. "You're too persistent for your own good."

"Well?"

"If I tell you, are you going to run off on me again, or am I going to have to tie you to the chair?" He grinned slyly. "There is rope in my bag, so don't think I won't."

Her eyes widened. "You wouldn't dare!"

He stood up and disappeared into the bedroom for a moment, returning with a bundle of rope in each hand. "So, are you gonna stay put like a good girl?" he asked. "I hope you say no because I really wanna try these out."

Her eyes locked with his and butterflies fluttered around in her stomach. Oh gosh, she couldn't really be getting turned on by the idea of being tied up, was she? The ache pulsating between her legs told her firmly that she was. The whole thing was absurd. Man! Her mind was becoming as strangely twisted as his was.

She shivered in response to his heated gaze, his eyes literally dancing with excitement. "I'm...uh...just going to sit over there." She pointed to the recliner, moving as far away from him as possible.

"Party pooper," he said, sticking his tongue. Placing the rope on the coffee table, he sat back on the couch, spreading his arms across the top. His left leg was partially crossed over his right, and his foot was resting just above the knee. A half grin played on his face as his eyes took on a dazed look, like he was imagining tying her up.

Or maybe that was her imagining what it would be like to be totally helpless and under his control. She shook her head, trying to shake her mind free of the alien thoughts that had taken over her entire being.

"Where were we?" she asked.

"Talking about tying you up."

It was her turn to stick her tongue out at him. "Get serious, Wade."

He feigned a look of offense. "I've never been more serious."

She rolled her eyes. "I'm not letting you tie me up. I'm not a hog."

They were getting so far off topic it wasn't funny. She had one question, and her husband was taking forever to answer it. It would be easier to find out where a lightning bolt would strike next than it would be to get the response she wanted.

"Who is my father?"

"Why do I suddenly feel like I'm on the set of Star Wars?"

"If we were, I'd use the force to get the answer out of you. Now answer the cotton-pickin' question."

"Your father is the King of Atlantis."

Her blood boiled, and her hands gripped the armrests. "What does it take to get a serious answer out of you? We aren't in a bloody movie."

He sighed as he leaned forward, resting his elbows on his knees. As his eyes burrowed into hers, he said, "Listen to me carefully, because I'm only going to say this once. You are Princess Nerina

Anastasia Albion, the only child of King Dathan and Queen Talise, the royal family of Atlantis."

When he finished speaking, his lips closed into a firm thin line and not once did he look away from her. She shrunk back into the recliner and diverted her eyes to the magazines sitting on the coffee table. Her reality had just taken an unrealistic twist.

Everyone on earth had heard about Atlantis. People have paid millions of dollars trying to search for the fabled myth—the technologically advanced city that had supposedly sunk beneath the ocean surface thousands of years ago.

Her body didn't know what to feel. It was virtually running on empty in the emotions category. Numb, if anything. "I think..." She paused a moment, wiping her sweaty hands on her pants. "I think I'm going to go lay down."

He went to help her up, but she waved him away. She needed to be alone and didn't want to be touched.

"Are you going to be okay?" he asked, still looking like he wanted to touch her.

She backed away from him, giving him a weird yes-no motion with her head. That's how muddled up her mind was. She couldn't even figure out how to answer him. *Sleep.* She needed sleep.

Upon entering the room, she collapsed on the bed. She pulled the sheets over her head, forming a cocoon around herself. And there, her tears found the freedom to fall. They kept falling until her body grew too exhausted to stay awake any longer, and she drifted off to sleep, hibernating beneath the sheets like a bear.

Chapter Twenty-Two

Two months had gone by, and they still hadn't heard anything from Kyle and Maggie. Wade couldn't help but assume the worst. However, he tried not to let his worry show. Nerina tried calling their cellphones, but she kept getting the "this customer is not available" message. Their phones were either turned off or the batteries were dead. Either way, things didn't look good.

Stepping outside the house, he called his friend Andre. "What have you found out?"

"Well, I stopped by their place, and it's been ransacked. Stuff is everywhere," Andre replied.

"And?"

"And nothing. That's it. Kyle and Maggie aren't there. By the way, thanks for making me pay a hundred dollars to get my car back from the impound lot."

Wade cringed. "I'll pay you back, I promise."

"You better believe you will. The police grilled me about you for hours before they finally let me go."

"Sorry, buddy. I didn't have time to explain what was going on." He looked back at the door to make sure Nerina was still out of earshot. The chill in the morning air cut him right to the bone. Colorado was colder than he was used to. They were tropical creatures, not polar bears.

Snow already covered the ground beneath his feet, and it was only the end of October. He didn't relish the idea of spending the winter in a cold climate, but at least they had wood to keep themselves warm.

The only heat sources in the house were a few portable heaters and a fireplace. Since it was a summer vacation house, the designers never bothered to integrate heat when they built the place. They must have thought that no one would actually use it when the temperature dipped into the minuses.

He walked along the dock, staring out over the water. Maybe he should try some ice fishing once it was cold enough, not that he had ever tried fishing on land before, not with a pole and bait anyway. It could be interesting, and they did need stuff to do to help pass the time.

"Hey, dude! You still there?" Andre asked.

"Ya, sorry. I faded out for a minute. Call me if you see or hear anything, okay?"

"Will do."

He clicked 'end call' and stuffed the phone in his pocket, rushing back into the house. Rubbing his frozen hands together, he brought them up to his mouth and gently blew into them, trying to ease the ache caused by the cold air. He walked over to the bedroom to check on Nerina, peeking his head in the door. She was still sound asleep, hadn't budged an inch.

It took her a few days to process the information he gave her shortly after they arrived, but when she did, she grilled him about her family. She became quite enamored with the idea of being an actual mermaid and a princess at that. Every girl's dream, apparently.

Her manners were anything but princess-like, but he wouldn't have her any other way. She'd said the whole thing reminded her of

The Princess Diaries movie, which she had made him watch endlessly with her.

If she made him sit through another girly movie, he'd need a testosterone injection. Next time, he'd make her sit through one of his movies, or she could sit on him. He liked the latter idea even better.

A soft moan caught his attention as his wife rolled onto her back. His body stirred at the sound, despite their sexual rendezvous last night. He loved being able to feast on her body any time he wanted, but he knew she needed her sleep. Quietly shutting the door, he went and made them some breakfast.

Her appetite had picked up since the morning sickness finally disappeared, giving her a little bit more energy for recreational activities other than living with her head in the toilet. He was also happy to be able to cook for her again and not have it upset her stomach. He loved cooking for her.

When the toaster popped, he placed two pieces of toast on a plate and covered them with scrambled eggs. After pouring a glass of milk, he added it to the bed tray. The perfect breakfast to surprise his wife with. Picking up the tray, he returned to the room and found her sitting up in bed, glancing at her phone. Her eyebrows drew together, and a frown marred her lovely face.

She glared at him, her nostrils flaring. Picking up his pillow, she threw it at him, knocking the tray out of his hands. The toast and eggs flew into the air and landed on the top of his head. The milk hit him on the chin, dribbling down his bright blue shirt.

"Figured your mood was too good to last," he mumbled, as he pulled his shirt over his, picking the scrambled eggs out of his hair. "I'm not cleaning this up."

"Jerk."

His chest tightened in frustration. "What the hell has gotten into you?"

"My parents won't answer their cellphones, and I can't even talk to my best friend because you took it upon yourself to delete her number."

"You're still pissed about that? It happened weeks ago."

"Ya, I'm still pissed. You told me she was okay."

"She is okay."

"Then why hasn't she called me?" She shook her phone at him.

He rubbed the back of his neck, shifting from one foot to the other. "Hell if I know." He did know, but if he told her now, it could mean trouble for them. And he wasn't about to risk her life just to let her talk to Jenny. No matter how much this would come back to bite him in the butt. Other things would take a bigger chuck out of his ass if he didn't cover their tracks. The look in her eye told him she wasn't buying his answer.

"What aren't you telling me?" she asked.

"She's fine. That's all you need to know."

"How can you possibly know that? She was with me when those men tried to abduct us. What if they came back?"

"Don't worry. I've got people watching out for her." Wade had a feeling they'd be back, which was why he had Andre and his other buddies checking in on her every now and then. Thankfully, they hadn't seen anything suspicious so far. "If they see anything suspicious, they'll let me know."

"I need to talk to her."

"That's not such a good idea."

She crossed her arms and glared at him. "You're not my boss, Wade."

"Actually, I am. Your father..." He snapped his mouth shut.

"Oh, heck no. You aren't doing that again."

"Leave it alone, Neri."

"Just because my father isn't here doesn't mean you're the boss." She got up out of bed and stood there in all her naked splendor. He couldn't help but stare at her. His gaze dropped, zoning in on the perfectly trimmed patch of hair between her thighs which hid the spot he loved to touch.

His groin throbbed, and he itched to touch her. *Keep a clear head. Keep a clear head.* He kept chanting that phrase to himself as she approached him. She had a way about her that always made him spill the beans. He was totally wrapped around her finger, and she knew it. Not today though, he'd be the man of steel.

"If you want to touch this body again, you're gonna tell me what I want to know." Slowly and tantalizingly, she ran her hands over her breasts and slid her fingers along her stomach to the spot he was looking at and touched her clit. She flashed a sexy smile in his direction.

"Oh, that's dirty." He ran a hand through his hair and grabbed the remaining bits of egg, squishing them on her head.

She shrieked and tried to brush the bits of egg from her hair, unsuccessfully. Looking around, Nerina picked up the soggy toast. "Two can play that game," she said, throwing it at his face.

He stepped to the side, and the bread flew out of the room instead. She went to pick up the other piece of toast on the floor when he grabbed her arm, pulling her against himself. "I think I'm already wearing enough food, thank you," he said.

Her breath hitched when her lower abdomen came in contact with his growing erection, barely contained behind his sweatpants, sticking out like a handle and ready for action.

"Don't even think about it." She pushed herself away and looked up at him.

"Why? I can tell you are." He took a step towards her and ran the pad of his thumb over her slightly rosy cheeks. She parted her lips as though she wanted to speak, but he never gave her the chance.

His lips closed over hers, swallowing whatever she was about to say. The next thing he knew, her right heel came crashing down on his foot, crunching his bones together mercilessly. Sharp jabs of pain shot up his leg, and his toes tingled. It was like he had hit his funny bone. He hopped up and down on one foot, swearing up a blue streak. Black dots invaded his vision.

For a moment, his wife was only a blur, a hazy figure beyond the pain. He hopped over to the bed and collapsed, massaging his aching foot. "You might not want to be standing here when I get my vision back," he growled.

Biting her bottom lip, Nerina hurried out the door and locked herself in the bathroom. She'd done it again. Her hormones had been all over the place lately, but there was no excuse for violence. She leaned against the door and placed a hand over her racing heart, willing it to calm down.

If she lashed out again, he would no doubt tie her up. And she wouldn't blame him in the slightest. He was a patient man, but she knew he had his limits, and by the look on his face, he had reached it. He had that animalistic glint in his eye, like a cave man ready to conk her over the head with a wooden club.

Walking over to the sink, she placed her hands on the edge of the off-white countertop and stared at herself in the mirror. The lights above the mirror shone down on her head, highlighting the yellow bits of egg in her red hair.

Her roots were already beginning to show but barely. Not that it mattered. It wasn't like she ever went beyond their backyard. It wasn't warm enough to spend much time outside anyway. While it was technically fall, winter had already made its appearance, and her body did not like the cold.

She liked sitting in front of the fireplace with a good book, cuddling next to Wade. Well, when they weren't angry at each other anyway, which didn't seem to be very often these days. She hated that they were going through a rough patch, but it seemed inevitable with all the secrets he wanted to keep. Life was one great big mess. And she had no idea how to sort it all out.

Nerina turned towards the tub, turned on the water and stepped in, closing the curtain behind her. She faced the shower and allowed the water to cascade over her head and down her back, pressing her hands up against the wall.

Looking down, she looked at her baby bump, which still wasn't that big yet. Tears pricked her eyes as she smiled. She couldn't wait until she felt the baby move. Sometimes she swore she could feel little flutters or bubbles but wasn't sure if it was gas or not. She could hardly believe she was going to be a mother soon. Nerina shook her head in disbelief as a giggle burst out of her mouth.

Everything still felt like a dream. The baby. Her being a mermaid princess. The men who tried to kidnap her. Nothing felt real. Maybe none of this was happening, and she had somehow fallen into a coma and was dreaming. Closing her eyes, she pinched herself on her arm. Reopening her eyes, the water from the shower shot straight into them. She sputtered and turned away from the spray. How was any of this real?

Mermaids were supposed to grow tails as soon as they touched water. No one had ever mentioned that it depended on the type of water they were in. He had to be pulling her leg. And yet, he did disappear right in front of her eyes. As she stayed there in the shower, washing herself and contemplating the situation, she heard a faint knock on the door.

"Neri?"

"I'll be out in a minute."

He continued to knock on the door, but she ignored him, attempting to finish her shower. Tilting her head back, she started to rinse the shampoo out of her hair. The pipes in the wall began to rattle, and the spray slowed down. Soon there was no water coming out of the shower head.

She leaned down and turned the hot and cold taps to no avail. For some reason, there didn't appear to be any water in the pipes. Brushing the shampoo from her forehead before it could drip into her eyes, she stared at the shower, puzzled.

The pipes continued to rattle and so did the door handle as Wade did his magic trick on the lock, strolling inside with a pleased look on his face. "Having trouble, are you?"

She grabbed a towel and wrapped it around herself, scowling at him.

He casually stripped down to his birthday suit, stepped in the shower and pulled the curtain closed, leaving her staring at the fish-covered shower curtain. The water started flowing again. He stuck his head out and smirked, saying, "Care to join me?"

Fuming, her hands balled into fists as she turned away from him. Suddenly the steam in the room intensified a hundred-fold, taking her breath away. Wade jumped out of the bathtub, his feet almost tangling in the shower curtain, as he shouted obscenities.

Her jaw dropped in shock. Multiple burns, on the verge of turning into blisters, covered his back. When she unclenched her fists, the water returned to normal, and the dense steam dissipated, as though nothing had ever happened.

"Don't just stand there bloody staring at me. Help me," he bellowed, trying to get a look at his back in the steamed-up mirror.

"We should get you to the hospital."

Grimacing, he turned towards her. "You are all the hospital I need."

She shook her head. "What on earth are you talking about?"

"Give me your hands." He reached for them as he half sat on the toilet seat—the other butt cheek had a burn the size of apple.

She held her hands up against his and sat on the edge of the bathtub. The edge was still hot, but not unbearably so. With no idea what to do, she sat there waiting for him to say something.

"Think about our connection until you can see me clearly in your mind as bright as day."

She closed her eyes and focused on him in her mind, concentrating on his voice. A warmth transferred between them. In the darkness, there were small lights moving around. Slowly, they gathered together in one spot, creating a faint image. The more she concentrated, the clearer the picture became until she could see him, shining like an angel. Only he had dark spots she couldn't see.

"Focus on my back."

The warming sensation intensified as she focused, pulsating like a heartbeat at the ends of her fingertips. She watched the light snake its way back into the dark spots until they all disappeared.

Knowing her work was done, she opened her eyes and saw Wade

smiling at her. He stood up and turned around. Not a single imperfection remained on his back. No burn. Nothing.

"How?" she gasped, as she ran her hands along his skin.

"Before we get into that, I think we need to wash the rest of the soap off, don't you?"

"I'd rather not step back into that wonky shower."

"Don't worry. Just focus on me, and we'll be done before you know it," he said, winking at her.

She highly doubted that, but she joined him anyway. She needed the release that she knew he would provide. The shower ran cold long before they were done, but neither noticed as their bodies were still humming with the energy of their connection.

In the back of her mind, though, something felt different. She couldn't pinpoint what exactly, but it was almost like something inside her had awakened. A new power was coursing through her body, and the strength of it scared her. She wanted to turn it off and go back to being who she was before, but she knew that was no longer possible. Whatever was happening to her was going to happen whether she wanted it to or not. All she could do was hang on for the ride and hope for the best.

Chapter Twenty-Three

For two months she was insatiable, eager to learn about her newfound abilities. She kept him going until he was ready to fall over with exhaustion. Where was all her energy was coming from? It was like the baby gave her a never ending well of the stuff.

The only good thing was it kept her from inquiring about Jenny and all the stuff that was going on back home. The novelty, though, was slowly wearing off, so today he wanted to blow the socks off of her and attempt to keep her excited.

Tossing a winter jacket at her, he said, "Let's go outside and play."

They put on all their gear and walked out the door. Being the end of December, the lake was completely frozen over and had been for weeks. The snow was falling as they made their way to the edge of Grand Lake. Nerina leaned her head back, catching a snowflake on her tongue.

Wade smiled. She had such an innocent air about her, and he hoped it would never disappear. Her heart was pure and untouched, and he worried about how these newfound powers would affect her if his worst suspicions came true.

Kyle and Maggie were nowhere to be found, and he had no way

of contacting Atlantis while he was all the way out here. Had they managed to meet with the king? A wreckage was pulled out of the water in the approximate area of their meeting place, but it was so badly damaged that there was no way of knowing who the boat belonged to.

He wanted to head back to San Diego to see for himself, but he knew that if he tried, she'd want to go too. He couldn't take her back there. Not yet anyway, especially not knowing what they would be walking into.

Jenny appeared to be safe at the moment. Andre said a young man was courting her. Thankfully, after he grilled him a bit more, he was relieved to find out it wasn't one of the men who had tried to abduct her.

"I'm ready," Nerina said, breaking him out of his trance.

"You remember what we were practicing before, turning ice into water?" he asked.

She nodded her head.

"Well"—he spread his hand out towards the water—"the frozen lake is your playground."

"But what if someone sees?"

"Just stay in control, and it will be fine."

"I don't think this is a good idea," she said, pulling the strings on her hood a little tighter so the wind couldn't blow it off.

"Do what I do." He walked down to the edge of the water and crouched down. Pulling off his glove, he slowly curled his fingers. The snow bubbled like boiling water in a pot, steam rising into the air around him.

Nerina watched as the snow and ice melted beneath his outstretched hand. Cracks in the ice branched out in a web-like design, stretching a few feet in front of her husband. She still couldn't wrap her mind around the idea of powers and abilities. The only word that came to mind was 'mutant.'

Wade placed his hands on his knees and stood up. "Now you try."

"Are my mom and dad like us? Kyle and Maggie, I mean."

"Let's finish the training, and then we'll talk about it inside over hot chocolate," he said, slipping his glove back on.

Nerina lived with a constant lump in her chest which grew larger with each passing day. She missed them and couldn't imagine living the rest of her life without them. Wade, thankfully, kept her too busy to think about it or at least tried to, but he wasn't always successful.

There were days when they were all she could think about. Sometimes it felt like they'd abandoned her and flew off on a plane to the Caribbean or something. At least, with those thoughts, they were still alive and not buried in an unmarked grave somewhere.

She glanced at the snow near the edge of the lake and contemplated how she'd crouch down with her belly in the way, being twenty-four weeks now. Off to the side, she noticed a log. Nerina brushed the snow off before sitting down.

Mimicking his actions from a moment ago, she concentrated on the patch of ice beneath her hand. The ice shifted, and the snow sizzled as it melted. Without thinking, she rapidly made a fist. A mini shockwave burst over the lake, causing the ice to break into pieces, rumbling loudly. Part of the lake looked like a gigantic flowing iceberg, with shards of ice sticking high into the air as they crashed together. The rest of it looked like a hot spring had risen out of the deep.

She snapped her hands back, holding them close to her chest. With heat rising in her cheeks, and a lopsided grin, she glanced up at Wade, chuckling nervously. "Uh...oops!"

He stood there with his hands on his head, mouth wide open. "I should have listened to you."

"Ya think?"

He grabbed her arm and rushed her back into the house, locking the door behind them, mumbling something about the five o'clock news.

~

165

"Mommy, Mommy, look at the lake." A young girl, with blond pigtails and a heavy red coat, grabbed her mother's hand and pulled her down the path towards Grand Lake. Her mom was too busy on the phone to hear or see the commotion, but it hadn't escaped her child's attention.

The girl's eyes widened as she watched the ice rise into the air, snow tumbling down the side. "Mommy, look!" She tugged on her mom's shirt and pointed to the icebergs.

"Just a second, dear," the mother replied. "No, Matthew, you can't join us tonight. You had your chance to take her, and you refused." Turning to face the lake, the phone dropped from her ear. Her eyes widened, and panic rushed through her. "Chrissy, get away from there."

Her precocious five-year-old daughter had already started climbing the walls of ice and giggling as she slid back down. With each slide, the woman's heart stopped, envisioning her daughter sliding through a crack.

"Now," she demanded.

"But, Mommy."

"No, buts. It's dangerous." She held out a hand to her. The ice was too unsteady for an adult to stand on, so she could only stand there, praying that nothing would happen.

Chrissy fell as the patch of ice shifted beneath her feet. She tried to stand back up, but another block of ice slid underneath it, tilting it dangerously high. The mother watched as her daughter slid down the ice wall and kept on sliding farther away from her, landing on a patch of ice that had cracked free from the rest.

The girl sat huddled on the small island of ice as it drifted away, tears streaming down her face. "Mommy, help!" she cried.

"Oh my god, my baby." Her mother frantically looked around for a stick, anything that could help her. "Someone help me."

Her cry echoed off the nearby buildings, and people filed outside to see what was going on. Gasps filled the air. Men tried to create a human line to reach the child, but the ice was too unstable, and it halted their efforts.

An off-duty firefighter jumped into the water and tried to swim out to the girl, but a patch of ice rushed in his direction, causing him to hurry back to the shore. "T-there's no way out there," he said, his teeth chattering together.

Sirens filled the air, but no one knew what good it would do because the fire truck couldn't get close enough to the shoreline to use its ladders or anything.

"Does anyone have a large boat that could handle the ice?" the off-duty firefighter asked.

"I'm part of search and rescue. Our boat should work," another gentleman piped up.

"Call it in, but we need a faster option."

A young man, with spiky brown hair and ripped blue jeans, stepped forward. He looked around twenty years old. "I have some rope and some ice-picks in my van. I was planning to do some climbing. Would that help?"

"Go get them."

The ice tilted, and the girl scrambled to hold on to the edge. "Mommy!" Her high-pitched cry filled the air.

Her mother cupped her hands around her mouth and yelled, "Hold on tight, baby."

The firefighter walked up to the mother. "I'm Daryl."

"Tammy," she muttered, chewing on her nail anxiously.

He put his arm around her shaking shoulders. "We are going to do everything we can to help your daughter."

Behind the crowd, a news crew was setting up shop, getting ready to broadcast the story nationwide. "Paul, set up off to the side. Get the camera on the girl." Katlyn, the resident news anchor, pointed to the area she wanted him to go, quickly following after him.

Pandemonium ensued the moment the camera was up and running. A large piece of ice rammed into the one the child was on, sending the girl tumbling into the water. Tammy fell to her knees and covered her eyes, praying.

"God, please help my baby."

Across the lake, Wade was standing in front of their door. His reckless wife wanted to go out and help the rescuers after hearing the story on the news.

"There's nothing we can do," he told her.

"Pardon my French, but bullshit." She crossed her arms and glared at him. "The girl is going to die if we don't help."

"You can't just go jumping into a lake and save her. People will ask questions."

"Watch me." She tried to push him away from the door, but he wouldn't budge. "Damn it, Wade. This is my fault."

"Think about the baby."

"That's why I need to do this. I can't let another mother lose her child because of something I did. Not if there is something I can do about it."

"You can't go jumping into the lake. It's too cold to go for a swim."

"We can't waste anymore time. She's already underwater." She placed her hands on Wade's chest and looked up at him with big puppy dog eyes. "If you won't let me help, will you help her? Please?"

He groaned, placing his forehead against hers. "You're gonna be the death of me, girl."

Upon saying that, he pulled open the door and took off to the edge of the lake. It was not steaming like a hot spring anymore, much to his displeasure. A warm swim would have been nice. He wasn't relishing an arctic one.

Knowing that he couldn't take the time to warm up the water, he took off his shoes and dove off the dock into the frigid waters. He gasped for air when the freezing waters knocked the wind out of him momentarily. Suddenly, he felt sorry for freezing Andy and Greg like human popsicles. This must be nature's way of getting back at him.

He swam through the water, heading in the direction of where the girl was last seen, warming up the water in his immediate surroundings, dodging fragments of ice that blocked his path.

In the distance, he saw the bright red jacket floating about ten feet below the surface. The girl wasn't moving. Grabbing her around the waist, he formed an air bubble around her head like a helmet, hoping it was enough for now and high-tailed it back to their place.

Chapter Twenty-Four

"H-here," Wade said, teeth chattering from the cold. With stiff and frozen arms, he laid the girl on the couch. "Y-your turn."

The young child's lips were blue, her skin pale. Nerina sat on the edge of the cushion and quickly removed the girl's clothes, wrapping her in a few large beach towels. She placed her palm on the girl's forehead but quickly removed her hand. "She's so cold."

"You'll have to warm her up slowly."

"How?" She looked up at him.

"Do you remember how you healed me earlier?" he asked.

Nodding, she let out a long breath and turned to look at her patient. She placed her hand on the young girl's chest and closed her eyes. As she connected with the girl, there was only a suffocating darkness. As her vision adjusted, she noticed a small pulsating light in the distance. The light was all that remained of the girl's life force. She willed her own light to reach out, but it fell short. The light grew dimmer with each passing second.

"Wade, I can't do this," she cried out, her heart racing as she shook with exertion.

"Use me." He placed his hands on her shoulder, providing her with his own strength and energy. His warmth spread through her, exactly as if she stood directly in front of a fireplace.

Returning her focus to the young girl, Nerina's light spread out in tendril patterns and followed the veins leading to the child's heart. The pulsating light grew brighter and slowly formed the pattern of a human. First the torso, then the head, followed by the limbs.

"Keep going, sweetie. It's working," whispered a faint voice in her ear.

The girl gagged and coughed, breaking Nerina out of her trance. Nerina quickly rolled her onto her side as water bubbled out of her mouth like a fountain. The child's eyes flickered open. As she became more aware, her eyes widened, and she scrambled to get away from them.

"It's okay, sweetie. No one's going to hurt you," Nerina said softly.

"Mommy?" she asked, her bottom lip quivering. "Where's my mommy?"

"Wade, can you throw her clothes in the dryer?" Grabbing the throw blanket off the back of the couch, she handed it to the girl. "It's okay. You accidentally got separated from your mommy, but we're going to take you to her once your clothes are dry, okay? What's your name?"

"Chrissy," she said, her voice barely above a whisper.

"Hi Chrissy, I'm Neri."

The girl blinked rapidly and tilted her head, tapping her finger on her chin. "Like the mermaid?"

Nerina smiled as she helped the girl wrap the blanket around herself. "You've heard of me?" After saying that, she clasped a hand over her mouth. *Shoot.* Wade was not going to be happy with her.

The child nodded. "You're my favorite mermaid."

Warmth trickled inside her at the young girl's words, and Nerina touched her pregnant belly. Hopefully, she'd be her child's favorite, too. Chrissy no longer looked scared. Instead, she sat bouncing on the couch, her color returning to normal. "Why do you have red hair now?"

Hoping to change the topic, she asked, "Would you like some hot chocolate?"

A grin spread across Chrissy's face, and she nodded her head so fast that Nerina thought her head was going to pop off.

"Just wait right here, and I'll get you a cup."

The girl cautiously peeked over the back of the couch and watched as Nerina moved about in the kitchen.

"How come you have legs?" Chrissy asked.

That was something she was trying to figure out herself. The idea she was a real mermaid with powers flabbergasted her. It was like she had jumped into an alternate dimension.

"Did a sea witch give you legs, too?" the girl inquired.

Nerina chuckled. Chrissy must have watched The Little Mermaid a million times, much like she did when she was little. "You like The Little Mermaid?"

"It's my bestest favoritest movie."

As Nerina continued to make the hot chocolate, the girl sang some of the songs from the show, and she couldn't help but join in. She had to admit it was one of her favorite movies, too, other than Splash.

The girl went silent and stared at her, mouth open. "Wow, you sing pretty."

"So do you." Nerina sat on the couch and handed her the lukewarm hot chocolate. "I even added marshmallows."

The girl shivered as she brought the drink up to her lips. "Smells yummy."

"Are you cold?"

"A little."

Nerina stepped into the bedroom and pulled out a blue shirt with a unicorn on the front and helped the child put it on while they waited for the clothes to dry. "Better?"

"Yep," Chrissy said, taking another sip of the hot chocolate. The girl looked down at Nerina's belly. "Is a baby in there?"

"Yes," she answered. Would her baby be a girl like Chrissy? So full of wonder and curiosity about everything? She hoped the baby was okay because she hadn't seen a doctor, didn't even get a chance to hear the heartbeat. The baby moved now and then which brought her some comfort, but worry still remained.

"When's it gonna come out?" The girl tentatively reached out with her tiny hand and touched Nerina's stomach.

"Not for a while, unfortunately."

Wade walked into the room, and Chrissy quickly cuddled up next to her.

"It's okay," Nerina pulled the child—blanket and all—onto her lap. "This is my husband Wade. He won't hurt you."

"The clothes should be ready soon, and then we can take you back to your mom," he said, taking a seat on the recliner.

"Should we call someone?" Nerina asked.

He shook his head. "We don't want them finding out where we live."

"But her mother must be worried silly."

She could imagine how she would feel if her own child went missing, and she hadn't even had her baby yet. If it was anything like what she was feeling about Kyle and Maggie's disappearance, she didn't even want to think about it.

"Give it another fifteen minutes. Her clothes should be dry enough by then."

The girl was more than content sitting with her. They talked about mermaids and the ocean. The questions shot out as fast as a machine gun, and Nerina loved every second of it.

She missed performing in front of the kids. The joy on their faces always made her smile. When she realized she'd never be able to perform again, a feeling of emptiness filled her stomach.

"Are you a mermaid, too?" Chrissy asked Wade.

Wade cast a glance in Nerina's direction, narrowing his eyes at her. "You weren't supposed to tell," he mouthed silently.

She shrugged her shoulders. When the girl asked her, it just slipped out, and she didn't have the heart to tell her that the mermaid show was an act. A child's imagination should be protected and not messed with. Besides, she was just a kid. What harm could she do? It wasn't like anyone would believe her.

"Hey boss, you gotta see this!" Andy yelled.

Russ walked into the room to find his men watching the news. He perched himself on the arm of the sofa and crossed his arms, listening to the reporter on the television.

"A small town in Colorado is mourning the loss of a young child who was visiting Grand Lake with her mother, Tammy Preston. A strange phenomenon swept over the town early this morning. The residents woke up to find the lake in a state of upheaval. Half of the lake was thawed out, while the other half contained broken chunks of ice, much like icebergs."

They switched to the footage of the young girl huddled on the ice as the news reporter continued speaking. "The woman's young daughter got trapped on a block of ice, and despite numerous rescue attempts, the child fell into the water. The rescuers were holding out hope that they could pull the child out in time, but so far, they have been unable to recover the little girl. Three hours have passed since she went under, and hope of finding her is waning. We will update you as information becomes available."

"Think it's her, boss?" Charlie pushed away from the wall and moved closer to the couch.

"Maybe," Russ replied.

"What else do you think could have caused something like this?" Andy asked, pointing to the television screen.

The man had a point. Russ didn't know of any volcanic activity in the area that could cause something like that. The nearest volcano was about two hours away. Not to mention, it would take something of immense power to be able to mess up the lake during this time of year.

From the looks of it, it had to be his wayward princess. And if it was, she was much more aware of who she was than the first time she'd met his men. They'd have to up their game. No more kiddie gloves. If only they could have captured her before she learned of her powers. It would have been so much easier. He had a feeling he'd lose a few of his guys before the battle was over.

At least he didn't have to worry about the guardian popping up out of nowhere, not since Charlie took him out. They just had to go in quietly and surprise them. The only thing they needed to figure out was her exact location, but thankfully, they had a general idea now.

However, he was still unsure why they would do something so visible. Were they trying to set a trap so they could fish his men out? That definitely sounded like something Wade would do. The man was too smart for this to happen accidentally. Russ ran a hand over his almost bald head. He'd recently got a buzz cut to hide his growing bald spot. Even though his men never said a word, they kept looking at the bald spot, and it annoyed him.

His daughter always kissed it, though, thinking it was some type of boo-boo. His heart twisted in his chest. Her health had deteriorated rapidly over the last few weeks, and the doctor confined her to strict bed rest. She had a few months left at the most, they said. He balled his fists as a brick settled in the pit of his stomach.

She was too young to face trouble like this, and all over some cockamamie decision that they weren't good enough for Atlantis. At least with the king gone, the queen was sure to give in and let them come back.

Queen Talise was a soft touch, always has been. But they still needed to get their hands on her daughter, otherwise it was all pointless. He couldn't get close enough to the queen to get her to heal his daughter, so Nerina was their only option. If she was in Grand Lake, they had to find her. Not that she'd likely still be there when they arrived, but it was the closest lead they had, and he wasn't about to give up now.

"Charlie, go round up a few men and meet me at the dock in an hour." Russ rubbed his hands together as a grin spread across his face. "It's time to go fishing."

And he knew just how to fish them out.

Chapter Twenty-Five

"Sit still, kid." Wade tightened his grip and balanced the girl on his shoulders, his boots sinking deep into the snow. They parked their vehicle a few blocks away from the rescuers' base camp and walked the rest of the way. That way, they could make themselves scarce as soon as the girl found her mom, hopefully avoiding the press.

He wanted to minimize Nerina's exposure, especially now that the girl knew who she was. Initially, he wanted her to stay at the cabin while he brought the girl in himself, but the little rugrat refused to go without her. That didn't impress him much, because the whole lake iceberg thing was sure to alert all their enemies.

As soon as they returned to the cabin, they would pack their stuff and head somewhere else. He had no idea where, but they'd figure it out. He was certain that the kid would blab their secret to everyone she talked to.

The only problem was that if they left, and Kyle made it to their location, he'd have no clue where they were or how to reach them if they had lost their phones. Wade was still hoping they were fine, but no guardian alive would have stayed silent for this long.

They were loyal to a fault, and that was what had him worried.

Where were they? What if it was only the two of them now? Could he protect her? Heck, after what she did today, she probably didn't even need protecting anymore.

He looked over at her as she walked alongside him. She had stuffed her hands into the pockets of her black parka—which they had found in the house when they arrived—and she hid her face behind the furry lining of her hood. He couldn't tell what was going through her head.

"We're just about there," he said, pointing up ahead. Base camp was inside the conference room of a hotel next to the lake. A bright orange tent had been set up with a portable heater in the parking lot. Food and drinks were being served, ensuring that everyone had the energy to keep going.

When it came to a small town, everyone played their part to help out. No one wanted their town to be the one known for losing a little girl. The search and rescue boat had been scouring the lake for hours, to no avail. That was all that had been on the news since it happened.

The girl on his shoulders squirmed again and yelled, "Mommy! I see my mommy."

Even amidst all the noise from the crew, a woman dressed in a gray fur coat turned towards them. Her hands flew up to her mouth, and she raced in her high-heeled boots through the snow in their direction.

"Nerina, go back and wait in the car." He didn't want anyone to recognize her like the kid did.

"But—"

"For once in your life, will you please listen to me and get the hell out of here!"

She let out a huff before turning on her heels and marching back in car's direction. He hated being curt with her, but she was too bloody stubborn for her own good. The last thing she needed was to have her face plastered all over the television again.

He placed the kid on the ground and put his sunglasses on, pulling his hood low over his face. Guiding Chrissy, they made their way towards her mother as she met them halfway. She picked up her daughter and spun her around in circles before losing her balance and tumbling into the snow. He had hoped to walk away without saying anything, but the news crews were already right on top of him.

"Who are you?" one asked.

"Where did you find her?"

"I'm sorry. No comment." He lifted his scarf to cover even more of his face. When he went to walk away, something grabbed his leg. Looking down, he saw that the kid had taken up residence there, wrapping her tiny legs around his calf.

"Don't go," she cried.

What a bizarre twist of events for the girl who wanted nothing to do with him. He reached down and tried to peel Chrissy off of his leg.

"Mommy, you have to meet them. They're mermaids and everything."

He picked her up in his arms and whispered, "That's supposed to be a secret, munchkin."

The girl pretended like she was zipping her mouth closed before turning to look at her mom. "Never mind," she said, giggling into her hands.

Wade handed her to her mom, backing away from the crowd and the cameras. "I have to go. Keep her safe, please."

Tammy nodded her head, tears glistening in her eyes as she hugged her little girl. The news crew pushed and shoved their way closer to him, shoving their microphones into his face, hoping for him to say something.

"We found her and brought her back. That's all that matters," he said.

"You and who else?"

He leaned his head back and groaned. "My wife and I found her floating in the lake, revived her, and brought her here as soon as we could."

The mother gasped and wrapped her daughter in a death grip,

kissing every square inch of her face. The crowd closed in on him in every direction, and the microphones were just centimeters away from his mouth.

"Are you saying she was dead?" one reporter asked.

His chest constricted and sweat perspired under his jacket, his t-shirt clinging to his skin. "I'm sorry. I have to go." He pushed his way through the crowd and rushed down the street, his boots kicking up the snow behind him.

Hell.

That didn't go well. A few of the reporters continued to follow him as he ran towards the car. Thankfully, their equipment slowed them down a little. Hopefully, he managed to get into the car and do a U-Turn before they could grab his license plate.

"You and your big mouth," he said, glaring at Nerina.

"What'd I do?"

"Are you seriously going to ask me that?"

"I don't know what you think I did. It wasn't like I blurted out I'm a mermaid. She knows me from my show. And if you know anything about my show, you know I never break the illusion with kids."

"You should have this time!" he snapped. "If she tells the news that mermaids rescued her, what do you think is going to happen then?"

Nerina folded her arms and stared out the window during their ride back, sinking into her seat. There was no doubt about it. She had messed up, and Wade was pissed at her. His posture was rigid, and his hands gripped the wheel so tightly she thought his knuckles were going to pop out of his skin. The veins in his neck greeted her with his pulsating heartbeat.

Yes, this was definitely going to be a lot of fun. He was either going to lecture her when they got back to the house or ignore her. The wheels locked as he turned a corner, sliding dangerously close to a car parked on the side of the road. He drew in a sharp breath, fighting to keep control of the vehicle.

She studied his face as he concentrated on the road ahead of him.

The snow was coming down harder now and obstructed their vision. He concentrated on the road ahead, keeping his jaw set, and his eyes fixed on the road, not looking away for a second.

She was thankful they weren't in a big city, trying to avoid all the other hazards of big city driving. Here, no one was on the road. Seriously, who would be crazy enough to drive in this weather other than them?

Sitting back in her seat, she pulled out her phone and noticed there was no internet service. Great, now she couldn't even surf the web. Staring at her call logs, she couldn't help but wonder why Jenny hadn't tried calling her. He either lied, and she was hurt or...

Wait a darn minute!

After a few clicks, her suspicions were confirmed. Jenny's number sat prominently displayed under her phone's block feature. Only one person had access to her phone, and he was sitting right next to her.

Wade pulled into their driveway and parked in the garage. She didn't even want to look at him. What gave him the right to do that? Anger welled up inside her like a star about to go supernova. Her heart raced, and heat emanated from her face. If she wasn't still in her twenties, she'd have assumed it was a hot flash from menopause.

She clenched her fists on her lap, desperately wanting to lash out at him. But she kept her cool as she watched him step out of the car. Opening her door, she got out and followed after him. Leaning over, she picked up some snow and packed it down hard between her palms. With her eyes narrowed, she lifted her arm and threw the snowball, hitting him in the back of the head.

"Bullseye," she said, smacking her hands together with satisfaction.

With his shoulders hunched over, he shook his head, trying to dislodge the snow that had landed in his collar. Grabbing the back of his jacket, he pulled it away from his back which allowed the snow to slide through and fall the ground.

Holding her head up high, she stormed by him, saying, "Jerk."

He grabbed her arm, pulling her to a halt. "Don't mess with me right now."

"Why? You've done nothing but mess with me this entire time!" She wasn't about to share with him what she found out. He'd probably take her phone away from her, but she didn't want to let him off scot-free either.

His grip tightened on her arm. "You may have just blown our entire cover with that little girl."

She tried to pull away. "Let me go. You're hurting me."

He refused to let go of her and pulled her carefully towards the house. Once they were inside, he let her go. "You need to stop acting like a child," he snapped.

"And you need to stop acting like my father," she jabbed back, tears stinging her eyes.

Wade turned away from her, breathing hard, as he ran both hands through his hair. No one could quite get under his skin like she could. And the way her attitude could flip from perfectly fine to absolutely crazy drove him bonkers.

He loved her, but never in his life had he ever wanted to have sex with a woman and throttle her at the same time. "You make me crazy," he said, turning to face her. In a sudden surge of his own hormones, he temporarily lost focus on the task at hand.

There she was. Her jacket in a crumpled heap at her feet, and her navy-blue jump suit hugging her curves, highlighting the new baby bump. Her eyes had a wild look in them, and her cheeks were the color of a tomato. She crossed her arms, pushing up her enlarged breasts. His mouth watered at the sight.

He wanted to go to her, but she was still holding her purse over her shoulder, and he didn't feel like being whacked up the side of the head. "Do you mind telling me what's gotten into you?"

"Forget it," she said, walking to the bedroom.

He watched her ass swing back and forth, desire quickly rising inside him. Pushing his urges into the back of his mind, he stepped into the kitchen and grabbed a beer. He needed to figure out what to do next, especially now that everyone in the world likely knew where they were hiding.

Plopping himself down on the couch, he took a large sip of his beer as he struggled internally. The infamous question was not *to be or not to be*. It was *to stay or not to stay*.

Chapter Twenty-Six

Giggling came from beneath the sheets in Jenny's bedroom. "Jason, stop that." She tried to pull herself out of bed, but he pinned her hands above her head, straddling her.

"Think I can get you hiccuping again?"

She squealed, bucking her hips into his crotch. "Don't you dare, mister."

He poked his fingers into her side, tickling her. "Say my name."

"Never," she said between fits of laughter, squirming beneath him.

He was already hard and ready for the third time that day. Who would have thought that a nerd like himself could have attracted a woman like Jenny? Cheerleaders and nerds really ever got together. He knew that. And if she knew the reason why he had mustered up the courage to talk to her, she'd mop the floor with him. He really liked her and was bowled over by the fact she actually wanted him. She even stated he wasn't like the others she usually dated.

Looking down at the woman under him, he felt a sense of pride. He was no longer the freaky science dude at the bottom of the sexual ladder. He had finally moved up a few rungs. Leaning down, he brushed his lips against hers as both of their phones rang in unison.

He leaned his forehead against hers and groaned. "Just when things were getting good."

"Ignore them." She reached up and linked her hands behind his neck, pulling his lips back to hers.

"I'm sorry. It might be my boss with some urgent news. He's a stickler."

Jason rolled off her, and they both grabbed their phones.

"Oh my god, Neri!" Jenny fumbled with her phone, knocking it to the floor. She slid out of bed after it, landing with a thump. "Holy shit, girl, what happened to you? You disappeared off the face of the earth."

Intrigued by her reaction, Jason said, "Boss, I'll call you back."

"No, don't hang up, you idiot," Craig said. "We know where she is."

"I can't talk now. Can we talk about it later?" He looked over at Jenny, making sure she wasn't paying attention to his call.

"She's in Grand Lake," Craig continued.

Picking up his boxers off the floor, he slid them on and stepped outside of the bedroom. "What makes you think that?"

"Haven't you been paying any attention to the news?"

He looked at the door to the bedroom and smirked. "Not really." He hadn't done much of anything over the last few days, except acquainting himself with the cute contours of Jenny's tattooed derriere. Even as he stood there talking on the phone, he ached for relief. He wanted to hang up and pull the phone out of her hand, taking her where she stood.

"Can you hurry it up, boss? I'm kind of busy here," he begged. Why he waited so long to explore this part of his life was beyond him. Hopefully, he'd never have to go back to being a single bachelor again. This was far too much fun.

"Turn on the news. They can't stop talking about it," Craig commented.

Jason leaned his head back and groaned again. "I can't do that right now. I'm with Jenny."

"Has she heard from her yet?"

"Oddly enough, I think she's on the phone with her right now."

"Then what are you doing on the phone with me, boy? Go find out what's going on," Craig ordered, ending the call.

Jason rolled his eyes. "Great idea, boss! Why didn't I think of that."

Craig was a brilliant man but a little slow on the uptake sometimes. He shook his head and returned to the bedroom. Jenny hadn't moved off the floor. Instead, she'd thrown her legs up on the bed and crossed her feet, chatting away on the phone. It didn't look comfy but whatever. He laid down on the bed and listened to Jenny's half of the conversation. Nerina's voice was too quiet for him to hear.

"I can't believe he took you all the way out there," she said.

He rolled onto his side and reached out, running his finger along the sole of her foot. He heard her sharp intake of breath and did it again.

"Stop that." She giggled, pulling her foot away. "No, not you, Neri. The man in my bed is trying to tickle my foot."

Neri must be talking because Jenny went silent again for a minute before saying, "His name is Jason."

After another long silence, she said, "Hey, I have an idea. Maybe he can drive me out there."

If she could get the address, his boss would flip. Maybe he would even give him a raise. His hopes were dashed when he saw her unhappy expression.

Her mouth curled into a frown. "Aw, okay. Maybe we'll come out there when the snow melts a little more."

Crap!

It's wintertime, and the snow over there would be nuts. It would probably reach the top of the wheel well of his car. Driving would be a little impossible. Well, *at* least they would have a location for the future when the weather cleared up.

He watched Jenny write down a possible address, sending a sexy smile his way. Her eyes were sparkling more than usual.

"Okay, I understand, Neri. Say hi to your bonehead of a husband for me." She put the phone down on the side table and climbed up off the floor. "You wouldn't believe what her idiot of a hubby did."

"What?" Jason asked, holding out a hand for her to come back to bed.

She shook her head and put on a nightgown. "That asshole blocked my number on her phone. I'm going to knock him on his ass when I see him."

He would hate to be that man right about now. "Is that why you couldn't get in touch with her for so long?"

"I'm so mad I could just spit."

"Now, now, ladies don't spit," he said, winking at her. "Did you want to go out and visit her?"

She nodded her head. "I'd love to, but the roads are impassable right now and likely will be for the next few months."

"You have her address, though, right?"

"Yes."

"Great."

His boss would want to fly in, but it would be pointless as they would need a four by four to conquer the roads over there. They could rent one, but there was no harm in waiting a little while longer. It wasn't like the two of them would be going anywhere, not by the sounds of things anyway.

He got up and walked over to the dress, picking up his cellphone. "What's the address?"

She grabbed the paper and read out the address. He quickly copied it onto his notepad app.

"We'll go as soon as the roads are decent."

Jenny tackled him. "Thank you, thank you!"

He fell back onto the bed with her on top. He'd send the address to his boss later. Right now, he had better things to do. As excited as he was to find their precious alien, having a woman on top of him was more immediately satisfying. He had a lot of time to make up for.

"Ready for round four?" he asked, running his hand up her nightgown.

"Looks like you already are." She ground herself against his cock.

Grinning, he tickled her sides, making her scramble to get away from him. Everyone else could definitely wait. This, however, couldn't. He quickly pulled her under him and had his wicked way with her.

A loud creak came from behind her. Nerina jumped and spun around with one hand on her chest, hiding her phone behind her.

"Who were you talking to?" Wade asked.

"Who, me?" she replied, stuffing the phone in her back pocket. "No one."

If he knew who she had called, he would never let her have the phone again. He'd probably toss it into the lake or something. And she wasn't about to let him take away her only outlet to the outside world. He'd already dragged her to the middle of nowhere.

"Let me see your phone." He held out his hand, wiggling his fingers.

"What are you, the data police now?"

He rolled his eyes and continued wiggling his fingers at her. "Give it to me, Neri."

"Last time I checked, it was my phone," she said, crossing her arms over her chest, "not yours. Go use your own."

He let out a growl and moved towards her. She gasped and rushed to the other end of the island in the kitchen, keeping it between them. If he went one way, she went the other. It was getting harder to move quickly these days with her growing belly getting in the way. She kept her eyes on him, monitoring his every move. The left corner of his mouth curled into a smirk.

"You're cornered. Where do you think you're going to go now?" he said, chuckling.

Darn!

He was right. It wasn't like she could outmaneuver him. She blew out a puff of air, contemplating what to do next. Go left, he'd catch her. Go right, same thing.

So, she merely studied him. The way his black hair curled just above his determined smoky blue eyes, and how his jaw was set with determination. He figured he was going to win this battle, but she had other plans.

She knew of one way to distract a guy, but she didn't exactly feel too loving or sexy at the moment. But there was, however, only one way out of this mess, and she knew it. Reaching for the link on the straps of her jumpsuit, she released one snap and let the strap fall over her shoulder.

Nerina glanced at him through lowered eyelids, licking her lips. She released the second snap which allowed her jumpsuit to fall to the floor. She kicked the pants under the overhang of the island. Hopefully, out of sight meant out of mind.

Moving out from the side so he could see her, she stood there in her pink panties and white belly shirt, her stomach extending out from below. It was a bump she hadn't quite gotten used to yet.

His mouth opened slightly, and his desire-filled eyes tracked her every move. That was when she knew she had him. Running her fingers along the edge of the counter, she slowly moved towards him and bit her bottom lip. When she was two feet away from him, a grin spread across his face, and the desire-laced look in his eyes disappeared.

"Ha." He zipped past her and grabbed the jumpsuit off the floor, pulling the phone out of her pocket. "As easy as taking candy from a baby."

"The jokes on you, darling." She turned away, tossing him a look over her shoulder. "That was my final offer. Consider the tunnel closed." With the flip of her hair, she sauntered towards the bedroom, adding an extra sexy hip swing to torture him.

He could sleep on the couch for all she cared. After locking the bedroom door, she placed a chair under the knob, just in case he decided to try his toothpick trick again. She still couldn't believe the jerk had blocked her friend's number.

In a way, she could understand why. They were in hiding, but to do it so underhandedly made her blood boil. He could have spoken to her about it. But, no, he invaded her privacy instead and made her worry needlessly about Jenny.

He had always hated Jenny, so he was probably just waiting for an excuse to cut her out of their lives. That ticked her off. How could she ever trust him after this? Tears welled up in her eyes. Their relationship was falling apart, and there didn't seem to be anything she could do to stop it. She wasn't even sure she wanted to anymore.

The man in the kitchen was not the man she married. Her parents weren't her parents. And she was apparently from a place she had no idea about, and Wade knew about it all along. Somehow, she knew there were more secrets. She could feel them. Sense them. And each one was pulling her further and further away from him.

As she lay there in bed, the connection that was usually strong between them was no more than a mere candle in the darkness. Tears rolled down her cheeks, soaking the pillowcase beneath her head.

She didn't know what the future held for them anymore. And that scared her more than anything. What do you do when you can't see a future anymore? A spirit of heaviness fell upon her heart, covering her in darkness. She wanted to cry out, but why bother? It wasn't like anyone cared about her pain.

In the solitude of the night, she had never felt more along and afraid. She could only hope that her fear was needless, and they would make it out of this okay.

Fingers crossed.

Chapter Twenty-Seven

Nerina looked at herself in the mirror and sighed, turning one way and then the other. The baby bump had grown considerably over the last while. By her calculations, she'd be about thirty weeks now, but it was hard to get excited about it.

Ever since Wade took her phone away, they had been at odds with each other. A few words in passing here and there, but he mainly kept to himself as she did. He had taken on the role of protector. Nothing more. He appeared to be more interested in guarding the house than having anything to do with her.

She was no longer 'babe' or 'honey,' but rather, he referred to her as 'Princess.' Sometimes she wished she could figure out what was going on inside that head of his. He hadn't even asked to feel the baby move or let alone touch her in any way, shape, or form.

What did he have to be mad about? All of this crap was his fault anyway. She wouldn't have cared as much if he would have been honest from the start. They really had to decide what they were going to be to each other because she couldn't take another month of this.

Thankfully, nothing ever came of the incident back in December with the lake. Initially, he had wanted to leave Grand Lake and go somewhere else, but they'd gotten snowed in and were unable to drive anywhere. If they wanted groceries, they had to use the snowmobile.

After two months of things being quiet on the home front, she thought he could take a break from this hard-core army role. He stayed up till all hours of the night, walking around the perimeter, dressed up like an eskimo.

She heard the door open, his boots stomping at the entrance. They had another fresh dump of snow during the night. It was almost like living in the Arctic. Hopefully, the snow would disappear soon because she didn't relish having the baby out here in the boonies.

Running a brush through her hair, she gave herself another quick glance in the mirror before heading out of the bedroom to face Wade. They were still married and couldn't avoid each other forever.

"Hi," she said softly. "Everything looking good outside?"

All he gave was a grunt in response as he hung his winter jacket up on the hanger. When he sat on the chair next to the door to pull off his snow pants, she walked over to the fridge and grabbed him a beer. He took it from her and grunted an almost unintelligible thank you, frustrating her even more. She snatched it out of his hand.

"Hey," he said, trying to grab it back, but she moved away from him.

"I do something nice, and you can barely give me a thank you," she complained.

"What do you want from me, Princess?" he snapped.

"For one, stop calling me that."

"Why? It's who you are." He pulled off his boot and threw it at the wall, hitting it with a thud. "And you're certainly acting like one."

She cringed. The corner of her eyes filled with tears. Cradling her belly, she walked to the kitchen sink and placed her hands on the edge. Her shoulders shook as she cried silently. If she had known marriage would be this hard, she never would have said yes. She had brushed off the advice of others at the time because she thought what they were saying was ludicrous. Even her parents had said that marriage wasn't all puppies and rainbows.

They actually likened parts of it to a beautiful snowfall that after a while turned to a muddy slush pile. They had tried to warn her that he had secrets. Why couldn't they have told her that they had secrets, too? She heard a deep sigh come from behind her before he disappeared into the other bedroom where he'd been sleeping for the last while.

After a few minutes, he re-appeared with something in his hand. It was her cellphone. He didn't toss it in the lake after all. Placing it on the counter, he stood there and watched her. A look of apprehension and worry spread across his face.

"Please talk to me before you call anyone, okay?" he begged. "I can't keep you safe if I don't know what to expect."

"Thank you," she said softly. "I'm sorry."

"You scared me by calling Jenny. Her phone could have been tapped after your experience with the kidnappers."

That was something she hadn't considered. In fact, she hadn't given it much thought at all because she couldn't really remember what happened that night. But now that he mentioned it, she felt bad for having put them in danger.

"I really didn't think that it would cause any trouble."

"I know." He picked up his beer and motioned her to the couch, where they sat down. Leaning back, he propped his feet up on the coffee table. "We came out here because a group called the Outcasts want to use you to regain entry into Atlantis. That's why they tried to kidnap you."

"Why me? What good would I do?"

"The royal family are considered to be the life-givers. You provide life to the heart of Atlantis for as long as you are alive. If they capture you, they'll force your family to let them return to the city."

"What's so bad about letting them come back?"

"They are a rebel group. They don't just want to return to the city. They want to take it over and use the Albions as slaves for their beck and call. Russ, their leader, lost his wife in childbirth after they got kicked out, and he's never forgiven them."

"That's so sad. Why'd they get kicked out?"

"He killed your grandfather in an attempt to take the throne."

"Oh." She paused a moment before asking, "Was his wife involved in it, too?"

Wade took another drink of his beer and then said, "She distracted the guards while her husband finished the job."

"Was she pregnant at the time?"

"It's actually how she distracted the guards. She faked being in labor."

Nerina looked down at her own preggo belly, watching as the baby flipped and rolled beneath her stretched skin. Using your own baby for such a despicable act was appalling. "I couldn't imagine doing something like that."

Wade brushed the hair back from her cheek, running the pad of his thumb along her cheekbone. "That's the difference between you and them. Not everyone has a pure heart like you." Not even me, he thought to himself.

Touching her made him realize how much he missed the feel of her skin. He hated the wall that had been built between them. He missed her gentle caress, but despite him making the first contact in a month, she didn't touch him back. However, she did lean into his caress, and that made him feel hopeful for their future.

"Were you there when he died?" she asked.

"Yes. I was a guard in your father's army. Well, just a rookie at the time." He dropped his hand to his lap, wrapping it around the beer can. The tin can crunched beneath his grip. They were getting dangerously close to a topic he always tried to avoid. A time he didn't want to remember.

"Was that when you were married before?"

He squeezed the can even harder. Beer squirted out the top, soaking into his clothes. "Shit." Standing up, he shook his arms, droplets of beer flying everywhere. The image of his wife flashed clearly in his mind.

They'd only been married a week when it all went down. If only he would have known she'd be the curious type. She decided to follow him to see what was going on without his knowledge. He didn't see her until it was too late.

Sharp pains radiated in his chest as the memory assaulted him. It wasn't his fault. Maya had startled him when she approached him from behind. He thought she was one of them. "Stupid, stupid," he muttered, smacking his forehead. She'd still be alive if it wasn't for him.

The guards found him hunched over her body, her blood all over his hands. He tried to say it was an accident, but no one wanted to take a chance on a youngster like him. Not with the rebellion in full swing. They thought he was one of the invaders and cast him out.

"Wade?"

Shaking his head, he tried to pull himself away from the thoughts. That was when he saw Nerina's hand waving in front of his face.

"Sorry, babe. I faded out there," he said, running his hands down his face.

"What happened to her?"

"You don't want to know. Trust me."

"It might help if you talk about it."

"How? Is talking about it going to bring her back? Or change what happened?" He wiped the newly formed tears from his eyes and turned away from her. "The past is the past."

She wrapped her arms around him, hugging him tight. "I'm here for you."

He pulled away and turned to look at her, an ache rising in his chest. "Really? And what if I told you I killed her? Would you still want to be with me then?"

Shock registered on her face, her mouth dropping open.

"Ya, I didn't think so," he mumbled, walking over to the door. It would be better for them to have a clean break now than for her to get tangled into his web any deeper. Once she finds out the truth about everything, she wouldn't want anything to do with him anyway.

Why did he even think this could work? She was way out of his league, and she deserved someone much better than his lousy ass. With his luck, he'd get her killed, too. Why the bloody hell did the king trust him?

"Wait...wait." She rushed over, grabbing his arm. "Just give me a second."

"Why? So you can figure out a way to tell me that you want a divorce?"

"Is that what you want?" she asked quietly.

"No, but your silence over the last few months makes me think you do."

It pained him to think he could lose another woman in his life, especially the one who meant the most to him. Was it even worth pretending that it was going to work out?

She rested her palms against his cheeks, forcing him to look at her. "Talk to me, Wade."

He closed his eyes and tried to push back the pain. The last thing he wanted to do was break down like a little baby. "Her name was Maya. We were childhood friends. Marrying her seemed like the natural thing to do when we came of age. We'd been married a week and we were working in the king's service."

Wade ran a hand through his hair, pacing the length of the living room. Maya wasn't the most beautiful girl in the kingdom, but she was courageous, fun, and adventurous. "She was a thrill seeker. I should have known she was going to follow me to try and find out what was going on."

"What happened?"

"We came under attack one night."

"The night my grandfather was killed?"

He nodded his head. The memory of that night was still crystal clear. No matter how hard he tried to forget, it was impossible. "All the personnel, except for the guards were to be taken to the safe room, while the rest of us tried to stop the outcasts. I'd taken out a few already and was monitoring a situation further down the hall when I heard a noise come from behind me. Being the trigger-happy kid I was, I acted first without thinking."

He plopped his butt on a seat at the table, cradling his head in his hands. "Before I knew what I was doing, my spear pierced her stomach. I didn't know. I didn't know it was her." His shoulders shook as he cried, loud sobs filling the room. "There was nothing I could do. She's dead because of me. I couldn't keep her safe." He smacked his palm on the table in frustration and pain.

Nerina's hands come to rest on his shoulder. "It was an accident, sweetheart. You didn't mean to do it."

"I've gotten pretty good at causing accidents apparently." He pointed a thumb over his shoulder at her belly.

That's when she dropped her hands to her stomach. "Are you saying our baby was an accident?"

Chapter Twenty-Eight

"By getting you pregnant, I triggered the mess we're in. You weren't supposed to be undergoing this change until you were thirty."

"What was I supposed to do? Wait until I'm an old hag to have kids? Let me tell you one thing right now, mister," she said, wagging her finger at him. "This baby is not, and never will be, a mistake."

"Boy, there I go again, getting you all upset," he muttered. "I seem to be doing a bang-up job of that lately, too."

"Stop, you sound like a grumpy ole gus."

"It's not like I have much to be happy about lately."

Instead of answering him with words, she lifted her shirt and grabbed his hand, placing it on her belly. Her stomach rolled beneath his palm, and a smile tugged at the corner of his lips, despite the tears still flowing down his cheeks.

"This baby is something to be happy about," she said.

"You're right. Sorry, babe." He leaned over and kissed her baby bump. The baby kicked and bopped him in the mouth. Pulling back, he rubbed his lips and chuckled. "That kid packs a wallop."

Nerina laughed. "Don't I know it!"

"Have you been keeping track of the weeks?"

"I thought you were doing that," she replied, all innocent-like, making sure her eyes were as wide as a dove's.

"Oh, please don't tell me—"

She laughed, cradling her belly as it shook with the force of her laughter. "Of course, I know. I'm about thirty weeks." Who wouldn't be counting down the days until they got their own body back?

Her body reminded her of the movie, 'Aliens,' where big gross alien creatures laid eggs inside the crew, and a short time later, they'd burst out of their abdomens in a blaze of glory. Hopefully, her baby wouldn't have any special powers that allowed it to do the same.

Nerina shuddered at the thought. The movie parallel was too close for comfort. She wasn't giving birth to a human either. *Boy,* she really had to stop staying up all night watching horror movies.

"Okay, good. We still have time," he said, trailing his hand over her stomach with a big goofy grin on his face. "I still can't believe we have a baby growing in there."

"I started believing it when the baby found my ribs." As if on cue, the baby jabbed a body part into her ribs. Nerina stretched to the side, hoping to dislodge the unseen body part. "It seems to be her favorite spot."

"Could be a boy."

"Well, I'm calling the baby a girl for now," she said, sticking out her tongue.

"I'll call it a boy then, to even the chances a little."

She laughed. "I don't think it quite works that way."

"Oh, well. I can dream."

"Well, we have another ten weeks to go till we find out." She rubbed her belly. The time left in her pregnancy felt like an eternity. The novelty had worn off, and she wanted the baby to be born already.

"I'm thinking that we should get you to Atlantis when you're around thirty-six weeks, so that our doctors can take care of you."

"I thought you were trying to keep me away from there?"

"It was only supposed to be until Kyle and Maggie arrived, and we talked about everything, but…"

He let his voice trail off. Sadly, the fate of her parents was still a mystery. She knew they would never abandon her, but thinking they were possibly dead, especially after they had parted on such horrible terms, tore her up inside.

"How would we get there? I don't even have a tail."

"Once we get you to the ocean, you'll undergo your first transformation."

She bit the bottom of her lip, remembering how her legs turned to jelly ages back. "Will it hurt?"

"Nah, you might feel a weird tingling sensation, but that's about it."

She stuck her leg out in front of her and wiggled her toes. Soon her legs were going to be gone, and she'd have a tail. Her old dream of swimming in the deep blue sea was actually going to come true.

"The most direct route will be if we leave from Coronado Beach."

"The beach where we met?"

Her mind went back to that day. His eyes had honed in on hers, and with that sexy 'I'm so cute' smile, he made his way over to where she had been standing. In those first few moments, he held her heart in the palm of his hand.

But something felt different now. She had assumed they never knew each other. She certainly didn't know who he was anyway. However, if he knew her family, that meant he likely knew all about her.

"So, you've known everything about me since the beginning?"

"Yes."

"Were you on the beach that day because of me?"

"Yes."

"How did you know that I'd be there?"

Wade swallowed the saliva that was building up in his mouth, choking it past the charcoal sized lump growing in his throat. If she didn't end up giving him the silence treatment by the end of this conversation, he'd be surprised.

"Would you believe man's intuition?"

"Do you have such a thing?" she asked, tilting her head.

He gave her a crooked, cautious grin. "I call it staying out of the doghouse."

She smacked his arm, hard. Wade laughed. He knew she wouldn't accept his answer, but he had hoped by not directly answering her question, she would move on to the next question. However, the fire in her eyes told him she wasn't about to set him free.

Shit!

"Well?" she prodded again.

"You always went there every week at the same time."

"How would you know that?" she asked. "Were you following me?"

He contemplated how to answer her without adding insult to injury. "Let's just say I had my eyes on you for a while."

"Why?" Just as he was about to give an answer, her eyes widened, and she smacked her forehead. "Of course, I'm so stupid. How could I have been so blind?"

Somehow, he had a feeling that the next few minutes would not be to his liking. He knew what kind of imagination she had, and that she would probably come out with something close to the truth.

"What do you mean?" he asked.

She turned her back on him and walked towards the couch before turning back to face him. "My father sent you, didn't he?"

"How do you figure that?"

"You knew everything about me," she said, "and given your history with my father, it only makes sense."

He rubbed his neck and stared at the floor. That wasn't the whole truth, but if she had to find out about any part of his past, he'd prefer that to be the one. He doubted he'd accept it anymore gracefully though.

"Well?" she asked.

"Sorta kinda?"

She cocked her hip and crossed her arms. "That isn't a real answer."

He wiped his sweaty palms on his pants and stood up, his heart pounding. Their relationship was about to get muddled down by his murky past, and it made him want to punch something. Nothing in this world meant more to him than her, but whether she'd believe that after the truth came out, he had no idea.

"He found out your life was in danger, and I offered to protect you."

Her eyes filled with tears. "Did he ask you to marry me, too?"

Her father had suggested marriage, but that was the last thing he wanted to tell her. If she knew it wasn't his idea, she'd push him away again. He may not have wanted to marry her at first, but he sure as hell wanted to marry her by the time he had asked her.

"Yes, but—"

She held up her hand and silenced him. "That's all I needed to hear."

He thought since they had started talking again they'd start moving forward from all this silent treatment and running away, but they just took a few steps in the wrong direction. "I disagree."

"I don't care if you disagree. You've lied to me from the very beginning."

She turned away again and was about to retreat to her cave of a bedroom, but he took a few quick steps in her direction and grabbed her arm. "We're not done talking."

"Kindly let me go."

"Not until you listen."

"Why?" she snapped, pulling her arm away. "So you can feed me more lies?"

"Please, Neri. We need to talk about this." He went to reach for her again but thought better of it when her eyes started sparkling.

"You are a fine one to talk about talking. You had years to talk to me, but you didn't." She clenched her fists by her sides. The water on the floor by the door sizzled.

He held his hands up. "I know you're mad, but please calm down."

Maybe it was a bad idea bringing her to a lake. The water would increase her strength, and she could level the town if she wasn't careful. He had powers, but nothing of the same magnitude as to what she was capable of.

"Don't tell me to calm down."

He watched as steam rose past their windows. "Look, if you don't settle down, you'll melt all the snow and lead everyone directly to us."

Nerina slowly loosened her fist and took a few deep breaths. Flexing her fingers, she walked over to the window and wiped the fog off the glass. He was right. There was no snow within fifteen feet of the window.

Biting her nails, she stood there silently and processed what he had said. Wade hadn't asked her to marry him of his own volition. Her father had asked him to. She rubbed at the ache in her chest, choking back a sob. Was there anything in her life that was real? Authentic? In a sense, she couldn't help but feel like a drama queen, but she was angry. Furious even. Everything they had built their life on was a farce.

She wanted to love and to be loved. But, instead, all she got was a game of charades. "How could you not tell me?" she asked, her voice trembling.

"Because you weren't allowed to know."

"It's my life, damn it."

"I know, Neri. The idea was to tell you when you turned thirty, but we kind of jumped the cue a little." He pointed to her stomach.

"Why thirty?"

"That's the age of ascent in Atlantis, and a sign that you are ready to lead our people."

Looking out the window, she said, "Thank goodness I'm not thirty yet." She knew nothing about being a leader. Okay, maybe she had organized and created the mermaid program at San Diego, but that was nothing compared to leading a nation.

If she was supposed to take over, shouldn't there be like queen lessons or something? Why keep her in the dark? Why keep her clueless about her own people? "Does everyone spend time on the surface, or was it just a me thing?"

"It's a royal family thing."

"Why? I mean, if I'm supposed to lead the people, then why send me up here?"

"To protect you."

"But the people who are after me *are* on the surface," she said, scratching her head.

"It's been that way since we arrived on this planet. Some people didn't agree with leaving our planet behind and dissenters grew in the ranks over the years. To protect the throne, the oldest child of the royal family was sent to live on the surface with the guardians.

"When you say the guardians, I'm taking that you mean Kyle or Maggie?" She walked over to the couch and sat down.

"Kyle, yes." Wade joined her, giving her knee a squeeze.

"Not Maggie?" she asked.

He shook his head.

"Who are they, though?" she asked. It was funny how you could live with someone and not really know who they are. That seemed to be happening with every single person she had lived with lately.

"They are a group of people known as the Lavantians. They come from our home planet. While we have power over water, they have power over fire and lava."

"What about Jenny? Is she involved in this somehow?"

"That's something I haven't been able to figure out yet. That's why it bothered me when you called her."

"I—" Nerina's words were swallowed by a deafening boom as the window behind them exploded into a thousand pieces.

Chapter Twenty-Nine

"Get down." Wade dove off the couch. A bullet zipped by, grazing his hair.

She wasted no time ducking for cover in front of the couch, hands over her ears. "Wade," screamed Nerina, her heart racing like a galloping horse.

He ran his hands along his head and then checked his palms. "No blood, I'm fine. We gotta move."

They hugged the floor, trying to stay out of sight. Another bullet flew past them, destroying their one and only television.

"Go. Now!" He helped her up, pushing her towards the bedroom. "Stay low."

She stumbled after taking a step. Her ears were ringing, knocking her equilibrium off balance. Shaking her head, she tried to focus, but the walls around her took on a mind of their own and began to spin.

Wade slipped his arm around her, helping her towards the bedroom. She heard shouting outside and then silence. No bullets. Nothing. When they reached the bedroom, he slammed the door shut, locking it behind them. How many times had she done that since they arrived here?

He rushed over to the window and peeked out the curtain. His back flat against the wall. "I can't see anything."

She sat on the floor at the foot of the bed, crying silently. If she wouldn't have phoned Jenny, none of this would have happened. Now their lives were in danger, and it was all her fault.

"I'm sorry. I'm sorry. I'm sorry," she said repeatedly, covering her face with her hands.

He came over and kneeled beside her. "Look, we can feel sorry for ourselves later. Right now, we have to find a way out of here."

"Ho-w?" she cried, hiccuping. Their opponents had guns, and the two of them had nothing. They were goners.

"The window."

"I'm a beached whale. I-I can't fit through there," she cried, peeking out from between her fingers.

Something hit the front door with a loud thud, causing the sound of wood splintering to fill the air. Nerina jumped, wrapping her arms around him when another loud bang rocked the house.

"We gotta move now." He pulled himself away and ran to the window. Taking a quick peek outside, he slid it open and climbed out. He landed silently in the snow. "It's all clear. Come on."

Soon, they hit the bedroom door, and it shook, loosening a hinge that was barely holding on. She stood there, watching it all happen. Her feet refused to move. Another thump against the door knocked it sideways slightly.

"Neri, now!" Wade yelled from the window.

"I-I can't move," she cried. Her legs refused to budge. It was as if someone had nailed them to the floor.

"You're afraid. Concentrate on my voice, sweetheart. I know you can do this."

Did someone forget to add freeze to the fight-or-flight response? She definitely hadn't heard about it. Nerina cringed when something hard hit the door again, cracking the second hinge. This wasn't happening. This couldn't be happening. She had to be dreaming. Yes, that was it. She was dreaming. Any second now, she'd wake up safe and sound in bed, wrapped up in the sheets.

Wade's face appeared at the window. He held his hand out, beckoning to her with both hands. "If you don't move now, we're going to lose our chance."

"This isn't happening. This is all just a dream," she said to no one in particular, plugging her ears against the noise. Slowly breathing in through her nose and out through her mouth.

"Damn it, Neri." Wade climbed back in through the window and shook her shoulders. "This is really happening. Now move your ass."

In a daze, she allowed herself to be pulled to the window. "I bet if we invite them in for tea, we can talk to them."

"They aren't here for a tea party," Wade growled, giving her a shake. "Snap out of it."

She shook her head to clear away the cobwebs. The ringing in her ears had settled, but the banging behind her did not. They were in danger, and she was standing there like an idiot with him glaring at her.

"Sorry," she mumbled, her feet finally moving of their own accord. As she stuck one leg out the window, the loud bang against the door made the last hinge fall off, and it fell to the floor.

At the entrance stood a well-toned man with a buzz cut. "Pull that leg back in the window now," he ordered, training his gun on her.

Wade stepped in front of her, becoming a shield. "Don't do this, Russ."

The man's brow furrowed as he glared her husband. His face red. "You nearly cost my daughter her life."

"You know this man?" Nerina asked Wade.

"Know me, dearie. He used to work for me." Russ said through clenched teeth. "Isn't that right?"

That was something he definitely forgot to mention. Nausea rolled around in her stomach, which was irritated by the baby deciding to beat her stomach into an uproar.

"Do you want to tell her or should I?" the man asked.

"Don't you dare!" Wade took a step towards him.

Russ discharged the weapon, the bullet narrowly missing her husband's foot. "I wouldn't do that if I were you."

If that would have been her, she would have dove for cover, but Wade stood there, unflinching. He did, however, stop moving towards the man. Was he used to getting shot at?

Her stomach bubbled and gurgled, acid rising high in her throat. "I'm going to be sick."

The two men continued their stand-off, ignoring her completely for the moment. She needed to get to the bathroom before she puked all over the floor. Raising a shaky hand like she was in class, she waited for someone to acknowledge her.

"How'd you find us?" Wade asked.

"I need the bathroom," she interrupted. "I'm gonna puke."

"Charlie," Russ called.

Her hope dwindled when she realized she'd have a dang chaperone in the bathroom. She wouldn't be able to come up with a rescue attempt with a babysitter.

A beefy boxer type guy walked into the room. He looked like he could take on Moose and beat him. "Ya, boss?"

Boss? Charlie looked like he could easily overpower Russ in a nano second. Feeling lightheaded, she placed a hand on Wade's shoulder.

"Take the lady to the bathroom," Russ ordered.

Charlie went to step towards her, but Wade sent him a warning glare and said, "Where my wife goes, I go."

"Not this time, hot shot," Russ said, waving his gun again. "Andy, get your ass in here. And bring the rope you found."

Her stomach muscles spasmed, and she rushed towards the bathroom. The man tailed closely behind her. Her whole body shook with each step. She wasn't sure whether it was from the fear or the cool air that whipped across her skin.

She collapsed in front of the toilet and emptied the remains of her stomach into the bowl. Her throat burned with each forceful heave as chunks spewed out of her mouth and nose. Her eyes filled with water, and tears rolled down her cheeks.

She waited for her stomach to stop churning before she stood up and flushed the toilet. Turning, she glared at the guy taking up space in the doorway. "Can I have some privacy, please?" she asked, motioning towards the toilet.

The guy's face reddened, and for a second, she didn't think he was going to move, but hesitantly, he stepped out of the doorway. She reached for the door and slammed it shut, turning the lock. She needed a moment to think. Alone.

Her phone call was likely the reason they were in this mess, so it stood to reason she should be the one to get them out of it. But what did she know? She'd only ever been in one fight, and that was when she was a kid. Even then, though, no one had gotten hurt as it was a cat fight with a bunch of slapping going around.

These men were carrying guns. A far cry from an open-handed slap. From what Wade was telling her, they wanted her alive, but she doubted they'd be so kind to him. There had to be something she could do.

Turning on the tap, she ran her hands under the warm water. Suddenly, memories of the lake resurfaced and how she almost killed that little girl. Her chest tightened at the thought. She had nightmares of that day, not quite as many recently, but it made her scared to use her powers again.

But that's the answer!

The only way for them to get out of this was for her to tap into her abilities. It was time to show them what she could do. Hopefully, she could stop them before something bad happened.

Chapter Thirty

"Are you going to drive me over there or not?" Jenny asked, placing her hands on her hips.

"Why are you in such a rush? We don't necessarily have to go today." Jason tried to pull her back onto the hotel bed, but she resisted.

"As much as I enjoy spending all day in bed with you, I need to know she's okay." She picked up her phone from off the desk and stared at the screen. "She hasn't returned any of my calls."

"Can't we spend one more day together before we go over there?" He knew the minute they went over there, things would change between them.

"Get your lazy ass out of bed or give me the keys. I'll drive myself."

"Okay, chill out. I'll take you," he said, rolling his eyes at her temper. She could fly off the handle at the drop of a hat. It was almost like navigating a minefield, but it was the price he paid for the passion she had buried under that tough exterior.

He rolled off the bed and strolled to the bathroom. Stepping into the shower, he pulled the curtain closed and turned on the water. He was itching to get the sweat off his body from their early morning sexual rendezvous.

The door opened and creaked close on the other side of the shower curtain. Maybe she had decided against going and was going to join him instead. But his hope was dashed when he heard the distinct flush of the toilet. He jumped out of the way, but not before the spray turned ice cold, pelting him on the back.

"Jenny!" he growled.

"Don't keep me waiting," she huffed before leaving the room.

That girl had a mean streak. He was beginning to think that bringing her was a bad idea. They left a day earlier than the rest of his gang. She didn't know about them or that they were coming to Grand Lake as well. They were arriving later, which was the main reason he wanted to wait until tomorrow to go for a visit.

The water finally warmed back up, and he stepped back under the shower to finish cleaning himself. His heart flip-flopped back and forth regarding his feelings for her. What they had in bed was incredible, amazing. But, as time went on, he could see that she was a high maintenance woman. He doubted he was ready for someone like her. Jumping out of the shower, he pulled on his clothes and joined her in the other room. She was ready to go, sitting there with a scowl on her face.

"Why is it you get ready so quickly when you want to go somewhere, but not when I come by to pick you up for a date?"

She shrugged her shoulders and tossed his shoes at him. "Come on, let's go."

"Geez, you're pushy, woman!" he mumbled.

But he did as he was told, and before long, they were in the car on their way to the house.

Wade stood in front of the window, contemplating his next move. He wasn't sure exactly how many attackers there were, but from his current head count, there appeared to only be three of them. To be honest, seeing Russ and Charlie out in the field surprised him.

"Where's Glenn and Moose?" he asked.

"Wouldn't you like to know," Russ smirked.

"So, what makes us worthy enough to grace us with your presence?" Wade asked. "Or didn't you trust your men not to mess up again?"

Andy walked into the room with the rope he had found in the closet. It was the rope Wade put there in the event that Nerina tried to run away. Now he regretted buying it.

"Tie him up," Russ ordered.

Andy looked between him and Russ, hesitantly taking half a step towards Wade.

"Don't be a chicken," Russ said. "Just do it!"

"Remembering your flash freeze, are you?" Wade said, smirking.

Andy's face and ears turned beet red, his lips stretching into a thin line. "I swear I'm going to turn you into an icicle one day."

Just when he thought Andy was going to storm him like a bull, Charlie shouted obscenities from the other room. The men glanced at each other, eyes widening as they moved towards the doorway.

Wade jumped on the momentary distraction and dove out the window, landing in the bushes alongside the house. Lifting his head, he spat out a small stem that had found its way into his mouth. As he ran his tongue across his lips, a metallic taste filled his taste buds. Spitting on the ground, he noticed blood mixed in with his saliva.

"Shit," Russ yelled. "Find him!"

Wade pressed up against the wall of the house and disappeared from sight with a simple hand movement. Out of the corner of his eye, he could see a vehicle blocking their driveway. *Damn.* They wouldn't be able to escape in the car.

The lights of the vehicle suddenly turned on and someone poked his head out the window. "Russ, he's outside!"

Glenn!

Wade ducked as he saw a gun being aimed in his direction. He had to move, but he couldn't stay hidden and move at the same time. "God damn it!" he mumbled, as he fought his way out from behind the bush, running towards the backyard.

A hundred red-hot needles dug into the flesh of his shoulder, as a loud bang filled the air. The force of the bullet made his upper body twist in agony, throwing him to the ground. His vision blacked out for a second before filling with bright white spots. Gripping his injured shoulder, he gasped for breath.

The snow began to sizzle beside him, steam rising into the air. His scared little princess must be rising to the occasion. Before long, the door swung open and out rushed Russ, Andy and Charlie, followed by a large water dragon. They stumbled over Wade, landing on the grass beside him.

Wade shook his head to clear the rest of the white dots away from his vision. The action caused even more pain in his shoulder. Blood squeezed between his fingers as he pressed his hand against the wound.

The blue, see-through water dragon opened its mouth, shooting ice at the feet of their attackers and freezing them in place. His wife stood behind a shimmering wall of water that formed the belly, her hair flying behind her and eyes glowing brightly.

"No one messes with my family and gets away with it." As Nerina raised her arms, the wings of the water dragon spread out, spanning the width of the house.

He'd never seen anything like it before, not even with the rest of the royal family. There were stories of the ancient Atlantians using dragons in battle, but he thought they were just fables to keep the children entertained.

Glenn rounded the corner with his gun ready to fire at her.

"Don't shoot," Russ ordered.

Nerina flung her arm out and the dragon's wing picked up Glenn, throwing him towards the lake. He landed hard, skidding across the ice. Looking down, she saw Wade wincing, his shirt covered in blood. Enveloping herself and her husband inside the body of the dragon, effectively shielding both of them from their attackers, she dropped to her knees in front of him.

Tears filled her eyes. "I'm so sorry."

Her hands came to rest on his shoulder, and he winced at her touch. The dragon faded slightly as her power was diverted to healing instead. As soon as the wound was healed, she stood up, swaying slightly as the sudden movement decreased her blood pressure. The dragon lost its shape, falling like water to the ground.

Wade stood up beside her, putting his arm around her waist to help steady her. The only two pieces of evidence that a wound ever existed were all the blood on his shirt and the bullet hole.

The touch of his hand against the skin of her waist revitalized her. "You don't know who you're messing with," Nerina said, facing her opponents.

"And you, darling, do not know who he is," Russ said, waving his gun at Wade.

"I know more than you think, jerk," she replied.

Russ lifted his head towards the heavens and laughed loudly. "Do you really think he's told you everything?"

Wade let go of her waist and stepped towards him. "Don't you dare!"

She looked at her husband. His shoulders were tense, and his fists were clenched by his sides. The snow began melting all around him. This wasn't the reaction of a man who had no more secrets to tell. From the looks of it, he still had plenty.

From the other side of the house, she heard a car door slam, and their voices carried in the direction of the wind. It sounded like...

No, it couldn't be.

She took a step towards the side of the building when Russ shot a bullet at her feet, making her jump.

"You aren't going anywhere yet. I haven't told you everything."

Wade took a step towards him. "Shut the hell up, Russ, or I'll—"

"You'll what?" Russ interrupted. "I'm the one with the gun." To prove his point, he fired another shot, this time at Wade's feet.

"Nerina," a voice called from the front of the house.

She never expected Jenny to come all the way out here, even though she said she would. She purposely didn't answer her phone calls to keep her safe.

"Stay there. Don't come back here," she yelled to Jenny, not that she would listen to her request. She was too much of a free spirit.

Charlie moved towards the side of the house. "Looks like only two of them, boss."

"Forget about them," Russ said, turning his head back in their direction. "So, princess, what did your lovely prince tell you?"

"None of your business," she said. Her stomach started to roll and not from the baby this time. There was a look in the man's eyes that made her uneasy. She felt like she was about to leave her stomach at the top of a very steep hill.

"Did he tell you that I sent him?"

"Shut up, you asshole." Wade created an ice ball, throwing it at the man's head.

Russ ducked and laughed again, like a mad man. "This is priceless. I'm so glad I get to see the fall of your relationship before I kill you."

Nerina stepped away from all their testosterone. When Wade went to walk towards her, she held up her hand to ward him off. He had done it again, kept another secret from her.

"Is what he said true?" she asked her husband.

"You bet your batootie it is," Russ said. "You've finally held up your side of the deal, Wade."

Her heart thumped erratically, pain radiating all over. "What deal?"

"I hired him to kidnap you."

Wade jumped at Russ, growling at him. Charlie tackled him to the ground and sat on him. She couldn't do anything but stand there, a wave of dizziness washing over her. Leaning over, she rested her hands on her knees. She trusted him, and he lied to her. He had been lying since the very beginning. She couldn't believe he had worked for that crazy coot.

Lifting her head, she looked at Wade on the ground, pinned by Charlie. "Is that true?"

Her husband smacked his fist into the ground. "Yes, but—"

"Stop," she cried. "Just stop with the excuses."

With one broad sweep of her arm, a thick cloud of fog rose between them. Hidden inside the fog, she turned and ran down the driveway, towards the voice of her friend.

Chapter Thirty-One

Nerina's mind spun in circles as she did the pregnant waddle down the driveway, as fast as her body would let her move. Had she really created a water dragon? How on earth did she know how to do that? Things were changing faster than she could keep up. And Wade, she didn't even know who he was anymore.

Looking up, she spotted Jenny standing beside a man she didn't recognize. She slid to a stop, almost landing on her butt. *Another stranger.* Performing a quick assessment, she decided he looked less dangerous than the men behind her.

"Get in the car, hurry!" Nerina shouted, rushing over to the car, cradling her belly.

"Why, what's wrong?" Jenny followed suit, motioning for the man to get behind the wheel.

"Men. Guns," she said, breathing heavily. "Need I say more?"

"Where's Wade?" the man asked, as they piled into the car.

"Drive, whoever you are!" Nerina ordered.

They'd barely pulled away from the house when the back window exploded. The women ducked, screaming.

"Holy Fuck!" Jason slid his body down in the seat, accidentally pulling the wheel too far to the right. The car swerved from side to side as he fought to re-gain control on the slippery roadway.

"Can't you do a better job of driving?" Jenny snapped.

"I'd be happy to pull over and you can drive instead," he said, putting his foot on the brake, making the car slide some more.

Jenny looked out the back window and slapped Jason's shoulder. "Take your foot off the god damn brake and drive."

"Make up your mind, woman!" he growled.

"Boy, you guys sound like an old married couple." Nerina forced out a chuckle, her entire body shaking with adrenaline. Her stomach had decided to get in on the action by contracting painfully. She winced as she stared out the back window.

After a few minutes, she spotted that they were being followed, but the car was quite a ways behind them, thankfully. Was Wade in the car with them? Was he really one of them? Would they have shot one of their own?

God!

She was so confused. The only thing she wasn't confused about was the fact that she fell in love with a figment of her imagination. He wasn't who he said he was. As soon as she was back in California, she never wanted to see his lying ass again. Shooting pains spread out from her chest and down her arm. She breathed in through her nose and out through her mouth, waiting for the pain to dissipate.

"What the hell was that about?" Jenny asked.

"Wade lied to me." Nerina didn't want to go into any more detail, not with a stranger in the car.

"I told you so. Good riddance," she said, clicking her tongue. "I can smell a liar from a mile away."

Jason coughed, smacking his hand against his chest, causing the two of them to glance over at him.

"Sorry," he mumbled. "Something went down the wrong way."

Nerina narrowed her eyes at him. He was another man with secrets, of that she was certain. As soon as she had a moment, she was going to voice her concerns to Jenny. They didn't need any more frauds in their lives.

"Looks like we've lost them," Jenny announced.

Jason glanced in the rear-view mirror, locking eyes with Nerina. "Do you want to tell me what the hell just happened?"

"It's a need-to-know kinda thing," she answered.

"I'm *kinda* the one driving the car, with a now blown out back window," he said, hooking a thumb over his shoulder. "I'd like to know who I'm running from."

"We need to call the police," Jenny said, pulling out her phone.

Nerina snatched her phone away. "No. No police."

Her friend sighed, grabbing her phone back. "What kind of trouble have you gotten yourself mixed up in, girl?"

"I'll explain later. I have to get back to San Diego." She needed to know if her parents were okay. They may have lied to her, but she knew more about the situation now and understood their place in her life. They could protect her more than Wade could.

"Well, we can't drive down the highway with a broken window," Jason said.

"There's a hardware place in town. We can buy some plastic and patch it up for now," Nerina suggested. The last thing she wanted to do was wait around town to repair a window when the bad guys would be looking for them.

"We could just bunk at the hotel and drive out tomorrow," Jason suggested, turning towards the hotel parking lot.

"No," Nerina said quickly. "That'll be the first place they look."

"Fine."

They set out for the hardware store and parked around the back. As they were fixing the car, Jenny and Jason pelted her with questions, but she kept shrugging them off as a 'tell you later' kind of thing.

She still couldn't wrap her head around the fact that Wade had been hired to kidnap her. Her heart hurt thinking about it. Was there such a thing as broken heart syndrome? If there was, she certainly she had it.

Tears threatened to fall again as she stood there, holding the plastic in place while Jason taped it down. "I'm sorry about your window."

"There was nothing you could do," he said, sighing, as he put the last piece of tape in place. "I'll be right back, ladies."

The two girls watched him walk towards the building, and as he was walking, he pulled out his cellphone. Why did he need to make a call? A shiver crept down her spine.

"Who is that guy?"

"His name is Jason. I met him after you disappeared."

"What does he do?"

"He's a scientist. Something to do with genetics, I think."

All the blood drained from Nerina's face. It had to be a coincidence. What were the odds of someone else finding out about her and using her best friend to get close to her? They needed to go. Just the two of them.

"We need to leave."

"We will as soon as he gets back."

"We have to leave without him. Get in the car." Nerina climbed into the driver's seat and went to turn the key. "Crap!" she said, smacking her hands against the wheel.

He'd taken the keys with him.

They had tied Wade's hands behind his back, and he sat between Charlie and Andy in the backseat. Glenn was getting reamed out by Russ for having shot at the car. Wade was relieved that they wanted her alive.

As for himself, he had no clue why they shoved him into the car and didn't just kill him. They usually killed traitors on the spot. Did they think they could use him to find her? He'd rather die than help them.

"Did you see the look on her face? It was just priceless," Russ said, his laughter filling the car.

"Shut the hell up," Wade snapped, kicking the driver's seat.

Charlie stuck his gun into Wade's ribs. "Play nice."

"I'm just returning the favor," he grunted as the barrel dug into his side. "Get that gun away from me before I make you eat it."

In response, the guy clocked him on the head with the butt end of the gun. Wade groaned, his vision blurring. *That smarts.* If his hands were free, he'd shove that gun up Charlie's ass.

"Charlie, will you refrain from hurting the help," Russ said, sighing, "please."

"Can't I hurt him just a little?"

"Once we get the princess, you can hurt him till your heart's content," Russ said, placating the man like a little kid.

It didn't surprise Wade that they were going to try to use him to locate her. He was the only way she'd be found. The connection his people had with their mates was unprecedented. Closing his eyes, he focused on his breathing until her image appeared in his mind. He was hit by a wave of fear and panic emanating from her spirit. His heart rate increased, and feelings of anxiety bounced around in his chest.

Something spooked her, and that could only mean one thing. Someone else had found her. That was all he knew. Her location had remained hidden from him. If their connection was partially severed, she must really pissed off.

"Shit," he mumbled.

"What was that, pretty boy?" Russ asked.

He bit his tongue to hold back the words he wanted to say. Goading them too much was not going to help the situation. Although he had to admit he enjoyed egging them on, it was far too easy to make them flip out. Moving his hands, the rope rubbed like sandpaper against his skin. There was no way he could free his hands while trapped between the two henchmen.

After a few minutes, they drove into the heart of town. Russ pulled to a stop in the parking lot of a gas station and glanced back at him. "So, mister hotshot, where's the girl?"

"I see a girl over there," Wade said, nodding towards a girl entering the store.

The boss picked up the gun on his lap and pointed it towards him. "Find her."

"You really think I'm going to help you?"

"If you want to live, yes."

Wade spat in the man's face. "Fuck you."

"I know who I want to fuck, but it isn't you," Russ said, wiping the spittle off his face. "I have every intention of making the princess mine, you know."

With his teeth bared, Wade lunged at the man's neck, intending to sink his teeth into the man's carotid artery. Charlie grabbed him by the collar of his shirt, yanking him backwards. His wrist landed awkwardly against the seat, sending a sharp pain up his forearm.

The two men placed their arms against his chest, holding him back. He kicked at the man's head.

Russ moved to the side, laughing like a hyena. "I figured that would get your panties in a twist."

"You touch one hair of her head, and I'll make sure you never see the light of day again." Wade kicked his foot towards him again, making a solid connection with the man's shoulder.

Pleasure rippled through him as Russ groaned in response. The man threw off his seatbelt and turned to face him, holding his gun inches away from Wade's nose.

"You do anything like that again, and I'll bury a bullet in your brain."

"You won't cause you need me."

"Where is she?"

"Bite me."

Russ' fist shot out, hitting him squarely in the mouth. Wade's teeth dug into his lips, and his head bounced back against the seat. Groaning, he licked his lips, blood dripping down his chin.

"Someway, somehow, I'm going to kill you," Wade said. "That's a promise."

"Not today, pretty boy," Russ said. "Shut him up."

The last thing he saw was Charlie's fist approaching his temple, then his world went black.

Chapter Thirty-Two

"He just saved your ass," Jenny said, crossing her arms. "We aren't leaving him behind."

"I don't have time to explain." Nerina flipped the visor down and then slammed it back into place. "Help me look for a spare key."

Her friend pulled a key out of her pocket and dangled it in front of her. "We aren't going anywhere until you tell me why."

"Just trust me. I'll explain along the way."

She was probably going to break some type of mermaid code here, but she had no other choice. Looking around, she made sure no one else was looking before she concentrated on the snow near her friend's feet. Lifting her arm, the snow melted, and she created a wall of water in front of Jenny.

Her friend's eyes widened, her jaw dropped, and she stumbled backwards. "What the hell? Who are you?"

As Nerina dropped her hand, the water splattered to the ground. "I'll tell you in the car. Can we go, please?"

Jenny froze, fear running rampant through her eyes. When Nerina took a step in her direction, Jenny turned and ran towards the store.

Nerina threw her hands up in the air. "Great, just great."

She hadn't counted on that. So much for being friends. What was she supposed to do now? She had no money for the bus, and it wasn't like she could walk back to San Diego. The only thing she could do was go back to the house and see if they had left Wade behind, but that didn't sound too appealing either. Out of the corner of her eye, she saw Jason emerge, dragging Jenny behind him. He was stronger than he looked.

"I'm not sure what's going on between the two of you, but we gotta go before they find us," Jason said.

"I'm not getting in the car with that thing." Jenny grabbed his fingers, trying to get him to release her hand.

"Would you rather be dead?" Jason asked, pushing her towards the car.

Nerina couldn't blame her for being frightened and leery. She felt the same way when Wade pulled out his bag of tricks and disappeared right in front of her.

"Jenny, I'm the same person I was before. I promise I won't hurt you. Please, we can't stay here, or they'll kill us," she said, all the while not taking her eyes off Jason. She didn't exactly want to get back in the car with him.

However, the other men had guns, and he didn't. Not that she knew of anyway. He was also the only person who could get her back to San Diego. She just wasn't sure if he had his own agenda. It couldn't have been a coincidence that the good doctor started going out with her friend right after the incident happened at the house.

"Jason," Nerina said, placing her hands on her hips. "I'll get back in the car with you under one condition."

He tilted his head and looked at her. "And what might that condition be?"

"That you give me the keys." She held her palm out to him.

He raised his eyebrows at her and hid the keys in his fist. "Over my dead body."

Nerina walked up to him and watched him swallow hard as he

backed up a step. That told her all she needed to know. "You know about me, don't you?"

Jenny stood there, scratching her head. "Wait...wait...wait. You knew all about her, Jason?"

"Well, I...um," he stammered, staring at the ground.

"Figures, just when I thought I met Mr. Right." Jenny walked towards him, with intent written all over her face, and kicked him in the crotch. "I can't believe you used me to get to her."

He doubled over, groaning. "Romance the girl. It will be easy, they said. He better pay me overtime for this."

That caught Nerina's attention. "Who's paying you?"

Jason held his crotch, keeping his legs crossed. "Can we just go before they find us?" he ground out between his teeth.

"I can't believe I'm going to say this to you." Jenny walked to the driver's side, climbed in and looked at her. "Get in."

Neri climbed into the passenger seat. "Thank you."

"You better tell me everything," she said, sticking the key in the ignition. "Every single juicy detail."

Suddenly, Nerina had a bad feeling about taking the car as the engine roared to life. Winding up in jail wasn't high on her to-do list. All she wanted to do was get back home and not have any more detours along the way.

"Maybe we shouldn't take his car," Nerina said, second guessing her grand theft auto decision.

A detour to the police station was not going to help the situation. The last thing she wanted was have her baby in jail. Nerina placed her hand on the door handle to step out of the car. "I can't go to jail."

"Don't be a wuss," her friend said, revving the engine.

"Jenny, get out of my car." Jason leaned into the car through the open window, attempting to grab the keys.

Her friend grabbed her purse, pulling out a can of pepper spray. She held it up to his face. "Back away, now."

He held up his hands and stepped away. "Don't do anything stupid."

"Bye, Jason." Jenny blew him a kiss and drove away.

Hopefully, he wouldn't call the police on them, but Nerina doubted they would be so lucky.

"So, Neri, spill it. Tell me everything."

"Well, it all started when I found out I was pregnant...

"Can't we get rid of mister golden boy?" Charlie asked, shoving Wade off his shoulder and into Andy. "I'm tired of him sleeping on my shoulder."

"We need him to find the girl," Russ replied.

Andy pushed him back towards Charlie. "Why don't we just park beside the highway? If they leave town, we'll see them."

"They might already be out of town," Russ commented.

"Doubtful. They are going to want to fix their window before traveling the highway," Andy said. "Otherwise, the police might stop them, so I figure if we wait on the side of the road heading out of town, they'll drive by eventually."

Russ contemplated the suggestion. It made sense. They'd be trying to avoid the cops, not drawing them out with a broken window. "Maybe we don't need this douche after all," Russ said, motioning to Wade. "Toss him out."

Once they were free of the dead weight, he spun the tires and pulled out of the gas station. The smell of burning rubber snuck in through the vents. Every once in a while, his men would come up with an idea that even he didn't think of, and that earned them respect in his books.

He spotted a pullout beside the highway southwest of the town. He pulled off the road and parked his car at the best vantage point to see any oncoming vehicles. They had to find her soon, or his daughter didn't stand a chance.

That was the only thing he cared about at this point. The doctor only gave her a week or two at the most now. She was no longer responding to them. Tears filled his eyes. He quickly wiped them away before the guys could see. His daughter was his strength and his weakness. He couldn't lose his only living memory of his wife.

His wife's laughter and her greenish-blue eyes lived on in his baby girl. She was all he had left, and he wasn't about to let this cruel world rip her away from him. Not when there were people on this planet who could help her.

His vision could see only red as he thought about having to bury her needlessly. Children weren't supposed to die before their parents, not in his world. And he wasn't about to let it start now.

His phone rang, making him jump. "Hello?"

"Sir, you must get back as soon as possible."

Russ sat up straighter in his seat. It was the doctor. "Why? What's going on?"

"I thought she had a few weeks, but we've been struggling to keep her going all morning."

His heart sunk into his stomach, and his shoulders followed. "The earliest we might be back is tomorrow evening."

"I'll try my best, but I can't make any promises. I'm sorry, sir," the man said softly.

"Keep her alive or you'll be joining her," Russ threatened, disconnecting the call. He needed to hit something. Someone. He punched the steering wheel, beeping the horn. If Wade had done the job he was hired to do, instead of becoming a traitor, they would already be back in Atlantis, and his daughter wouldn't be suffering with a stupid earthly disease.

There were things on earth he'd never heard of before, and because their people didn't have the right antibodies, they got sick on land easier than humans. Also, the air quality sucked near the big cities, which was why he loved the island. There, you could stare up into space and watch the stars without all the lights and pollution getting in the way.

"You okay, boss?" Glenn asked.

"Just keep watching," he snapped, his voice wavering slightly as he wiped a solitary tear off his cheek. Tears were a sign of weakness, and if he wasn't careful, some cocky guy would cash in on it.

It angered him to no end that his only hope was in a woman who continuously eluded him. This time, she wouldn't get away. His daughter's life depended on it. Russ popped the trunk of the car. "Time to bring out the tranquilizers."

Charlie opened the door and walked around to the trunk, pulling out the dart guns. It was something Russ had been trying to avoid since discovering she was pregnant. It was complicated enough with just her, let alone adding a baby into the mix. He knew that if she died, there would be no Atlantis to return to.

When the guns were handed out, Russ said, "No belly shots. We don't want to risk hitting the baby."

They'd been sitting there for over an hour when a vehicle approached them. The setting sun cast a shadow upon the upcoming vehicle, so it was hard to see whether it was them or not.

"Does anyone know the license number?" Russ asked.

"I think it started with a 3RY," Andy answered.

"It's them, boss. I recognize the car," Charlie said, smacking the front seat.

Allowing them to get at least a block ahead of them, he pulled his car onto the highway. There was no need to follow them too closely and alarm them. He wanted them to feel safe enough to put their guard down. Without any traffic lights, it was easy to keep up with them. If the doctor could keep his daughter going for another day or so, he should be able to get back with Nerina by then.

After three hours of driving, he saw a state patrol vehicle parked on the side of the highway which had turned its lights on as soon as the other vehicle passed them.

"Well, boys, I think our chance has finally arrived."

Chapter Thirty-Three

"Sir, are you okay?" a muffled voice asked, as something tugged at Wade's wrist.

"Don't worry. Help is on the way."

It sounded like a woman's voice, but the ringing in his ears made it difficult to determine who it was. Groaning, he tried to sit up, but his arms wouldn't cooperate. Opening his eyes, nausea filled his gut as the blurry world spun around him. He quickly closed them again and took a deep breath.

"One second," the unfamiliar voice said.

Someone tugged at his wrists again, and then he could finally move them. His wrists burned with pain as he rubbed them.

"Boy, we've been having far too much excitement in our small town lately."

With his stomach settling, he tried to open his eyes again to see who was talking to him. The spinning had settled slightly, but he still had blurred vision. He shook his head to clear away the cobwebs and instantly wished he hadn't. A heavy band of pressure wrapped itself around his skull. Groaning, he covered his eyes and tried to sit up.

"It looks like you took quite the blow to the head. Do you remember what happened?" the woman asked.

"Who are you?" he asked, slowly testing his speaking ability. At least that didn't seem to be affected, but it made the pounding in his head worse.

"I'm Rebecca. One of the gas station cashiers."

A police car and an ambulance pulled in beside them. He struggled to stand up to prove he was fine but fell back to his knees when the world spun again. *Stupid son of a bitch.* He was going to kill that bastard.

"What happened here?" the cop asked, as the paramedic leaned down to help Wade.

"I'm not sure, sir. I came outside and found him passed out on the ground, with a rope tied around his wrists." Rebecca said.

"Hi, sir, I'm Joe. Can you tell me your name?" the paramedic asked.

"It's Wade Douglas," the woman answered.

Wade and the paramedic glared at her.

"Sorry," she said, her face turning a bright shade of red. "I looked in your wallet."

It was the twenty-question game that the paramedics usually asked to see how alert you were, but he didn't exactly want them to know his name. When he looked up at the cop, he saw a look of recognition pass over his face.

Shit!

His day was just getting better and better. The cop turned and walked back to his car, taking a seat as he checked his computer. He needed to leave before the cop got back out of his car again.

"I'm fine. I can walk it off," Wade said, swaying slightly as he stood up. His stomach picked that moment to join in on the fun. Hunching over, he puked all over the paramedic's shoes.

"Brian, we need the stretcher." Joe yelled, shaking off his shoe.

"No, it's okay." Wade turned away from them and started walking, his legs pulling him in every which direction. It had been ages since he felt as drunk as a skunk. It was not a nice feeling, and he never even had anything to drink to make it worth it. If he didn't get his head back on straight, he would be sitting in the back of the police car any second now.

"Hold it right there," the cop said, stepping in front of him. "Get on the ground now."

"I was held hostage, and now you want to arrest me? What gives?"

"We'll sort it out down at the station."

"Captain, sir, with all due respect, this man should be going to the hospital." Joe stepped between them. "You can put him under house arrest there."

Wade raised his arm into the air. "If I can interject, I'd rather not go anywhere."

Joe leaned towards him and whispered, "Just play along."

He tilted his head and looked at the paramedic. A familiar fiery sparkle appeared in the man's eyes, and the corner of his mouth curled into a grin. Another guardian, he thought with surprise. He'd been curious as to who prepared the safe house for their arrival. Now he knew.

Pretending to faint, he fell into the man beside him. The paramedic grabbed him, slowly lowering him to the ground. "You're heavier than you look," Joe whispered to him before looking at the cop once again. "Sorry, sir. You're going to have to meet us at the medical center."

Quickly, they piled into the ambulance, leaving the frowning cop behind.

"You let her do what?" Craig shouted through the telephone.

Jason held the phone away from his ear as he stood in the hotel lobby. "I didn't let them do anything."

"Why didn't you stop them?"

"Why didn't *you* stop them at the hospital?" Jason shot back.

Craig sighed. "You should have just waited for us before racing over there, like a hero on your own."

"Shoulda, coulda, woulda."

"I swear if you've messed this up for us, you'll be finding another job when you get back."

Jason rolled his eyes. No wonder Craig never dressed up in a Santa Claus costume at any of the Christmas parties. He was far too grumpy to pass as jolly ole Saint Nick. Here Jason was, going out of his way to help him and the man couldn't even say thank you.

"Next time, you can do it all by yourself," he said, ending the call. Why had he even bothered getting involved? Now he had no car and no girlfriend. She'd torn his heart in two when she pulled out the pepper spray. It served him right, though. He shouldn't have been so stupid.

Walking up to his room, he shoved his hand in his pocket to grab the room card and came up empty. After checking all his pockets, he pulled out his wallet and looked inside. His room card was nowhere to be found. Thinking back, Jenny was the last one who had it. They had only received one.

Smacking his forehead, he returned to the lobby. "Excuse me, miss?"

"How can I help you?" Lisa, the front desk clerk, asked.

"It would seem that the woman I was with took the room card with her when she left," he said, his face burning with embarrassment. "Do you have a spare?"

"Generally, we charge for lost cards, but since this is your first stay with us, we'll waive the fee," the lady said, smiling. "Just give me a moment and I'll program another one."

"Okay, thanks." He turned around and leaned against the front desk, resting his elbows on the counter. He shook his head at his own stupidity. He really had to stop letting others tell him what to do. Was he that much of a pushover?

No. He refused to believe that. He had to own up to his own

stupid decisions, like getting too close to Jenny. He had started to let his other head make the decisions for him. He was in it for the girl. They knew something that no one else in the scientific world was aware of. A triple helix human—or, at least, she looked human. That much they knew. Just sitting in the car with her had been a rush.

It was weird that Jenny didn't know anything about her, though. She had worked with the girl for a while but seemed to be about as clueless as everyone else. Pulling out his phone, he searched for Jenny's number, but then his phone rang.

"Hello, Jason speaking?"

"Hi, Mister Carlson, this is Officer Roberts calling you back. We've found your car. It's being towed to the nearest impound."

"And my girlfriend?"

"That's what we need to speak with you about. There has been an incident."

His heart thumped in his chest, and his throat tightened, causing him to squeak as he spoke, "W-what happened?"

"Our officers pulled your car over near Grand Junction, but they came under attack. Do you know if they had any enemies, or do you know of anyone who might want revenge on you or your girlfriend, an ex, perhaps?"

The front desk clerk returned to the desk and handed him the room key.

"Thanks, miss," he mouthed to her before returning to his phone call. "Is she okay?"

"We'd like to come by and ask you a few questions. Are you still at the hotel?"

"Yes, I'll be in room 202."

"Thanks. An officer should be arriving shortly."

Jason hung up the phone and wandered over to the elevator. Things were getting weirder by the moment. His team would do better forgetting about the whole thing before someone got hurt. There would be other chances to win a Nobel Prize, at least for him anyway. He had his entire career ahead of him.

His hands shook as he clicked on Jenny's number in his contacts. Her phone kept ringing until it went to voicemail. With a sinking feeling in the pit of his stomach, he couldn't help but feel that something terrible had happened to her.

She was a handful to deal with, but regardless of everything that had happened, he cared about her. What if the cops thought he had something to do with the attack? The last thing he wanted to do was wind up in jail and have his PhD revoked or something.

He had worked too hard and too long to have it taken away because of some fanciful quest that his boss had sent him on. When he joined genetics, the last thing he expected was to get shot at while doing his job. He didn't want to die before he had even lived. If Craig wanted her, he'd have to go after her himself from now on.

God!

He needed a drink. Walking over to the bar fridge, he grabbed himself a rum and coke. Thankfully, he'd have his vehicle back soon and would be able to go home. Everyone else could stick around and do their own bidding. He was finished.

Before long, there was a knock at the door, and he opened it to find himself facing four police officers, and none of them had a smile on their face. "Uh, hello?"

"Jason Carlston?"

"That's me. Please, come on in."

"Thanks. I'm Lieutenant Thomas. We need to talk to you about your girlfriend, Jenny Peters."

"Is she okay?"

"I'm so sorry. She passed away at the scene."

He stood there dumbfounded, and his drink slipped from his hand, landing on the tan carpet. Dead? That couldn't be possible. Not her. They were safely in his car, driving down the road. How could that have happened? Why couldn't anyone save her?

"Wh-wh...what happened?" he asked finally, sitting down in a nearby chair.

"After you reported your car stolen, one of the state patrols saw it and pulled it over. When they arrested the two women, they were attacked from behind."

"By who?"

"We were hoping you might have the answer to that question," said the only female cop in the group as she hooked her thumbs in her belt loops.

"I have no idea."

"We noticed that there were bullet holes in the body of your car, as well as a broken rear window. Can you tell us what happened?" asked Lieutenant Thomas.

He swallowed hard. His throat dry. "Am I under arrest?"

"Not at this time, but other than our police officers, you are the last person to see Jenny and Nerina alive."

"Is Nerina dead, too?" he asked, holding his breath.

"Her condition and whereabouts are currently unknown, so we need you to tell us everything you know."

"How long do you have?"

With that, he told them everything that had happened, right from the very beginning. Maybe by working together, they might find her, and he wouldn't get arrested.

Chapter Thirty-Four

"You're lucky that the baby is okay. What were you thinking?" the unfamiliar voice said, as it floated into Nerina's consciousness, like a ghost hovering above her.

She tried to open her eyes, but a sharp pain bounced around inside her brain at the simple movement. Her body shook at the intensity, causing her stomach to lurch unexpectedly.

Her eyes shot open. She tried to roll over, her mouth filling with puke. She couldn't pull herself onto her side because her arm was trapped. She turned her head as her body heaved uncontrollably. Her mouth filled faster than she could spit it out. She banged her fist on the surface beneath her, gasping for air in the dark room.

"Let me untie her arm, or she won't be able to help you at all," the voice said again.

"Fine, but as soon as she stops, tie her back up again," said another voice.

Her arm fell free, and she rolled onto her side as another heave rocked her body. A hand came to rest on her shoulder, while another gently patted her on the back. Shrugging them off, she blew chunks out of her nose.

When her stomach settled, she rolled onto her back, catching a glimpse of light under her nose. She must be wearing a blindfold. Suddenly, a flood of images filled her mind. The last thing she could remember was driving down the road with Jenny, and then the cops stopped them.

She remembered the cops handcuffing them, walking them to the squad car and then...nothing. Her mind drew a blank. Now she was...she was...where? With who? Where's Jenny? Her breathing grew ragged, and her pulse jumped beneath the skin of her wrist. She reached for the blindfold, but her hand was immediately pulled away.

"Let me go," she cried as she tried to pull away, but they wrapped something around her wrist, securing it in place.

Shaking her head rapidly, she tried to dislodge the blindfold, but only succeeded in making herself nauseous again. "Please," she whimpered. It was dark. She hated the dark.

Groaning, she laid her head back on the pillow. If it wasn't one thing, it was another. Couldn't people just leave her alone? One minute she's normal. The next, she was a freak, and suddenly everyone wanted a piece of her.

"Please, let me go," she whimpered again.

"No can do, Princess Nerina," said a slightly familiar voice. She felt a rush of wind beside her head and off came the blindfold, taking a piece of hair or two with it.

"Ouch," she cried, massaging the tender spot. She blinked her eyes rapidly, trying to bring them back into focus. Her vision came to rest on a man with a bald head.

"You!"

The man from the cabin stood there, grinning at her. "I've been waiting a long time for you."

"Screw you." She kicked her foot out, hoping to hit him, but he jumped backwards.

"Don't make me tie them down as well." He picked the rope up off the chair. "Your husband was kind enough to supply us with more than enough of it."

Her stomach rumbled again just as the baby woke up. Tears filled her eyes. This was not the life she had imagined for them. How could she have been so stupid? She couldn't believe she had allowed herself to get so enamored by Wade. Look at the trouble it got her and Jenny into.

"I want to see Jenny."

A look passed between Russ and the unnamed black-haired gentleman on the other side of her bed, and her heart dropped. The black-haired man had on a lab coat, but no name tag. His face looked as if it had seen many battles won and lost. His wrinkled skin and bloodshot eyes told her that he didn't want to be there anymore than she did.

"Please, I need to see her," she pleaded, looking up at the dark-haired man.

Russ grabbed her chin and forced her to look at him. "You don't talk to him. You talk to me. You want something, you ask me. Do you understand?"

Upon seeing the fury in his eyes, she swallowed hard and quickly nodded her head. She went to wrap her arms around her belly, but she couldn't. Someone had tied her wrists to the bed posts. It made her feel so exposed. Almost like being naked.

"Please untie me?" she begged. The rope dug into her skin as she tried to pull her arm free.

A young woman with long golden blond hair appeared at the door, wringing her hands in front of her as she looked at the ground. "It's your daughter, sir. She's taking her final breaths. If Nerina's going help, she needs to do it now."

"Do? Do what?" Nerina asked.

Russ ripped the ropes off the bed and pulled her to her feet. Her legs collapsed beneath her, weak and wobbly. Sweeping her into his arms, he marched out of the room and down the hall.

She pushed at his chest. "Put me down, please!"

His hand shifted slightly, coming to rest dangerously close to the corner of her breast. "Would you rather I drag you?"

Shivering at the contact, she moved his hand away. Her stomach grew increasingly nauseous as he continued their trek through the building, moving from corridor to corridor and then up a flight of stairs.

"Please put me down. I'm gonna be sick." She slapped a hand over her mouth, acid burning the back of her throat.

Placing her on her feet, she quickly leaned over and puked all over his shoes, intentionally. Well, the puke was coming whether she wanted it to or not, but she might as well say hello in her own way.

"Shit." He tapped the tip of his shoe on the carpet and then turned to the young woman behind them. "Kara, get Ariella here to clean up the mess."

"Yes, sir."

When Nerina finally stopped puking, Russ grabbed the ropes still tied around her wrists and pulled her behind him. After turning down another corridor, she could see a group of people mingling in the hallway about halfway down.

She dug her heels into the carpet and brought the two of them to a halt. "What's going on?"

Russ stopped and looked at her, his eyes swollen and red, cheeks wet with tears. He must have started crying during their walk.

"My daughter is dying. I need you to save her," he said, tugging on the ropes to get her moving again.

This time she went willingly, despite the fear lingering in her soul. If she could help heal his child, then maybe he would let her go. She still didn't know how this whole thing worked, but she'd give it her best shot. Hopefully she had the energy to help. Her body was still out of sorts from whatever they gave her.

She'd barely been able to help Chrissy, and that was when she had energy. It had been only because of her connection with Wade that she was able to bring her back. What would Russ do if she couldn't save her? That was something she didn't want to find out.

He pulled her into his daughter's bedroom. Every stuffed animal in the world filled the room. There was barely room on the bed for her. In her arms, she held an Ariel mermaid stuffy.

Nerina approached the bed and sat beside the youngster. The child's skin was a pale-yellow color, and her breathing was labored. For a second the child stopped breathing, and Nerina's heart raced, thinking she was too late.

A moment later, a horrible gurgling noise filled the room as the child took another labored breath. Nerina immediately wrapped her arms around her stomach as if she could somehow protect her own child from such a fate.

"Help my baby." Russ pulled a gun out of the back of his pants and pointed it at her. "Please," he begged.

She placed her hands on the young child's chest, closed her eyes and focused on finding the child's life force. In Chrissy, she was able to see a light in the distance. But here, there was only darkness. She could feel every soul in the room back away from her as a ball of light formed in her hands, lighting up the room. The warmth of it trickled throughout her body, but nothing changed.

Why wasn't it working? Her heart shattered into a thousand pieces as she realized there was no hope for his daughter. The damage inside her little body must be too much to fix or Nerina simply didn't have the strength to help her on her own. Her cheeks were once again home to a waterfall of tears, and a bloody metallic taste coated the back of her throat. She must have bitten her cheek without realizing it.

How could she be the life of Atlantis when she couldn't even wish life back into this child? Was everyone confusing her with someone else? She didn't and couldn't understand it. Pulling her hands away, she allowed the light to fade, along with her hope of freedom.

"Why...why are you stopping? Damn it." Russ cried, shoving the gun into the back of her head.

"She's gone. I'm sorry." Every muscle in her body tightened as she waited for him to pull the trigger.

"No. Help her, please!" he cried, dropping to his knees beside the bed. The gun clattered to the floor as he pulled his daughter into his arms, burying his face in her neck.

Kara came up behind him and placed her hands on his shoulders. "I'm sorry, darling."

He pushed her away, then returned to cradling his daughter. His body shook violently as his cries filled the room. In the distance, the dogs howled, joining him in his despair. One by one, everyone filed out of the room, giving him much needed time to say goodbye to his baby girl.

Biting her bottom lip, she quietly stood up and tiptoed to the door. She almost made it out the door when she heard a click behind her. When she turned around, she came face to face with the barrel of his gun.

"If she can't go on living, why should you?"

Chapter-Thirty-Five

Wade rallied the troops. Their mer-team broached the surface of the ocean just beyond the island. Thanks to Joe, he was able to get back to San Diego in record time. One had to love a good old-fashioned ambulance ride to speed things along.

Joe and his buddies were going to approach the island from the east, while the mer-troops entered through the underground entrance on the west side. The entrance was behind a waterfall, or so it appeared. The waterfall was actually a fake 3d holographic projection; the joys of being rich.

He tried to see if he could see her via their connection, but things were still as dark as they were before. There was no way he could find her using that method, not until she opened up to him again. His heart has never felt so empty. It was stupid of him to think he could have kept all this a secret from her.

"We are going to have to do a section-by-section search. I've given you the layout of the island, and the potential locations where they might be holding her prisoner," he said to the mermen around him. "If possible, try not to be seen. Our friends on the east side are waiting for our signal before they engage with the enemy. If you find her, get her back to the entrance. Kill anyone who gets in the way."

He stared at the island. The house sat in the heart of it, surrounded by a dense forest that was almost impossible to walk through without a machete. Under the house, tunnels ran in every which direction. The previous leader was a paranoid lunatic who had gone all out and created an underground maze. One in which only a few people knew the way out—Wade being one of them.

"Remember, she's pregnant. We can't afford to lose her. I need to you to help me bring her home," Wade said.

The mermen around him nodded in agreement. The queen had ordered him to take as many men as he needed and bring her daughter home. There were matters to discuss, she said. With a flip of her tail, she disappeared behind her seaweed door before he could ask any more questions.

That was how he found himself here, staring at the island of the outcasts. A place he knew like the back of his hand. There wasn't a corner he didn't know, and he hoped he could use that to find her before she got hurt.

"If you see a bald-headed man, do not engage. He's mine."

If he had hurt a single hair on the top of her head, Russ would never see the light of day ever again. Wade would make sure of it. His eyes narrowed as he stared at the island, his heart pounding inside his bare chest.

"He may have added a new security system since I left the group, so keep your eyes open," Wade warned. Beneath the surface, his black tail gently moved back and forth, keeping him afloat. It was time to bring his wife back to their true home. No more holding back. No more secrets.

"Let's do this." With a swift kick of his tail, he dove under water, speeding towards the island. His army followed suit.

His anger was building as he approached the underground entrance. They were going to pay for kidnapping her. She may not want him anymore, but that didn't mean he was going to give her up without a fight. She was worth fighting for, and he was going to show her he loved her, even if he died trying.

The cavern had a few boats inside it, but it was relatively empty, like everyone had gone on a break or something. Russ usually had a man or two guarding the area, but it was eerily quiet. Looking upwards, he saw a camera facing the entrance. Creating an ice ball, he threw it at the camera and took it out on his first try. "Okay, the coast is clear. Let's go."

They climbed onto the smooth stone walkway. After drying off, they stood up and slipped into some clothes that were in the bags on their back.

"The weapons cache is this way," Wade whispered, pointing down one of the hallways. They didn't have any guns as they were pointless in Atlantis, so they had to raid Russ' personal stash to even the odds.

With each step, the muscles in his body tightened, tensing to the point they felt like a springboard waiting to snap. Why was it so quiet? He didn't like this. Not one bit. Were they hiding somewhere, getting ready to ambush them?

Relax, dude. Remember what happened before.

He breathed in through his nose and out through his mouth as he moved silently down the hallway, his buddies close behind. If he learned anything from the last time, it was that he couldn't be gung-ho about this whole operation. He needed to be smart. Otherwise, he could lose her the same way he lost Maya.

It wasn't going to end that way this time. He wasn't going to be stupid. Facing the access panel, next to the weapons locker room, he inputted the specific code for the month and opened the door. His jaw dropped.

First, there were no guards at the entrance, and now he opened the weapons cache with the same code as when he was here years ago. Something didn't add up. Standing off to the side, he sprayed the camera with spray paint before going inside.

"Stand guard outside," Wade said to two of his men. "If you see anyone, let us know."

As soon as they crossed the threshold and stopped in the center of the room, he knew he'd made a mistake. Bright lights filled the room, blinding them. The door creaked behind him. He tried to reach for it, but it was too late. It slammed closed, locking them inside.

"Please don't kill me," Nerina begged, holding her hands up in front of her face.

Russ grabbed her by the hair and pulled her head back, shoving the barrel of his gun under her chin. "You don't know how much I want to make you pay right now. Make you all pay."

"I'm sorry," she whimpered. "I really tried to save her."

"Shut up." He pushed the barrel into her neck. "Don't ever talk about her, or I'll blow your pretty little head off, just like I did your friend."

A mangled gasp tore from her throat. "Jenny!" She started to cry, but no tears would form. Her tongue was dry, and her scratchy throat right along with it. "I-I need water."

Pulling back even harder on her hair, he said, "Do you think I'm stupid?"

"Please, I don't feel well."

"Shut up." He tightened his grip on her hair and pulled her down the hallway, back to the room she was in before. Yanking on her hair, pulling strands out by their roots, he threw her onto the bed. She cried out in pain.

"I'm not asking you to give me the ocean. I need a drink. You know I do," she said.

He growled and bared his teeth at her, tying her wrists to the bedposts. She thought for a second he was going to bite her or something. Shivering, she tried to move as far away from him as possible.

Pressing his knee down on the bed, he leaned over her body to check the rope on the other side, his crotch coming freakishly close to her face. She gagged and turned her face away from him. He pulled the rope tight. She cried in pain as it dug into her skin, bringing a cruel smirk to his face.

"You deserve to feel the pain that I feel inside," he snarled.

"Why, why me?"

"It's your fault she's dead," he said, tugging at the rope again.

She winced. "I'm sorry."

He raised his arm and smacked her across the face, her head whipping to the left. With a mind-crunching crack, his knuckles connected with her cheekbone a second time. Her face stung like the dickens, and her eye pulsated as the world blurred around her.

Grabbing her chin, he lowered his face to hers. "I'm going to make you and your people pay."

She tried to spit at him, but her throat was completely dry that it came out as a mouth fart instead. He lifted his hand to smack her again, but the radio on his belt squawked, temporarily distracting him.

Standing up, he pulled it off his belt. "Talk to me."

"We have company," a voice said.

Russ looked down at her with fury building in his eyes. "Is it him?"

"We don't have a visual feed in the weapons locker, but I think it is."

"Is he secure?"

"For now. We've taken out the two men who were standing guard."

"Don't open the door till I get there," he ordered. Clipping the radio back onto his belt, he stepped towards the door before turning and looking at her with hate-filled eyes. "Looks like your hubby decided to pay us a visit. Before all this is over, you are going to feel the same pain I do."

She didn't respond. Her head was spinning from him using her as a punching bag. Giving her head a light shake, she tried to bring her eyes back into focus, but tears thwarted her attempt. Even after she had abandoned Wade in the middle of danger, he still came to rescue her.

Ha. Ya right! He probably just came to get paid for fulfilling the mission. But none of this made any sense. If he had agreed to kidnap her, wouldn't the king have killed him or at the very least, refused her hand in marriage?

God! Her head was a jumbled mess. She didn't know what to believe anymore. If he really had the intention of turning her over to him, wouldn't he have brought her here before the man's daughter died? Maybe she had misread the situation.

Walking to the door of the room, Russ turned and smirked at her. "Life's a bitch, isn't it?"

Chapter Thirty-Six

"What do we do now?" one of his men asked.

Wade gripped the back of his neck and smacked his forehead against the door multiple times. He should have figured Russ would have booby trapped the room. It was far too easy to get into the most well-guarded room on the island. The only upside to this was that they were on the side with all the weapons.

Turning in slow circles, he studied the room. The room was made of solid rock, and the only way in or out was the vaulted door in front of them. They had no cutting tools. Nothing that would be of any use against a steel door.

"Damn it!" he yelled, punching the door. Burning pain shot up his forearm as he shook his hand in front of him. He flexed his knuckles as they turned a bright shade of red.

Malik placed his hand on Wade's shoulder. "Hey, you might need that fist later."

"If that bastard hurts one hair on her head, I'll..." He pulled his arm back again to strike the door, but Malik covered his fist with his hand.

"We'll find her, don't worry," his oldest buddy said softly. He and

Malik have known each other since they were kids. He was about the only person who believed that what happened to Maya was an accident.

"Guys, I'm feeling a cool draft over here," another of his team stated. The man was standing beside a huge wooden storage cabinet, storing a variety of firearms, in the northwest corner of the room.

"See if you can pull the cabinet away from the wall," Wade said, motioning to it.

A few of his men wandered over and dislodged it from the wall. It was only hanging on by a hook to keep it from falling over. Behind the cabinet, there was a vent. He ran a hand through his hair and stared at it. Only a child would fit through the narrow opening.

Stomping his foot on the ground, he spun around and punched the cabinet, shattering the glass. "Shit." Bits and pieces of glass embedded themselves into his skin. Cringing, he pulled out one of the larger pieces, blood dripping down his hand. It stung like hell.

"Dude, you aren't going to be able to help her if we have to take you to the hospital." Malik stepped between him and the cabinet. "So, shape up."

"Malik," Wade said, with a hint of warning in his voice.

The man backed off, hands in the air, instantly making him feel bad. Malik was only trying to help and even offered to come on this mission to rescue Nerina when he didn't have to.

"Sorry," mumbled Wade.

"No sweat."

Wade paced the length of the room, thinking of what to do next. They couldn't get out through the vent, and the only other way out was the door. He knew Russ would come in with guns blazing, even if they used their abilities to hide themselves.

They couldn't shoot first because it could be an innocent person standing in the hallway. The only thing they could do was position themselves on either side of the door, and then see what came through it.

The only problem with that idea was that Russ could toss a stink bomb or some other type of bomb into the room, making them run out into the open and become target practice.

Damn it!

Every scenario he came up with had them on the losing end. They were in a jam of his own making. He was failing everyone left, right and center. The battle they had listened to on the other side of the door told him his men standing guard were dead. It killed him to know that his people wouldn't be in a life-or-death situation if they weren't trying to fix his screw up. He should have protected her better.

She must be so scared and confused right now. His heart felt empty without her presence filling it. Her light and love filled him like no other. He needed to get her back, and not just get her back, but win her back. Wade wanted her in his life, and without any secrets between them.

"Okay, guys, listen up," Wade said, turning to face his men. "We've been in tight jams before, so this is no different. My guess is that they are going to try and fish us out with some type of gas grenade, so we need solutions."

"We could open fire as soon as the door opens, then run like a bat out of hell," Jerry suggested. It was his first ever mission on land.

"I thought of that, too. The only problem with that idea is that Nerina could be on the other side or some other innocent person." Suddenly, an idea flashed in his head. "Okay, here is what we're going to do.

Within moments of explaining his plan, the door clanged behind them, creaking as opened.

"Show time."

Nerina tugged at the ropes tied securely to her wrists. No one had checked on her for a while. It didn't even look like anyone was guarding her either. They probably had their hands full managing her husband.

Twisting her wrist to loosen the ropes, she felt it give slightly and gave an inward shout of joy. If she could get one hand free, the other would be a breeze. Her hand was about to slip free when the door to her room opened and in walked Kara with a glass of water.

"Hel—"

The woman held a finger to her lips as she wandered over to the bed. She sat down, holding the water up to Nerina's lips. Grateful, she smiled before taking a sip, mouthing a thank you.

"We don't have a lot of time," Kara whispered as she offered her some more water. "The guards are all dealing with your group, except for the one outside your door."

Nerina's eyes widened as the women reached for the rope, freeing her from the bedposts. "Why are you helping me?"

"The less you know, the better," Kara replied, helping her stand up. "I can't help your hubby, but I can get you out of here."

"No, I can't go without him."

"Princess, this is what your husband would want. We need to get you home."

"We are here because of me. I have to help him."

"Darling, look at you," she said, pointing to Nerina's belly. "Do you really want to risk your baby?"

Suddenly, the guard standing outside pushed the door open, and upon seeing her free, went for the gun on his belt. "What's going on..."

An ice bullet flew past Nerina's head, imbedding itself into the guard's forehead, silencing him. In shock, she stared at Kara, her mouth hanging open. The woman shrugged before grabbing her by the arm and dragging her towards the door.

"Please, I've been dragged around enough. I really am capable of walking," she said, pulling her arm free.

"Fine, but hurry," the woman said, "and be quiet."

Nerina followed Kara down the hall, sticking close to the wall.

"It won't be long before security informs Russ that you're gone. Hopefully, we can get you outside before the news gets around."

Then what? Was this the end of her quiet life? It was like the universe didn't want to leave her alone and coughed her up for everyone to see. Everyone was thrusting her into a forgotten world that no one on the surface knew much, if anything, about.

She had no idea what to expect when she arrived in Atlantis. Would she even fit in after living on the surface for so long? Would the people accept her or see her as a freak just as people did here? What if—

"Nerina, don't zone out. Stay with me!" Kara said, shaking her slightly.

"Sorry," she mumbled.

The woman grabbed her sleeve and pulled her down the hall into another bedroom. Kara walked over to the mantle above the fireplace and twisted what looked like a crystal ball. In the fireplace, Nerina heard a creaking noise as the back panel swung open, and they crawled inside.

"You seriously couldn't have found us a door?" She had to almost do the splits to crawl down the passageway with her belly in the way.

"This is the only unguarded entrance into the catacombs, short of that camera." Kara pointed above their heads once they exited the crawl space and stood up in the underground tunnels.

The rocky walls of the hallway, littered with dim lights, reminded her of the secret tunnels one would find in a castle. They must have paid a fortune to build it.

"Who built this place?" Nerina asked.

"It was designed by the first official leader of the Outcasts. I think his name was Nitan Pukai. When the first split of Atlantis happened, the people settled here. They didn't quite feel at home in the villages or the cities."

"It's really quite something."

"Come on, let's go." Kara started to walk down the deserted hallway.

Nerina followed her around corners and down staircases, through more hallways, each blurring with the last. She didn't know which direction they were heading or where they were going.

As they turned this way and that way, she couldn't help but wonder whether the woman was leading her into a trap. The deeper they went, the more eerie things became. They rounded a corner and stepped into darkness. Something brushed against Nerina's face. She gasped and stumbled backwards.

Kara's arm shot out to steady her. "It's just a spider web."

A shiver slithered down her spine as she pulled the cobweb off her face. "Is there another way we could go?"

The woman opened her mouth to speak, but a loud bang echoed down the hallway, shaking the ground. They pressed their backs up against the wall. An unseen creature landed on her shoulder, walking its way across her neck. Nerina screeched and whacked her neck.

"You do realize they can't hurt you, right?"

She stuck her tongue out at Kara, not that she could see it in the dark. "Lead the way, fearless leader."

Kara chuckled and took her by the hand. Step by gingerly step, they made their way down the darkened hallway, towards a light they could see at the end. When they stepped into the light, the relief was almost instant, and Nerina let out a long breath.

"Please tell me we're close?" Nerina begged.

"Not too much longer."

Kara didn't say it with much enthusiasm, and it made her heart falter. If it took them much longer to escape, she couldn't shake the feeling that they'd come face to face with someone soon. The odds were stacked against them.

Another bang, louder this time, echoed down the hall. A few moments later, when the sound stopped vibrating along the walls, they heard voices...followed by footsteps.

Nerina looked at Kara, and their eyes widened.

Chapter Thirty-Seven

Kara placed her finger to her lips and motioned for her to disappear. Nerina nodded, and she grabbed Kara's hand as they faded away. Their disappearing trick came in handy now and then. She didn't quite understand how it worked. Whether they manipulated the water particles in the air or created some type of mirror shield, but it was awesome and definitely came in handy.

The trick would explain why humans rarely saw her kind. When someone thought they spotted one, they would quickly disappear, leaving the person wondering if they were losing their mind.

If only she could have learned this earlier, she could have avoided all the bullying. She would have disappeared around a corner and faded into nothing, instead of having the girls follow her into the bathroom as she tried to hide.

Returning to the present, Nerina listened as the footsteps and voices got louder. It sounded like they were right around the corner.

"Why do we always get stuck on patrol duty? I want to see the man who's caused Russ so much trouble." The grumbling tone made the person sound like a teenager rather than a man old enough to be in an army.

They rounded the corner, and sure enough, the kid looked no older than maybe a senior in high school. The two men were standing a short distance away from them when the radio squawked, letting them know the girl had escaped, and that Kara was helping her.

"Looks like you might see some action soon, boy," his older companion stated.

When the men walked by, a cobweb fluttered across her face. She tried to silently blow it away as a tickle rose in the back of her nose.

Uh oh.

Not good. So not good.

She tickled the roof of her mouth with her tongue, hoping to stop the sensation, but it only made it worse. If she didn't have bad luck, she wouldn't have any luck at all.

She swallowed the sneeze, only allowing a slight squeak to break free from her lips. Hopefully, they would assume it was a mouse. The youngster jumped at the sound and spun around.

"I heard something."

"You're always hearing something. It's just a mouse."

"That wasn't no mouse."

The man held his fist up to the boy's face. "Are you questioning me?"

Nerina's muscles tensed at how the man was treating the boy. She wanted to give him a piece of her mind but stayed silent, reminding herself that they were both enemies, no matter the age.

The two men continued down the hallway until another sneeze slipped out unexpectedly, and this time there was no stopping it. The saliva that squirted out of her mouth fell like snow to the ground.

"I told you. I told you!" the youngster said, grinning from ear to ear. "I knew someone was here."

"Shut it!" the other man growled to the boy, lifting his gun in their direction. "Okay, reveal yourself."

Kara squeezed her hand before letting it go, revealing herself to the men. "Cool your jets, boys. It's just me."

"Where is she?" The older man asked.

"I told you. It's just me, Clay."

Why would Kara reveal herself? They could have stayed hidden and hoped for the best. Now, Nerina would have to figure out how to escape on her own, and she had no idea which way to go. Kara hid her hand behind her back and pointed down the hall, signaling to go right as if she had read her mind.

Kara sniffled. "I had no choice. She made me do it."

"Why were you hiding, then?" Clay kept his gun trained on her.

"I was scared you'd kill me before hearing my side of the story."

A deafening gunshot pierced the air, and Kara's body jerked backwards. Her head slammed into the rocky floor, and her white shirt turned red with blood. Nerina stifled a gasp and squeezed her eyes closed. She tried to keep her hand in place, despite it shaking horribly.

A third member of the team had fired the gun. Nerina hadn't noticed him until now. The guy had long brown hair and was dressed in army styled clothes. He walked over to Kara's body on the floor, blood pouring out of her mouth.

"Why?" she gurgled, gasping for air.

The man kneeled down, trailing his gun across her cheek. "Darling, darling, darling, you gave yourself away when you appeared to us. You're no outcast. All of our powers are gone."

Nerina looked down at her newfound friend, her stomach twisting and turning. Nausea raced around inside her like a ping-pong ball. She couldn't let someone die right in front of her.

She wanted to stomp her feet, scream and yell, because she knew that if she revealed herself, she'd be putting her baby in danger. But if she didn't, then this woman wouldn't make it, and Kara put her life on the line to save her. Dropping to her knees, she revealed her hiding spot.

"And that, boys, is how you get the princess to reveal herself," the army guy said, smirking, training his gun on her. "Step away from her."

Glaring at the man, Nerina held her position, placing her hands on Kara's chest. Turning to the woman, she closed her eyes, only to be yanked backwards by her hair. She cried out in pain and grabbed the hand holding onto her hair, trying to ease the pressure as he yanked her across the dirt floor.

"Please let me help her," she begged.

"She's a spy."

"Don't let her die, please." The ache in her stomach was now in her chest, ever expanding as she watched Kara take a raspy shallow breath, with a strange hissing sound coming from her chest.

She wasn't a paramedic, but the bullet had to have hit her lung. "You have to let me help her."

"We have a rule on the island. Death to all spies and traitors."

Her eyes widened, and her spirit yelled with every ounce of strength she had.

"*Wade!*"

Pressing the plastic sealed pager, Wade signaled the guardians. He wanted to wait until he'd found Nerina, but they were between a rock and a hard place, literally. After the initial gun fire, Jerry, who had volunteered to be the eyes on the door, was sprawled on the floor behind one of the cabinets. Alive or dead, he didn't know. He couldn't check.

He and Malik were on the left side of the door. Ari and Dalis were on the right. It had become a stand-off. Each party wielded enough firepower to kill each group three times over.

The room lit up and Wade lost his balance, falling back into Malik. He caught a spiritual glimpse of Nerina. She was sitting on the cavern floor beside another girl who appeared to be dead. Then, just as suddenly as she appeared, the vision vanished.

"What was that?" Malik asked. "You okay?"

"I just saw Nerina. She's alive," he said, his body still jittery from the jolt of adrenaline that pumped into his veins as her emotions hit him like a freight train. "No one is going to keep me from her."

Wade took a step towards the door, but Malik pulled him backwards as another shot was fired into the room. "Are you crazy?"

"They're going to hurt her."

His buddy shook his shoulders. "They won't hurt her, not unless their demands aren't met. You, on the other hand..."

Malik didn't even bother to finish his sentence. He didn't have to. Wade knew what he was about to say. Russ would love to wipe him off the face of the planet and wouldn't think twice about killing him.

If the last thing he did was get Nerina off this island, he would die a happy man. She was all that mattered to him. Ever since the moment he laid eyes on her, he knew she was someone worth dying for. Not because she was a princess, but because she meant everything to him. She was his lover, his wife and his best friend. Well, when he wasn't being a dickhead.

He'd never met anyone like her, and he had to go and blow it. He was going to do whatever it took to make it up to her, and he would be there for her until he took his last breath. That was a promise. It was written in his marriage vows, and he intended to keep them, for better or worse.

"You can't stay in there forever," Russ taunted.

He was right. They were going to get dehydrated very quickly, as opposed to the team on the other side of the door. If that happened, they would lose strength rapidly. They had to do something and fast.

Wade leaned forward and quickly fired a gunshot out the door, and then he pulled himself back inside, flattening his back against the wall. He heard a groan and a thud as a body hit the floor. It probably wasn't Russ like he was hoping, but it was a damn good shot, if he said so himself. All of a sudden, he heard a bark of laughter and some gasps from just outside the door.

"Do you realize who you just shot?" Russ bellowed.

No. Not again. The gun slipped from his hand, and he leaned over, resting his hands on his knees. The walls of his throat caved in, and his head started to spin.

Malik rested a hand on his back. "They are just playing with you. Don't let them get to you."

"But what if I killed her?"

"Do you really think Russ is so stupid as to bring her down here? He knows what's at stake if she dies."

All he could see were his hands covered in blood and the body of his beloved laying dead on the ground, eyes open, unblinking. He gasped for air as panic and fear set in. "I can't. I can't do this again."

Malik whacked him up the side of the head, drawing him back to the present moment. "Pull yourself together, man. She isn't dead and you know it. See for yourself."

Wade took a deep breath and glanced towards the door before leaning back against the wall. He was right. There was only one way to know for sure. He closed his eyes, and within seconds, he felt her presence, and a grin spread across his face.

She was scared silly but alive. Relief flooded his soul. And, at the same time, a newfound anger built up inside him, fueling him with adrenaline. "That's it. We're getting out of here."

"Right behind you, buddy."

He hated the idea of rushing. He knew it was never the best idea. People always said patience was a virtue, but time wasn't something they had a lot of. They couldn't wait them out. Raising his hand in the air, he proceeded to countdown.

Three

Two

One

Just as he was about to run out of the room with guns blazing, a loud bang shook the entire room. Rocks from the ceiling rained down on them.

"Watch out!" Wade yelled, diving into the corner of the room. He curled into a ball and wrapped his arms around the back of his head.

Chapter Thirty-Eight

Silence filled the room as the dust settled. No noise emanated from the hallway either. Whatever the explosion was, it was sure to draw attention, even from people on the mainland.

Using his elbow, Wade shoved a rock off of his back and groaned, "Did anyone get the license plate of that truck?" He felt like he'd been run over by the biggest truck on the market. No one responded to his half-hearted joke, and alarm ripped through him.

"Malik?" he called. "Give me a roll call, people?"

Some fingers moved from under a pile of rocks. "Get me out of here," Malik moaned.

Wade grabbed the hand and pulled as hard as he could, but Malik didn't budge. "Hang on." He started picking up the rocks and tossing them to the side, trying to find him under all the debris.

"Ari? Dalis? Talk to me," he said, continuing to help Malik.

Still nothing. Craning his ear towards the door, he paused to listen for a moment. There didn't appear to be any activity from out in the hallway yet. He let out a breath of relief and then grabbed his friend's hand again and pulled hard. This time, Malik made his way out from under the rubble.

Climbing over a pile of rocks, they began to dig the rest of the team out. Uncovering Ari's head, Wade checked for a pulse. He shook his head at Malik and sighed heavily. Moving to Dalis, they struggled to get free.

"About time," the guy mumbled.

Wade picked up a gun and poked his head out the door. So far, none of the attackers were moving. Quietly, he motioned for the men to follow him. As they stepped into the hall, he could only spot a few bodies, and Russ wasn't anywhere to be found unless he was buried underneath everything.

Slowly, they made their way up to the house and found her tied to a chair in the ballroom. A fitting place for the last dance. Russ had a hand on her shoulder, and a large group of his men stood gathered behind him. The odds weren't exactly in Wade's favor, as only two of his men had made it this far.

"Let her go," he demanded. "You don't want to do this."

"On the contrary, it's exactly what I want to do. That's why I have her and you don't," Russ said, jeering at him. "Now, she gets to watch me kill you. I'm sure she'll take pleasure in that, won't you, darling?" The man leaned in and planted a kiss on her cheek, keeping his eyes on Wade.

"Well, can you at least let me say one last word to my wife?" he said solemnly, trying to sound a little resigned to his supposedly inevitable death, but his hands clenched as anger built inside him. He needed to smash one of his fists into the guy's face.

The man motioned for him to come forward, but when Wade's men started walking with him, Russ raised his gun. "Just you."

He approached his wife and stopped in front of the chair, staring at Russ, eye to eye. "Can we have a minute of privacy, please?"

Russ and his men took a few steps back, and Wade kneeled down in front of her, brushing the hair back from her eyes. She deserved the entire truth, and he might not have any other time to tell her. "Babe, I'm so sorry about everything. Yes, I was hired to kidnap you, but when I met you and looked in your eyes, I couldn't go through with it. Your smile. Your laugh. You as a person, knocked me off my feet."

He cupped her face with his hands. "After we met, I went to the king and told him all about the plan. And yes, he suggested that I marry you to protect you, but I didn't ask you out of a sense of duty or because he wanted me to."

Tears rolled down Nerina's cheeks. "Then why did you?"

He brushed her tears away, struggling to keep control of his own. "Because I fell head over heels in love with you. And that is the god-to-honest truth. I swear. There has been no one else in the world that I've ever wanted more than you."

"Okay, enough of the sentimental feely crap," Russ said, stepping forward.

Standing up, Wade leaned over and whispered in her ear, "The guardians are coming."

He watched as her eyes widened and filled with hope. He knew she was thinking about Kyle and Maggie, but he hadn't heard any news about them beyond the boat being destroyed.

Standing up, he faced his arch nemesis. Russ still appeared to be none-the-wiser about the guardians coming if the haughty look displayed in his eyes was anything to go by. The man wasn't stupid, though. The wheels had to be turning in that brain of his trying to figure out where the explosion came from.

"You killed my daughter, and now you've almost destroyed my home," Russ said, raising his gun towards Wade.

"You seem to be awfully reliant on that gun," he said. "Have you forgotten how to fight?"

"I could take you down with one hand tied behind my back," the man said, handing his gun to Charlie.

"Why don't you put the island where your mouth is?"

If there was one thing he remembered about being part of the Outcasts, it was the way their leadership worked. It was much like an alpha male thing. A person would fight their way up the ladder. To his knowledge, no one else had ever challenged the great Russell. The man knew how to fight, even without his powers. He was a black belt and could whip the ass of everyone on the island.

Wade had probably just signed his death warrant, but he had to do something to delay the time a little until the guardians arrived. That was if they were still okay. He had no idea if the explosion was their calling card or if it took them out. It could very well just be him and his men.

Nerina wiggled in the chair, trying to get free. "Wade, no!"

"You should listen to your wife," Russ said, glaring at him.

Cradling her face in the palms of his hands, Wade kissed her. Long and hard. "Take care of my baby."

"Please...please don't do this," she cried, fighting with the ropes that were tied around her limbs. "Don't leave me."

"It will be okay, Neri," he said, giving her another quick kiss before backing away, keeping his eyes on his opponent.

"If any of his men interfere, kill them," Russ ordered.

The men backed up, giving the two of them room. They circled each other.

"You really want to do this?" Russ asked, doing a spinning jump kick in the air. "You know I'll wipe the floor with you."

"That remains to be seen," Wade said, widening his stance a little and bringing his arms up to a defensive position.

Russ threw a punch at his head, which he easily dodged. That wasn't the punch of a seasoned fighter. It was almost like he was testing him.

"Come on. Quit toying with me," Wade said. "Let's do this."

Russ grinned and pulled off his dress shirt, handing it to one of his men. For a minute or two, he flexed his muscles, which gained ooh's and ahh's from his audience. It was impressive, but Wade wasn't intimidated. Muscles weren't everything in a fight. Patience was sometimes the most important skill, knowing when to strike and when to dance.

Russ fired a sidekick towards his abdomen, and Wade deflected it away with no problem.

"Ah, you've been practicing?" the man said with a grin.

"Just a little." Wade watched him closely for any weaknesses in his movements that left him vulnerable. He also knew that Russ was aware of that tip and would be watching closely too. That was what all this playing around was for.

Russ did another spinning kick, aiming it at his head. Wade grabbed his leg and slammed him to the ground. Charlie stepped forward to intervene.

"Don't," Russ growled, slowly standing back up. "I got this."

"Okay, boss."

Russ took a few steps backwards and stopped beside Nerina, grabbing her by the hair and tilting her back.

"Let her go," Wade demanded, stepping towards him.

"Ah, I wouldn't move if I were you." Russ closed his hand around her neck. "It would be so easy for me to snap her pretty little neck."

"What happened to your honor?"

"You aren't one of my men anymore." Russ leaned down and planted one right on her lips, never taking his eyes off Wade. "But I'm gonna make her mine."

"Like hell you will." Wade rushed him, seeing only red, aiming a flying sidekick at his chest. He knew he had made a mistake the moment his feet left the ground. Russ hooked his arm around his leg and body slammed him to the ground, knocking the wind out of him.

His men could do nothing but stand there, as everyone else had their guns trained on them, not allowing them to interfere. Wade tried to get back up, but Russ kicked him in the gut. He groaned and held onto the man's leg.

Spinning like a top, Wade knocked Russ' other leg out from under him until they were both on the ground. Russ swung his arm and elbowed Wade in the face, rolling away from him.

With blood dripping down his chin, Wade jumped to his feet as did Russ. They circled each other again. This time Russ purposely passed by Nerina, running his hand through her hair.

Wade's hands itched to rip his arms from their sockets. No one was allowed to touch her that way but him. Running towards him again, he sent a punch towards Russ, which was easily deflected. Russ landed one of his own in Wade's ribs.

Wade bent over, cradling his side as he groaned. Russ took that moment to do a street fighter move—an upper cut that knocked him flat on his back. He kicked Wade's head, knocking it back against the hard tile. He was about to do it again when Nerina screamed.

Chapter Thirty-Nine

Her cry pierced the air, and thunder shook the building. Everyone's attention returned to her. No one moved a single muscle. Her hair, which had been dyed red, had changed to a pure shade of white, and her eyes sparkled like diamonds.

In a flash, bolts of lightning disintegrated the ropes around her limbs, leaving a gaping hole in the skylight. Fog rolled in, spinning around her like a tornado.

"Have you forgotten who I am?" Nerina said, approaching Russ.

"Shoot her," he yelled.

Before they even had a chance, a funnel of wind pulled them through the roof, leaving her alone with Wade's men and Russ.

"I'm not just the princess of Atlantis. The ocean is mine and everything in it. Everything that holds water." Holding her hand out, she sensed the water in his body. She lifted him off the ground without laying a hand on him. She walked towards him, her hair flying behind her.

Joe and his men slammed open the doors to the room and skidded to a halt when they saw her. She turned to face them, still keeping Russ suspended in the air.

"Wow, it's okay. We're with him?" Joe pointed to Wade.

Nodding her head, she returned her attention back to Russ. With a swift flick of her hand, she could send him into oblivion. When she saw Wade almost die, it appeared to unlock the final piece of the puzzle inside her, allowing her to reach beyond the realms of humanity and become one with the ocean surrounding them, above and below.

"You killed my friend," she said, twisting her hand slightly and slowly closing it into a fist.

Steam surrounded him as his skin began to wrinkle, turning him into a human prune. "Please stop," he begged.

"This is my island now. My world. And I won't let you hurt another soul ever again." With a quick flick of her wrist, he burst into a million droplets of water, which all disappeared before they hit the ground.

After all was said and done, she stood there and stared at her hands. Her entire body shook with adrenaline. Wade approached her cautiously. When he reached her side, she collapsed, breaking into tears.

"I j-just...I j-just k-killed someone," she stammered, her teeth chattering away. "I j-just killed someone." The words played over and over again in her mind like a broken record. She was a murderer. A cold-hearted murderer.

Oh god!

How could she have...

Oh god!

Covering her face with her hands, she rocked back and forth on the floor like a rocking chair. "I'm a m-murderer."

Wade wrapped his arms around her, hugging her close. "You did what you had to do, sweetheart."

"Don't you get it?" she said, shoving him away. "I just killed someone. I could kill you. Get away from me."

Kneeling in front of her, he placed his hands on her knees.

"Sweetie, I know how you feel. Remember what I told you about Maya?"

"That was an accident. I chose to kill him. I wanted to kill him." She buried her face in her knees as she continued to rock. "Oh god. I'm a horrible person."

"I've done the same. You are not a horrible person. You did what you had to do to survive."

"But—"

"No buts." He stood up, holding his hand out to her. "I think it's time to see all the lives you saved today."

She looked up at him, wiping the tears away from her eyes. "You mean..."

A noise overhead caught her attention. There was an FBI helicopter hanging in the air above the wrecked skylight.

Wade looked up as well. "I think it's time to go home, our real home." Turning to the guardians, he said, "Will you guys be okay?"

"Ya, we've got this. Get her out of here," Joe said, shaking his hand.

Wade went to take her by the hand and walk towards the door, but she dug her heels into the ground and brought him to a halt. She turned back to the newcomers. "You guys are the guardians, right?"

The man nodded.

"Do you know where my dad is?"

Joe shrugged his shoulders. "I'm afraid not. We haven't been in contact with him for months. I know you have a lot of questions, but you need to get going, Princess."

This time she allowed Wade to lead her back down into the catacombs. Her mind was in a daze over all the events that had taken place, and her chest ached over the life she had snuffed out. As they reached the underground entrance way, Wade turned to her and placed his hands on her shoulders. "I need to warn you about something."

"What?"

"I didn't want to tell you before, but—"

Wrapping her arms around herself, she pulled away from him. "How many more secrets do you have, Wade?"

"I'm sorry for all the secrets. I really am. And I promise I'll spend the rest of my life making it up to you, but this one I wanted to tell you when I was one hundred percent sure. I still don't know yet, but now that we're heading to Atlantis, I don't want you walking in unprepared just in case."

"Just tell me the damn news already." She had an inkling of what he might say, and even her heart appeared to know what was coming, as it thumped desperately beneath her ribcage. Her body shook as she leaned back against the rocky wall for some support.

"A while back, Kyle's boat was destroyed, and no bodies were ever recovered. Rumor has it that the king, Maggie and Kyle were on board at the time of the explosion," he said, resting a hand on her shoulder.

She shook off his hand and leaned over, gasping for air. The ache in her chest now filled her entire body. "No, please no. They can't be dead." More people may have died, and it was all because of her. Her stomach muscles contracted furiously, hardening like a rock. She gasped for air as pain wrapped around her abdomen.

"Easy, Neri. Take a deep breath," he said. "We don't know anything for sure. I just didn't want you walking in unprepared for the possibility that they might be gone."

"I hope you just scared me to death for no reason," she said, sticking her tongue out at him, all the while freaking out inside. If they had died because of her, she didn't know what she would do. How do you live with yourself after something like that?

Sitting down on the edge of the underground dock, they dangled their legs in the water. She wished she could be more excited that she was about to pop a tail, but she couldn't stop thinking about her parents. Her chest was tight, and the walls of her throat felt like they were closing in, not allowing her to take a deep breath.

"It's time," he said.

She took off her shoes and dipped her feet in the ocean. She watched as the lower half of her body glowed bright blue and the tips of her toes tingled. Mesmerized, she watched as a silver ribbon swirled around her legs.

Then, as soon as it started, it was over. Her legs were gone. And in their place sat a bright silvery-white tail with scales highlighted in a brilliant shade of blue. Wade's tail was all black. He was right. The change didn't hurt. It did tingle, though.

"Wow," she whispered.

"Well, my princess, are you ready to go?" he asked, slipping into the water.

Was she? Was she ready to leave everything she knew behind? There were unknown voices echoing down the hallway behind her which helped her make up her mind. She carefully slid into the water beside her husband. She hadn't quite forgiven him, but she did believe she could trust him with her life. That much she knew and willing dove under the water with him, hand in hand.

They swam for what felt like forever. She was deeper than she'd ever been beneath the ocean surface before, and her legs—her tail was aching. "Can we rest for a moment?" she said.

"We're almost there," he said.

She took a seat on a rock. "I have to rest."

Nerina rubbed her tail as she looked around. The only light to penetrate the darkness were the jellyfish that swam ahead of them, guiding the way to Atlantis. The sun didn't penetrate this deep into the ocean, and it showed by the lack of plant life in the area. It was eerily empty, and a little spooky.

"Check that out," Wade said, pointing to something beside her.

It wasn't very big, maybe two inches or so. It looked like a glow in the dark comb. She wanted to reach out and touch it, but she knew enough to respect its personal space. "If I remember, that's a comb jelly?" she asked.

"Yep," he replied, grinning. "So, you ready to go?"

Riddled with nerves, she took his hand and held it tightly. "I think so."

They swam another few feet until they reached a trench. Nerina tightened her grip on Wade's hand and followed him down into the darkness with the jelly fish lighting the way. They kept descending until they came to a cave in the stone wall. "This way."

As he swam towards it, she pulled him back. "Do we really have to go in there? It's darker than a tomb, even darker than out here."

"You'll be okay, I promise."

It only took them a few minutes to get through the cave. The guards at the entrance to Atlantis moved to let them pass. When she swam into the open, it was like a whole other world. Bright lights filled the underwater cavern. The size of the cavern was immense. It had to be hundreds of meters wide and probably just as deep.

In front of her was a huge pulsating disc shaped building, if you could call it that, with tendrils that disappeared into the ground. It looked like it provided light for the entire city. Surrounding it were coral buildings with every dazzling color you could think of.

Mermaids and mermen were swimming around, acting like it was just another day for them. It was a bustling underwater city.

"I, uh...am I dreaming?" she asked him.

"Welcome to Atlantis, Nerina."

"How do places like this even exist without people finding out about it?"

"Come. It's time to learn all about your people."

As they neared the disc shaped building, the pulsating pattern grew stronger as did the strength of the light that filled the city. A wave of warmth flooded her being. It felt like a presence was reaching out to her.

She looked at Wade. "It's alive?"

"In a manner of speaking."

They crossed over a bridge and the guards in front of the building bowed slightly, moving out of the way. As a door opened in front of them, Wade said, "After you, mi 'lady."

She followed Wade down a pure white hallway. Flashes of what looked like tendrils of light followed them along the wall. "Your life force is already lighting up the place," he said.

They quickly entered a large room. She saw seahorse-shaped thrones on a platform along the back wall. One seat was empty, but someone occupied the other. The older woman looked much like Nerina. She had long, flowing white hair and a silvery-white tail. She was talking with a man beside her.

As Wade and Nerina approached them, the white-haired woman turned to face them. A big smile spread across her face. Gingerly getting up from the throne, she swam towards them. Nerina couldn't make her tail move.

"Welcome home, darling!" The woman reached out and kissed her on both cheeks.

"Princess, I would like you to meet Queen Talise," Wade said. "Your mother."

"My mother." She swallowed hard, staring at the woman in front of her. Ever since this all started, she dreamed of this moment. And now that it was here, it seemed too unreal.

"I can't believe you're here," Queen Talise exclaimed, pulling her close. When Nerina didn't respond, she pulled away. "I'm sorry. I can't imagine how incredibly confusing this must be for you."

"It's a little overwhelming," she admitted, moving closer to Wade. He was the only person she knew at this point.

"One second." The queen swam back to the man next to the throne and said something to him. When she was done, she swam back to them. "Come, let me show you to your room."

Nerina followed the queen but then paused for a moment. "Can you tell me if everyone is okay? Wade told me about the boat."

The queen's face fell. "Not here. I'll tell you everything once we get to your room."

When they approached a seaweed door, it swung open. And

inside the room was someone she never expected to see sitting on the bed. Her mother. Well, it looked like her, except she had a bright green tail.

"Mommy!" she cried, rushing towards her. "Is it really you?"

"Neri." Her mom wrapped her arms around her, holding her tight, tears filling her eyes.

"I can't believe it's you, and you have a tail," Nerina said, laughing with joy. "Where's Dad? Is he here, too?"

Her mother started sobbing into her hands. Queen Talise sat on the other side of Nerina's mom and wrapped her arms around her shoulders. The queen's face was downcast, and sadness filled her eyes.

The look on their faces told her everything she needed to know. "He's gone, isn't he?"

Maggie turned towards her, taking Nerina's hands in hers. With a shaky voice, she said, "Someone attacked the boat. Kyle died in the explosion. The king..." Her mother's voice cracked, and she started crying too hard to continue.

"The king died saving your mother's life." Queen Talise said, giving Maggie a slight squeeze. "He used his last bit of strength to change her."

Unable to take anymore, Nerina fled. She swam down the endless corridors with Wade hot on her tail.

"Nerina, stop," he begged, grabbing a hold of her arm. "Please."

"Let me go," she cried, hitting him with her fists. But he didn't listen. Instead, he pulled her into a tight hug. As he held her close, she lost the last of her resolve and buried her face against his chest, crying. "He's gone. He's really, really gone."

"I'm sorry," he said, rubbing her back.

"I won't even get to meet my real father," she said, her shoulders convulsing "I hate this, and I hate that you kept all this from me. We're supposed to be a team."

He tensed slightly, but he still held her. "I hate that you have to go through this. I'd do anything to take your pain away."

"I can't believe Dad's gone." She couldn't imagine never seeing him again, never being held by him. His tender voice was now one with the wind or the waves, depending on how she looked at it. Her heart felt empty. Nothing would ever again be as it used to be. He'd never call her his little girl anymore. She'd never be able to kiss his cheek and tell him she loved him.

The last thing she did was run away from him. He probably died thinking she hated him, and that made her heart shatter even further, sending a wave of despair through her. It was something she'd never be able to change.

"He died thinking I was mad at him. That I hated him." She cried even harder. Immense pain shot through her chest.

"He knows you loved him."

She looked at him, not wanting to feel hope. "How? The last thing I did was run away."

"Don't guilt yourself like this, Neri. He loved you and you loved him. He's loved you ever since you were a baby, and nothing could ever get in the way of that."

"You think so?" she asked, sniffling. "I don't suppose there is such a thing as toilet paper down here, is there?"

"Only seaweed or kelp," he said, brushing her cheek with the back of his hand.

She scrunched her nose up at the idea. "Ew."

He laughed and brushed her cheek with his thumb. "I love you, Nerina."

"I..." She struggled to find the words to respond. After everything that had happened to them both, there didn't seem to be any words in the world that could adequately describe the emotions coursing through her.

"Look, I can't change what I did in the past. I can only make up for it. And I promise you, I'll spend the rest of our lives doing whatever it takes to prove how much I love you."

"Wade, I..."

He placed his finger over her lips. "You have every right to hate me, to not trust me, but I hope you will find it in your heart to give me another chance. I will never love anyone else as much as I love you."

She reached up and removed his finger from her lips. "You came back for me, even when you didn't have to. You were willing to die for me. I saw how much you loved me when Russ was about to..." She paused, taking a deep breath as she shook her head. Now was not the time for morbid thoughts. "No one has ever looked at me the way you do."

"Are you saying what I think you're saying?" He crossed his fingers.

She suppressed a grin as she stepped away from him, crossing her arms. "That depends. Do you have any other secrets you're keeping from me?"

"Only one," he said, pulling her into his arms again. Her body stiffened in his embrace. "It's a good one, I promise." He leaned down and whispered into her ear, "I desperately want to make love to you right now."

Her body melted into his as their lips met. In that moment, he knew that he had won the most important battle of his life, and the prize was priceless—a woman that he would treasure for the rest of his life, and one that was his to hold forever.

Taking her hand, he led her down the hall to his room. And for the first time in their lives, they made love in their true form beneath the blues of Atlantis. How? well, that was one secret Nerina didn't mind keeping.

Epilogue

Months later...

"You ready?" Wade asked.

"Ready as I'll ever be," she said, staring down at the bundle in her arms. Their baby had decided to make an early appearance. Two weeks early, to be exact. As she stared at her precious jewel, she couldn't imagine ever giving her up. How did her parents find the strength to do it? The love in her heart for her daughter was beyond words. Nothing in the English language or their own came close to describing it.

Life was so funny. A year ago, she believed she would never have a baby, and as far as she knew, she was human. Now, here she was, part of a royal family of mermaids, and it blew her mind. She was still trying to wrap her head around that fact, and the fact that she was the mother of a newborn, who was wrapped in kelp, of all things.

Wade opened the door in front of them, which led to a platform overlooking the great hall. Crowds gathered in the room, awaiting their appearance. The queen was already addressing the crowd, wearing in her royal seashell crown.

"Today, we celebrate my daughter's twenty-fifth birthday. As you know, we sent her to the surface shortly after she was born, due to the threat from the outcasts. My hubby, may he rest in peace," she said, the crowd echoing her sentiment, "made a spur-of-the-moment decision years ago that brought her back to us a little earlier than planned. Thankfully, the threat of the outcasts has been eliminated. My daughter and her mate Wade Douglas fought the outcasts and defeated them."

The crowd cheered at her pronouncement.

"Thus, we welcome them home with great joy," Queen Talise said. "And now, as we gather to celebrate her birthday, we also want to take a moment to introduce the newest addition to the royal family. So, please join me in welcoming home my daughter, Princess Nerina Anastasia Albion, her mate, Wade Douglas and their firstborn daughter, Princess Nixie Cordelia Albion."

"Here we go," Wade said, holding out his arm.

She stepped out onto the platform, staring at all the faces in the crowd. They were her people. This was her kingdom. And one day, she would rule over them. Hopefully she could live up to the family name and honor the men in her life—Her father, King Dathan, whom she never had a chance to meet, and the man she would never forget, her dad, Kyle Winters.

To be continued in The Cowboy's Heritage

The Cowboy's Heritage

"Joey?" Reid McCloud called as he pushed a branch out of the way and continued riding down the trail. "Where are you?"

Their prize-winning lamb had gone missing during the storm that had hit their island last night. If he couldn't find the animal, his cruise-faring parents were going to kill him. They would never entrust the farm to him again, especially his father, who was often a recluse, and rarely, if ever, went on vacation.

As Reid was riding, a hawk screeched in the air above him, making him look up at the massive trees towering over him, with branches and leaves so thick it blocked the sunlight from hitting the forest floor. He placed a hand on his brown Stetson to prevent it from falling off. He couldn't tell what the hawk was squawking at, but it must have found something good to eat.

Grabbing the feed bucket, he rattled it. Joey had started responding to the sound recently. The bushes rustled beside him, causing him to look down as two rabbits scampered out—young ones by the size of them. There was an overabundance of rabbits this year, always eating his mom's carrots. It would seem they had gotten used to the sound of the feed bucket too.

"Not for you, sorry," he said, pressing his heels gently into the side of his horse Midnight to get him moving again. Where could the little guy be? Hopefully, he hadn't made it to the cliffs.

Reid stopped his horse at a fork in the path, debating which way to go. The path to the left would take him towards the northern portion of the island where the cliffs jutted out over the water, while the right would take him to the sandy beach. He might as well start with the beach, as it was the closest place to the farm.

After a few minutes, he ducked under a low-lying branch and emerged on the beach. Branches and leaves littered the area. His bright blue eyes scanned the honey-colored sand, hoping to see a hoofprint or anything that indicated that Joey had been there, but there was nothing new to be seen, except some greenish sea glass.

Cantering his way down the sandy shore, he checked the shrubs lining the edge to make sure Joey wasn't cowering underneath them. After making two passes, he tugged on the reins to the left to steer the horse back into the thick forest.

Maybe he should have brought their dog, Frisky, but he was getting old and was in the house napping. His dad hadn't bothered to train another sheep dog yet, and it was beginning to look like Reid would have to do it himself. Carefully, he made his way through the bush, looking this way and that.

"Joey, where the hell are you?"

He was about halfway back to the fork in the path when a resounding crack echoed around him. Reid glanced up in time to see a branch falling. "He-yah," he cried, flicking the reins as he ducked his head forward, squeezing his calves and his heels against the horse.

Midnight bolted forward, and the branch crashed to the ground behind them. Reid let out a breath of relief, and then continued down the trail until he reached the same fork again. A few skinny trees were leaning against the more robust ones, having been cracked from the high winds and heavy rain. He really needed to talk to his dad about finding another island or buying a place on the mainland away from the hurricane-force winds.

Taking the opposite trail this time, he scoped out the cliffs, but there was nothing that led him to believe Joey had ventured out this way. There were no hoofprints in the wet dirt, and no wool caught in the thickets. Glancing up at the sky, he noted that the sun was beginning its drop on the horizon, making him realize he'd been out longer than he had thought. Time was slipping through his fingers. Thankfully, he still had a few hours of sunlight left. It was the first part of August, and it didn't get dark too early yet.

When he reached the rocky terrain on the west side of the island, he hopped off Midnight and tied his reins loosely around a tree. He'd have to go on foot to check the area. A horse would never make it down the wet incline safely.

Taking one careful step after another, he moved from boulder to boulder down to the beach. There was a path between the large rocks, but he couldn't get to it without sliding down, and he wasn't about to get his pants wet. As he continued making his way towards the water, his radio squealed. "Joey's back. He was hiding behind a hay bale, shaking like a leaf," Chris said, his voice barely audible over the crashing waves.

"Thanks, Chris," he groaned, pinching the bridge of his nose. Coming out here had been a colossal waste of time. He could have been doing other things instead.

As he turned to go back towards his horse, something shiny and fishlike caught his attention bobbing in the water. It was half-hidden by a large rock. Reid hopped from one boulder to the next to get closer to it. On the last rock, his foot slipped and down he went, sliding to the ground on the other side. As he was falling, he caught his first glimpse of what had washed up on the beach, and his jaw dropped with the rest of him.

"It's a...it's a." He couldn't even say the word as he sat there dumbfounded, staring at the shiny, silvery-white tail, with diamond-shaped scales highlighted in blue. Reid reached out and poked her tail, then looked out over the ocean before turning back to check out the latest visitor to his island. It was a...a fish and a woman. Well, half of each anyway.

Hell! He must have hit his head on the way down, along with his aching ass. She couldn't be real. Mermaids don't exist. They just don't. Rubbing his eyes, he opened them again, only to find the *mermaid* still there. Her eyes were closed, half hidden by long, pure white hair which was partially covered in blood.

"It's not real. It's not real," he muttered, his head reeling at the discovery. His gaze ran the length of her body, past her seashell bra, to where her tail began. He couldn't help but run his hand along it, trying to find a seam or an opening that would show him it was fake, but it blended perfectly with her skin. Her fluke, much like a dolphin's, was floating in the water.

Reaching out, he gently checked her neck for a pulse. It was faint, but she was alive. He sighed in relief and then closed his eyes, shaking his head. This was too crazy. He had to be unconscious. Yes. It had to be a dream. Or the knock to his knoggin' had him seeing things that weren't there.

He needed Chris. It was the only way he'd know if what he was seeing was a figment of his imagination, or if she was actually lying there. Grabbing his radio, he said, "Chris, get to the rocky beach as fast as you can. I need your help with something." He didn't want to explain why because he had a sneaky suspicion Chris would call for help, thinking he'd injured his head.

"On my way," came his friend's reply.

Dropping the radio to the ground beside him, Reid took a deep breath, inhaling not only the salty smell of the ocean but a coppery one too. He glanced down at her, brushing the hair back from her face. Hopefully, Chris wouldn't be long because she needed someone to look after her wounds, and he didn't have his first aid supplies with him.

He ran his finger along her smooth, pure as ivory skin. It was like it had never seen the light of day, nor been damaged by the sun. "Where'd you come from?" he asked in a quiet, inquisitive voice.

Around her neck, she wore a necklace made of sea glass and pearls with a seaweed braided chain. There was something authentic about her. Something more than just a woman being a professional mermaid, which he found out was actually a thing. Standing up, he slid his hands under her armpits and tried to pull her across the rocky shore, but it was harder than he'd expected. Her slender upper body was easy enough to lift, but her tail weighed a ton, like it was one big muscle.

Reid maneuvered the mermaid between the enormous boulders along the pathway to the back of the beach. There was no way he'd be able to get her up the incline and over the big rocks without Chris' help. Setting her down gently, he waited for him. They had to get her inside before the next storm hit.

While he sat there, the woman began to shimmer brightly, and silvery ribbons of water swirled around her, making him shield his eyes. When the glare dissipated, and he could finally look at her, he saw she had legs instead of a tail. *Oh god.* He was becoming a chucklehead—a fool. Maybe he'd been alone for too long, and his mind was spinning some bizarre fantasy about being with a mermaid.

He was sitting there, scratching his head, when his friend's face popped over the boulder above him. "Well, I'll be darned. Look at what the storm rolled in."

Reid was too flabbergasted to answer him. "She had...she had a..." he stuttered as he continued to stare at two very sexy legs, and her naked womanhood. Her tail was long gone.

"Is she okay?"

"She's alive," he replied finally. That was much easier to say than what he'd been attempting to say. "We have to get her back to the house."

"Where do you think she came from?"

Reid shrugged, looking down at her. "Not a clue."

"Are we going to take her to the mainland or call for help and get them to bring a medivac in?"

That was a good question. If she was a mermaid, then she'd

become part of a freak show in a circus, and he couldn't do that to someone...even if she was the discovery of a lifetime. His grandmother taught him to do unto others as you'd have them do to you, and he most certainly wouldn't want to be studied inside and out, as she was sure to be. Mind you, he still wasn't sure whether he saw what he thought he saw, or whether he'd imagined it, because she had legs now and not a tail. As he was staring at her, he heard a click and looked up at Chris, who still had his phone in his hand.

"Really, dude?" Reid quirked an eyebrow.

The man grinned and shrugged as he put his phone in his pocket, and then held out his arms. "You can't tell me you didn't think about doing the same thing."

Reid shook his head and lifted the young woman towards Chris. Seeing as she was much lighter now, he had no trouble lifting her high enough for Chris to grab her.

"Careful," Reid said, as he tried to prevent her hip from scraping against the edge of the rock. He didn't want to scratch her beautiful, alluring body. Chris pulled her up the rest of the way and carried her over to the horse as Reid worked his way up the incline carefully, his mind reeling. Was he dreaming? How could she be real? It was like he had stepped into a movie.

They laid her over the back of Reid's horse and slowly made their way to the house, her breasts bouncing with each step, making his body wake up and take notice. He averted his eyes, hoping it would ease the ache building inside him. When had he turned into such a pervert?

"She's really quite something, isn't she?" Chris said, breaking the ten-minute long silence.

"I hadn't noticed," Reid murmured.

Chris laughed. "Is that why you've been staring at her rack since we left the beach?"

"Shut up." He released the branch he'd just pushed out of the way, hitting Chris on the knee with it.

"Ow," Chris said, rubbing his knee.

Reid turned back to face the trail, a smirk playing on his face, until he ran into a branch, knocking himself to the ground with an oomph.

Chris doubled over with laughter on his horse. "Serves you right, asshat."

Reaching up, Reid gingerly touched his forehead where a large goose egg was forming. Now he matched the woman castaway who had a bump on her head. This was definitely not another normal day on the farm. After a short while, they reached the house. Chris turned to tend to the horses while Reid took the unconscious mermaid inside.

If his mom were here, she'd admonish him for not having already given the young woman the jacket off his back. Stepping into his living room, he came to a stop. He wasn't sure whether to lay her on the couch or put her upstairs in the spare bedroom. But he knew he hadn't made up the bed in the guest room yet, and it didn't seem right to put an almost naked woman on the couch...not with Chris' peeping eyes.

So, he took her to the one bed that was ready to sleep in.

His.

Continue reading on Kindle Unlimited today

About the Author

Patricia Elliott lives in beautiful British Columbia with three of her children and her amazing, incredible partner. Now that her kids are all adults, she has decided to actively pursue her passion for the written word.

When she was a youngster, she spent the majority of her time writing fan-fiction and poetry to escape the harsh reality of bullying. Writing allowed her to escape into another world, even if temporarily; a world where she could be anyone or anything...even a mermaid.

Dreams really can come true. If you believe it, you can achieve it!

For more titles and to join her newsletter, please visit Patricia Elliott's website:

https://patriciaelliottromance.com

www.ingramcontent.com/pod-product-compliance
Lightning Source LLC
Chambersburg PA
CBHW061056100726
47911CB00012B/251